If I Were a Boy

Erin O'Reilly

Affinity
eBook Press
NZ
2014

If I Were a Boy
© By Erin O'Reilly 2014

Affinity E-Book Press NZ LTD.
Canterbury, New Zealand

1st Edition

ISBN: 978-1-927328-17-0

Editor: Ruth Stanley
Cover Design: Irish Dragon Designs

Acknowledgements

First and foremost, I want to thank my dear friend Julie for all her input in the creation of this story. Without her help, this story would be a train wreck.

Thank you Nancy for the final beta read.

Next, I'd like to thank Ruth for the wonderful editing job. She showed me the light and made this book so much better.

Thank you also goes to my son Bill for the Photoshop help even when he really didn't have the time.

Thank you Irish for the wonderful cover that captures the essence of my story exactly.

Last but not least, thank you Affinity eBook Press for taking the chance on my story and publishing it.

Although Padre Island National Seashore is an actual place, I did take some literary license with some of the settings.

Dedication

For Lisa
You do make me smile

Table of Contents

Also by Erin O'Reilly

Through the Darkness
Revelations
Deception
Fearless
'55 Ford
Fractured
Wolf at the Door
Sandcastles

With JM Dragon
Earthbound
When Hell Meets Heaven Series
New Beginnings
Atonement

Chapter One

Katie McGuire watched out the RV window as her husband parked the monster house on wheels so it faced the Gulf of Mexico. She didn't agree with buying the thing and hated every moment in it. The only saving grace was that Jack had bought the best money could buy. That meant the inside was spacious, as far as RVs went, and had rich wood accents, top-of-the-line appliances, and a larger bedroom than most with loads of drawers. What she disliked even more than the RV was the trip to Padre Island National Seashore. Every year for the past six years they traveled here to join five other couples whose only commonality was that the husbands were all pilots in the same fighter squadron in the air force.

Jack, like the rest of the squad members, was retired. He spent thirty years in the air force and reached the rank of colonel. His retirement pay along with wise investing was enough to keep him in his toys. To Katie, all of the other men were braggarts and most of the women were snobs who loved to gossip. What the women had to talk about was a mystery since none of them lived near enough to each other to form a bond outside of this yearly trip. The only woman she found remotely interesting was Helen Swenson, who, the year before, looked as bored as she was. Remembering the time they spent together, albeit for only a few days, made her smile. She was nice but seemed a bit guarded because it was her first time there as the new wife of Bobby Swenson. Definitely she was a fish out of water.

"Looks like we're the first ones here," Jack said. "I'd better get the car unhitched and park it in another site. If we work it like last year we can all be on the Gulf side."

The camping area that Katie looked at was deserted. "Lucky us. Maybe the others aren't coming." Katie couldn't keep the sarcasm out of her voice. *One can only hope.* She shook her head. *If I'd only gone through with the divorce last year, I wouldn't have to be here.*

"Don't be that way." Jack opened his door. "Why can't you just enjoy yourself while we are here for once?" He climbed down the steps before turning back to his wife. "Take care of the pop-outs while I drop the stabilizers."

Katie saluted. "Sometimes he can be such an asshole," she muttered. After unbuckling her seat belt, she stood and walked to the back of the RV to start opening the pop-outs.

†

After cranking out the awning, Katie set up a few folding woven beach chairs and sat down to enjoy the sun on her body. She looked around and shook her head. Why they picked this place for their RVs was a mystery to her. The building that housed a bathroom had cold-water rinse showers and there were no hookups for the RVs. If they wanted to dump their wastewater, they had to drive the RV to the dumping station where they could also fill their water reservoirs. The fact that the wind blew in from the Gulf meant they wouldn't have to suffer without air-conditioning since they couldn't run their generators after ten at night or before six in the morning.

Katie stretched out her legs and looked up at the deep blue sky where a few cumulus clouds were towering high into the atmosphere. A loud RV horn brought her out of her reverie. *Damn. No, they can't be here yet.* She sucked in a deep breath. *It's showtime.*

The rest of the day Katie spent watching the others arrive along with other campers who were not part of their group. She'd greet each couple, gave them all hugs, and told the wives to come to her RV for drinks and snacks once they settled in.

Jack was grumbling. "The others better get here soon or they won't be on the Gulf side," he said before rushing off to greet the newest arrival and help set up their rigs.

Since Jack was the commander of the squadron Katie was, by default, relegated to playing hostess to all the other wives. Over the years, she found the wives to be snobs and gossips who freely shared their opinions of people, politics, and religion. She didn't relish the job but she'd put on a happy face and do her best not to offend anyone. If she could, she would stay inside and let them fend for themselves—that was not an option. One by one the women brought their folding chairs and set them up under the awning of the McGuire RV. A gray-headed Rachel Matheson was the first to arrive. Saying she was plump was kind. The woman had a foul mouth and no trouble expressing her thoughts to anyone within hearing distance. Next, Brandie Markus, who was as thin as a reed and had the most annoying cackle for a laugh, arrived. Cassie Walton, an older woman and someone Katie considered a wannabe unfolded her chair and sat, causing the chair to groan. Erica Ellison, who had big blond hair and was by far the most obnoxious of the group, came right behind Cassie.

Hail, hail the gang's all here, what the hell do I care, what the hell do I care, Katie sang silently to herself.

She half listened as the four women prattled on and on about nothing remotely interesting but nevertheless smiled and nodded at the appropriate moments. She watched with anticipation for the Swenson's fifth wheel and let out a sigh of relief when they finally arrived. All the Gulf side spaces were full so Bobby Swenson parked directly across from the McGuire RV.

Thank God, they arrived. The last thing I want to do is spend the next five days alone in the company of these blithering idiots. At least with Helen she's an ally and we can actually talk about real life not gossip.

"I see the Swensons finally arrived," Rachel Matheson said. "She certainly is the coldest and most distant woman I've ever met. I can't believe Bobby dumped Karen for a trollop like her."

"She's only after his money," Brandie said.

Katie shook her head, wondering if any of them knew that Helen, as an investment banker, probably made more money than all their husbands combined. *Of course they don't. They haven't bothered to be pleasant or get to know her. She was the lucky one*

3

and her husband didn't make her sit with them. "Unlike Jack," she said under her breath.

"She is a slut. Karen told me all about how she lured Bobby away from her. I don't understand how Bobby puts up with her. Karen is such a sweet woman yet he threw her out for that bitch. He is so outgoing and happy and she is just the opposite," Brandie Markus added.

"I think she drinks. That's why she always has her sunglasses on," Cassie Walton added.

"She always looks like she has a pole up her ass. She never smiles." Erica Ellison shook her head. "Lord knows I've tried to befriend her."

"Maybe she is on some kind of antidepressants or maybe she smokes pot," Cassie interjected.

"What is your opinion of her, Katie?" Brandie asked.

Katie looked away from the Swensons' arrival and studied the group of women sitting with her. She wanted no part of their gossiping. "I think clucking like a bunch of chickens about Helen isn't going to let you get to know her. Is it?" Katie could see the surprise in the four pair of eyes watching her. "We know nothing about her except for a few days last year. Why don't we make a better effort this year?" Her heart was pounding in her chest for confrontation wasn't her strong suit. She'd rather listen than speak to save any kind of aggravation.

"She's a whore who stole Bobby away from Karen right, Brandie?"

"Yes, that is what Karen herself told me," Brandie said.

"She's certainly not the type of person I want to associate with or get to know. We need to go," Erica said. She stood, folded her chair, and then walked away with the others following close behind.

Katie's heart rate slowed, she chuckled, and relaxed into her chair. She gave herself a mental high five for getting rid of the obnoxious women and defending Helen.

"Hi there."

Katie looked up to see Helen standing near her. She had to suck in a breath. Helen's light brown hair that had blond highlights flowed around her shoulders. The blue tank top with matching

4

running shorts fit her perfectly. Her tanned legs seemed to go on forever before they ended in multicolored running shoes.

"Hi. I'm so glad you made it."

"I saw the invincible four all leave together with their chairs in hand. Did you offend them by any chance?" Helen grinned.

"No, not really I told them I thought they should get to know you better."

"Really," Helen said with a twinkle in her eye. "What will you ever do without them around you?"

Katie shrugged. "Suffice it to say, I don't think they will be asking us to join them anytime soon so it will be just the two of us. Do you mind?"

"Their loss." Helen settled into a chair next to Katie.

"I saw the Waltons are setting up their grill just like they always do on the first day."

"Yeah, that's steaks from Nebraska for tonight right? How can anyone forget that tradition?"

"We can go over there together and see if they really don't want to talk to us." Katie grinned.

"What the hell is going on?" A man's voice boomed across the campsite.

"Jack, what are you talking about?"

"Those women came to visit you at your invitation and it was clear when they all left they were not happy." Jack glared at his wife. "I'm the commander, and you know how important spending time with the squad is to me each year. I know you don't like those women and I understand why. What the hell happened now?"

Helen cleared her throat then stood. "I will catch up with you two later."

Katie watched Helen's retreat then turned to Jack and frowned. "Those women are so full of themselves that they can't wait to trash others." Katie's voice rose. "They sat here speculating if Helen was a drunk or on drugs and it was malicious. They don't even know her and I suggested we all get to know her and they walked off." Katie held up her hands. "Do you think that's fair of them? Do you condone that kind of attitude? Do you?"

Jack shook his head. "I wasn't here. All I have is your word for what was said."

"That should be good enough for you, Jack. They have been after Helen since last year. They are just making speculations about her and I did my best to make it work, just like you would want me to but it didn't happen. They obviously have other ideas. If you are so keen on making them happy you sit with them," she growled.

"Keep your voice down."

"Why? So your buddies won't hear how intolerant their wives are?"

"Katie, I hear what you're saying, but that is how they are. Can't you just go with the flow? I consider these men my closest friends. I don't want to get in the middle of a squabble between you and their wives."

"There won't be a squabble. I will be polite to them but I will not pursue their friendship. I will, however, spend time with Helen, who they have ostracized and needs a friend here. Perhaps the others will come around after that."

"Good enough," Jack said.

Katie stood and walked away toward the Gulf.

†

"What was that all about?" Bobby Swenson asked his wife.

Helen shrugged. "Don't know."

"You don't know," he repeated with a sneer. "Do you think I'm blind? I saw Jack go over there and you leave." He stepped closer to his wife. "What did you do?"

"I did nothing. I went over there to say hi to Katie. It was after the other women left. Then Jack came and asked why they left." She held her ground. "When they started having words I left."

"You better hope I don't find out otherwise."

Helen saw her husband's hand curl into a fist and she forcibly held back, refusing to let him see her shrink away. He had an awful temper and they'd had heated arguments in which she thought he might hit her but he hadn't. Still, she wasn't taking any chances. "You won't."

†

Helen sat on the outskirts of the gathered group picking at her steak, corn on the cob, and roasted potatoes. To her surprise, Katie sat next to her with her meal in hand.

"How's dinner?"

"Better than I thought it would be." Helen looked down at her plate. "I don't usually eat a heavy meal like this." Her eyebrows met. "Why aren't you sitting with Jack?"

Katie smirked. "The meal is over for the men so it is squad time...women are not allowed."

"Did you notice how throughout the meal the mighty four kept looking at us and covering their mouths to say something, and then laugh like a bunch of school girls?" Katie asked.

"Yes. How old are they, two?"

They looked across at the four women.

"Can you believe with all this beauty around us we have them front and center?"

"Indeed," Katie replied before she began laughing with Helen.

†

Rachel, Brandie, Cassie, and Erica, sat together in a tight circle. The men had moved into a group of their own, no doubt to relive their glory days.

"I'm surprised Katie didn't come over to sit with us. Now she's over there with that woman," Cassie said.

"Look at her over there glaring at us," Brandie said. "It's like she thinks we did something wrong."

"Bobby's new wife is a slut, we all know that. I can't imagine why Katie would stick up for her. She used to be so sweet," Rachel said. "Just look at that Helen sitting over there so smug like she thinks she is too good for us. I bet she's drunk."

Erica nodded. "I think you're right. I can see her glassy eyes from here. She's definitely a drunk."

"Well, I was taken aback when Katie said we should all get to know her. Like hell we will. Surely, she believed us when we told her about that whore stealing Bobby away from Karen. How can she condone something like that? I thought she was a God-fearing woman," Erica said.

"That's what I thought too," Brandie added. "Just look at Katie over there with that scowl on her face. It is sooo unattractive. She would be so much prettier if she just smiled."

"Maybe it is her time of the month and that's why she's bitchy," Cassie interjected.

All four women turned and looked at Katie and Helen before giggling.

Erica's eyes glanced at the two women across from them. "Katie will come crawling back tomorrow wanting to be friends again. Why else would she invite us to join her if she didn't want to be friends."

"Some friend. I'd rather have no friends than be associated with the likes of Helen Swenson." Cassie looked across the way and began laughing.

†

"Enough about them," Katie said. "They are too exhausting."

"I agree." Helen looked away. "I want you to know how much I admire you."

Katie's brow furrowed. "Me." She touched her chest. "Why?"

"They are rather obnoxious and here you are with your head held high despite their obvious taunting."

"There is no way I will let the likes of them rule my life or make me bury my head in the sand. But, I've always found that being nice to them throws them a curve and they don't know what to do."

Helen looked away. "At least you speak to them," she said and shrugged, "I just avoid them."

Katie chuckled. "I think avoidance is the wiser path. In so many words, Jack told me I had to be nice to them because they were part of the squad." She shook her head. "The *squad*, as he calls it, is nothing but sixty-something men who have nothing but old war stories to share."

"Isn't that the truth?" Helen looked at Katie. "I like you, Katie. Unlike those other four," she nodded in the direction of the women sitting on the other side of the grill, "you have a clue as to what life is all about. Tell me about your work."

Katie smiled. "I love my work. I love helping people."

"Even if they are gruff?"

Katie reached out and touched Helen's hand. "Please don't let this get around but my goal in life is to make everyone happy."

"Even the likes of them?"

"No, I will be pleasant toward them but that is all. I have no use for people like that. With me, it is either black or white. I either like someone or don't and if I don't then they fade into the background."

Helen tilted her head and looked at Katie.

"In case you were wondering I do like you."

A brilliant smile crossed Helen's face. "The feeling is mutual."

"How is the banking world?"

"To tell you the truth it is going very well. The market is at an all-time high and that is very good news for our firm."

"You like it don't you?"

"Yes."

"I can hear it in your voice. If you couldn't do that what would you do?"

Helen didn't speak for a few minutes. "Actually, I don't know. Work, my job, is all I've ever really strived for." She shrugged. "Nothing has ever interested me enough to think about anything else."

"Mhmm. I hear what you are saying. It is how I feel about what I do."

"Do you have any regrets?"

"About what?" Katie asked.

"Choices you've made in your life. Do you ever wonder if things would be different if you had taken a different path?"

Katie looked away. "I do wonder sometimes what my life would've been like had I made different choices."

Helen patted Katie's arm. "Me too. Would it embarrass you if I told you the only reason I agreed to come to this gathering this year is because I knew—no hoped—you'd be here?"

Color reddened Katie's cheeks.

"Sorry. I guess it did embarrass you."

Katie's heart skipped a beat. "Nothing to be sorry for...I am honored that you think that..."

Jack shook Katie's chair.

Startled, she frowned. "What?"

"It's time to turn in," he said. "Remember we're going golfing first thing in the morning."

Katie pointed to the other men still seated. "What about them?"

"Oh, they will stay up and drink, which means I will have the best round and win the pot."

Helen looked up at Jack and saw his smirk. "How much is at stake?"

"A hundred bucks each. I figure it will be easy pickings." Jack chuckled. "I've done that every year and they haven't caught on yet." He looked at his wife. "You ready to go?"

Katie shook her head. "No. You go on. Helen and I are having an interesting conversation."

Jack shrugged. "Okay, then." He turned and walked toward their RV.

"Don't you want to go with him?" Helen asked.

Katie frowned. "Not really. He can get ready for bed all by himself. I'll be damned if I leave here before those four go and I won't leave you to fend for yourself against them."

"What do you think about giving them their own treatment?"

"Like what?"

Helen grinned. "I loathe the idea since it is so childish, but we can look at them then giggle."

Katie laughed. "As tempting as that sounds...do we want to sink to their level?"

"No, we don't."

Off to their left came boisterous laughter and loud voices.

"Sounds like they are still going strong." Helen stood. "As much as I'd like to stay here I need to go, and hopefully I will get to sleep before they are done. Otherwise I will have to listen to Bobby snore all night long."

"There's nothing worse than drunken snoring." Katie grinned. "I guess I should have left sooner."

"One consolation is that they will all be gone by seven and we can go back to sleep." Helen shrugged. "Can we catch up in the morning?"

"I'll look forward to it."

"Sleep well, Helen. I'll see you tomorrow."

✝

Helen quickly undressed then put on shorts and a T-shirt and hurried to bed. She wanted to be asleep or at least look as if she were before Bobby came in. She knew exactly what would happen when he came back to the RV and she wanted none of it.

The slamming of the door pulled Helen out of a light sleep. "Crap," she whispered. She could hear Bobby stumbling down the long hallway before he banged into the door.

"Fuck," he growled.

He kicked off his shoes and the sound resonated around the room.

Next, Helen heard his zipper and she slowed her breathing to simulate sleep. She felt the bed dip as he slid under the sheet and then his hardness against her back. Helen had been down this road before and did not move.

"Frigid bitch," Bobby slurred.

When Helen felt him go soft, she struggled not to let out a sigh of relief. It wasn't long before he was sleeping and snoring and she could let out the breath she'd been holding.

Chapter Two

Helen woke up at six o'clock as she did every morning. She stood by the coffee machine with a cup in her hand, waiting impatiently for the machine to finish its task. Bobby's snoring had made her sleep pattern one of starts and stops. Just as she reached for the pot after its last gurgle, a hand grabbed her shoulder.

Helen froze in place.

"Next time I come to bed and want to fuck you'd better not be sleeping," Bobby snarled.

Helen turned around and faced her husband. "We agreed that is what your whore is for...you should have brought her if that's what you wanted to do." She didn't see Bobby's hand coming toward her until it was too late to duck.

One hand went immediately to her cheek that had the sensation of burning spreading across it. Her other hand instinctively pulled a knife out of the knife block and pointed it at her husband.

"Don't you ever hit me again," she screamed. "When you started screwing around with Madeline I told you that I would never be with you again." Helen wielded the knife so that it touched his stomach.

"You haven't the courage to use that on me."

"That's where you are wrong." Helen gave the knife a push. "Would you like me to prove it to you?"

"Bitch." Bobby took a step back before walking toward the bathroom.

Once Helen heard the water of the shower, her shaking hand placed the knife on the counter. She took a bag of frozen peas out of the freezer and held it against her cheek.

The shower water stopped and Helen picked up the knife again. *There is no way I will let him hit me again. I'll kill him first.* She froze when she heard the sound of his shoes moving in her direction.

"Hey, babe, I'm sorry. I don't know what got into me." Bobby lifted the bag off Helen's face.

She pulled away.

"What can I do to make this up to you?"

Helen shook her head. "There's nothing you can do. When we get back home I'm filing for a divorce."

"You will not embarrass me that way," he growled.

Helen saw his fist ball. "I should have left you when you took up with Madeline but I was happy you had someone else to maul." She sighed. "I was a fool to stay."

"You will not..."

There was a knock on the door. "Get a move on, Bobby," a voice from outside yelled.

"I'm coming."

"Go on and play the part of the good old boy that you do so well."

"You're nothing but a frigid bitch that hasn't a clue about how to please a man. Good riddance." Bobby grabbed the truck keys and stomped out the door before slamming it hard.

"No, *good riddance* should be my words."

Helen wasted no time in turning on her computer. She was glad that she insisted on getting the best satellite service possible for the RV. Initially it was for work but now it took on a new importance. Once she connected to the Internet and her email, she typed a quick message.

Sally, I need to speak with you. Please join me on Skype.

It didn't take long before Helen heard the familiar ring notifying her that someone was calling her on Skype.

"Sally, I have a situation."

"What's wrong? Are you ill? Has something happened?"

"I wish it were that simple." Helen steadied her voice and refused to let her emotions overtake her. "Bobby hit me this morning."

"I told you he was bad news, sis."

"I know, and you were right. I regretted it the moment I said *I do*." Helen shook her head. "I should have run when I met his wacky sister, Ingrid. She was so damn possessive that she told me once if I hurt him she'd make me regret it. She definitely is more than one card short."

"Do you want me to come and get you?"

"No. What I need is for you and Fred to help me."

"You name it and it is done."

"First, I need Fred to draw up divorce papers."

"Okay. I'm sure either someone in his firm or he can do that without a problem."

"Great. Next, I need all the locks in my house changed, the alarm system upgraded to include all the windows, and the garage door code changed. Oh, and can you get all my valuables out of the house and into storage in case he retaliates and burns the house down."

"I'll get started on that today," Sally said.

"I will also need Fred, with his power of attorney, to remove Bobby's name from the one credit card I have that I added his name to."

"Okay. What about bank accounts?"

"That is all separate. Basically, tell Fred that anything I have with his name on it needs to be changed or canceled."

"Are you sure you don't want me to come get you?"

"No. I don't want to alert him as to what I'm doing. I did tell him after the fact that I would be filing for divorce."

"What was his reaction?"

"As you would expect."

"Knowing him, that doesn't sound good. Are you sure you will be safe?"

"Yes. He won't do anything around his buddies. Besides, one of the other wives is being very supportive so I'll be fine."

"Okay. I'm not happy that you're staying there but I will do what I can at this end so everything will be in place by the time you get back."

"I need the element of surprise so I can walk away and not have to look back."

"Okay. Be safe and if you need anything please don't wait to let me know."

"I won't. Thanks, sis, I owe you, big-time. Bye."

"Bye."

Helen logged off the computer and sat in front of it for a long time holding the bag of peas against her cheek.

✝

Katie exited her RV and stretched her arms. It was a glorious morning with bright blue skies and light winds. She picked up her shell bag and began walking toward the boardwalk that would lead her to the beach and the water's edge only to stop and turn around. "I think I'll see if Helen wants to join me."

With a gentle rap on the door, Katie moved back anticipating the opening door. When no one answered, Katie frowned. "Maybe she's gone back to sleep or is in the shower." She raised her hand to knock again but thought better of it. She turned, took a few steps, and heard the door open. She turned and saw Helen and couldn't help the smile that came to her face.

"Good morning, Katie."

"Good morning to you, Helen. I hope I didn't wake you."

Helen waved her hand. "No, I've been up for a long time."

Katie glanced quickly at Helen's rumpled hair. "You sure?"

"Yes, I'm sure. Is there something you needed?"

Katie grinned. "It is a beautiful morning, the *ladies*, and I use that term loosely, are not to be seen. On top of that, the tide is out and that means it is prime shell hunting time."

"And, you want me to go with you."

"Yes. I can't think of anyone else I'd rather go with."

Helen nodded. "Come on in and have some coffee while I get dressed."

Katie followed Helen inside and watched as her friend poured coffee in a cup. When Helen turned around, Katie's hand automatically shot out to put her palm on Helen's cheek. "What happened to you?"

Helen moved a few steps backward. "Nothing, I ran into the door in the dark last night."

"He hit you didn't he?"

Helen couldn't help the tears that she'd been holding back from spilling out of her eyes.

Instinctively Katie reached out and pulled Helen into a hug. "Do you want to talk about it?"

"No, not really." Helen stepped back with a forced smile on her face. "I don't know what's wrong with me. I never cry." She looked away. "Let me get ready and I'll be right out."

†

Katie and Helen began walking toward the water only to detour to Katie's RV.

"What are we doing?" Helen asked.

"Helen, I can't very well invite you on a shell hunting date and not supply the right tools."

"So this *is* a date?"

"Of course it is. I invited you and you accepted, so it's a date." Katie grinned.

Katie unlatched a storage door located below the RV and lifted it open before she began pulling things out. "First," she held up an onion bag, "we need the proper bag for carrying our findings. Here's yours."

Helen let out a genuine laugh. "Why thank you." She peeked inside the cargo hold. "What else do you have in there for hunting shells?"

"Well, I just happen to have not one but two shell digging sticks." Katie held up two five-foot sticks that had a crook at the top.

Helen snickered.

"You may laugh now but wait until there is the perfect shell sticking out of the sand. Without the stick, your fingers will get full of sand and believe me there is nothing worse than sand under your fingernails."

"Do I get a choice of which one I use?"

Katie creased her forehead. "What kind of shell date would I be if I didn't let you choose first?" She laughed.

Helen clapped in delight and grinned. "Excellent. I will take the one on the right."

"Great choice. The end is more pointed than the other." Katie held her finger to her lips and tapped them. "Now, all we need are bottles of water and we will be on our way."

†

The tide was out almost as far as it would go when Helen and Katie stepped out on the sand. The only other people on the beach were a man throwing a ball for his dog to chase and a couple walking hand in hand.

"Doesn't that sand feel delicious under your feet?" Helen asked.

"Yes. *Delicious* is the exact word to use. We've been here later in the summer and the seaweed is so bad you have to step over it to get out this far."

"Yuck, that sounds disgusting."

For the next several minutes, the two women looked for shells, picking up quite a few.

While looking for shells Katie tried to find a way to get Helen to talk about her husband hitting her. She didn't seem the type of woman who would stand for that kind of treatment. "What gives?" she mumbled.

Helen looked at Katie and creased her brow. "What?"

"When I was twenty-two I graduated with a BS in nursing. I spent the next two years working ICU before I applied for graduate school to become a nurse practitioner."

"Really? I knew you had something to do with medicine but not what."

"I met Jack when his father was in ICU for a cardiac problem. He was active duty at the time but we managed to date a few times a month." Katie shrugged. "He was steady and reliable—probably because he was twelve years older than me."

"I think there is a *but* in there somewhere."

"Not really. He asked me to marry him and a week after I graduated we were married. I had my first miscarriage followed by two more before my gynecologist said I'd probably never be able to carry a baby to full term." Katie looked out at the waves as the tide came in. "It wasn't until the doctor told me that news that I realized the deep and abiding love for someone would be something I'd never know."

"Didn't you feel that for Jack...the deep abiding love part?"

Katie shook her head. "No. I loved him but..."

"He doesn't rock your world."

"Yeah, something like that."

"Yet you stay with him? Why?"

"I was brought up to believe that I'd get married and live happily ever after. As I said, Jack is steady and reliable for the most part. He does have his flaws. Like all flyboys he has had more than his share of indiscretions and he definitely has the commander role down to an art."

"He cheated on you?"

"Don't they all? I've thought about divorcing him for years now. In fact, I saw a lawyer six months ago, after he cheated again. You know I still think he's going to change but they never do— leopards never change their spots do they. My lawyer has nagged me to stop dithering and make a decision. I guess I should have known that the only things he is passionate about are flying and the *squad*. For some reason he thinks that because he was the officer in charge of the squad it means that he is still responsible for them all these years later." Katie shrugged. "I've discussed divorce with him but he is so controlling he doesn't believe I will."

"I hear you, although I think at some point you need to draw the line."

"Like him hitting you?"

"Yes," Helen whispered. "On the plus side for you...you aren't married to Bobby."

"That bad?"

"We've had more than our share of arguments. But after last night and this morning, yes it's that bad."

"Has he hit you before?"

"No. This morning was the first, and it will be the last time. I told him when I realized what a temper he had that if he ever hit me we'd be over."

"When I saw you this morning I thought he might have hit you. I've had patients who were the victims of beatings. I'm sorry it happened to you. I know we don't know each other all that well, but you don't strike me as the type of woman that would stand for that."

"Thanks. I'm not." Helen bent down and picked up a piece of sea glass.

Katie pulled a plastic bag out of her pocket. "I brought this for glass."

Helen deposited her find in the bag.

"Did you have any hint that he was violent before you married him?"

"No. You know how charming he is. He's the good old boy that everyone likes. He was like that until we exchanged rings." Helen picked up a sand dollar.

"That's cool. I've never found one of those before."

Helen pulled the sand dollar out of her bag and handed to Katie. "Here take it. It's my way of saying thanks."

"Nope, I won't take it." Katie pointed her stick out in the water. "There are a lot more over there."

The two women quickly picked up seven more sand dollars.

"You think they are ganging up like those bitchy women?" Katie asked.

"No way. Sand dollars are too classy for that."

"Did you know if you break one open you'll find bird-like parts inside?"

"Really? Why would anyone want to break open something so beautiful?"

"I don't know." Katie looked at Helen and turned serious. "So when did it start to go downhill? Your marriage I mean."

"At *I do*. It didn't take too long before I realized he had a hair-trigger temper." Helen stopped and took a drink from her water bottle. "I know what those other women say about me—that I was the other woman who stole him away from Karen, who is the most wonderful woman. Right?"

Katie nodded.

"The truth is that I did not intend to ever get married. I liked my job and my home. I was happy."

"Tell me about your job?"

"Okay. I'm a director of an investment banking firm." She looked at Katie. "My name there is CH Dunham and I do very well for myself so divorcing Bobby won't impact me financially."

"What does the C stand for and why don't you use Swenson?"

Helen smiled. "The C stands for Catherine. In the business world I am known as CH Dunham and I saw no need to change that."

"Understandable. Won't you have to give him half of everything?"

Helen shook her head. "Nope. Prenup."

Katie grinned. "I'm guessing you didn't get as far as you have by being stupid."

"Marrying Bobby was stupid. I know the others think I was the reason he divorced Karen but I didn't meet him until their divorce was over."

"They are idiots."

"I just might be the bigger idiot."

"Why?"

"Our neighbors, who we socialized with, divorced and she kept the house." Helen eyed Katie. "Know where this is going don't you?"

"Um, I'll take a wild guess. She kept calling Bobby for help with this and that, and before long he was spending most of his day with her. Been there done that and worn the T-shirt with Jack. "

"You will understand then. I was at work most of the time so I didn't really know but I suspected. He'd always talk about her and his desire to have sex with me thankfully became nonexistent. One day I saw them kissing in her backyard and confronted him. I told him he could keep her but not to expect me to let him touch me again."

"You didn't leave him?"

"No. Like you, I am comfortable where I live. Being married was good for me businesswise and frankly there was no spark when we *did* have sex before his affair." She grinned. "I was happy he was getting it elsewhere. I had him move into a bedroom of his own, which he objected to but I didn't give him a choice."

"What does this neighbor look like?"

"Madeline's a bleach-blond bimbo who has boobs that float."

Katie regarded Helen for a minute. "Helen, look at you. You're gorgeous, sexy, have a great body, and the most beautiful smile I've ever seen. If I were a boy, I'd never look elsewhere. I'd have only eyes for you."

Helen moved toward Katie and pulled her in for a hug. "Thank you. That's the nicest thing anyone has ever said to me."

Katie could smell the clean fresh scent of Helen's hair and wrapped her arms around her back. "I meant every word."

Helen let go of Katie and lifted her bag of shells. "What do you say we call it a shell day and go out for lunch?"

"That sounds yummy but how will we get there? The *squad* took two trucks—yours and mine—to go to the golf course and the bitches took their own so they could go and watch them."

The water was beginning to lap at their ankles and Helen moved toward the shoreline. "Did they ask you to go with them?"

"No, and I wouldn't have gone with them even if they did. The only reason they go is to have lunch at the clubhouse and to be seen. By whom I don't know but that's why they go. Also, by being there they can start drinking sooner."

Helen slapped Katie's shoulder gently before she laughed. "You're so bad."

Katie shrugged. "I made the mistake of joining them once and I vowed never again. The headache lasted for two days."

Helen chuckled.

"Why not let me put something together and we can have a picnic, then sit in the sun and read the books we brought."

"How do you know I brought a book?"

"Easy. I watched you last year sitting by yourself and reading."

"You did?"

"Yeah. That was before we met, during my stay-inside phase."

"I would love for you to make us lunch. It sounds wonderful."

"Great. Go get your bikini on and I'll meet you by that little dune over there."

"Why would you think I have a bikini?"

21

"You had one last year. If I recall correctly, it was the color of your eyes."

Katie looked at the woman as a chill ran up her spine. "You remembered that?"

"Of course I did. You, my dear, are the most," Helen cocked her head to one side, "fascinating woman I've ever met."

"Really?"

"Really. In my line of work, I have acquaintances and very few friends. There was something about you that called to me." She lifted one shoulder. "I meant it when I told you that you were the only reason I came to this horrible place." Helen grinned. "It certainly wasn't the luxury of an RV that had me eager to be here."

Katie grinned. "Thank you. I'll go get my bikini on and meet you in a little bit." Katie stepped forward and hugged Helen. "I'm glad you came too."

†

Helen hummed while she put together two turkey rolls before cutting up some carrots and adding some grapes to the lunch containers. Her mind wandered to the morning outing with Katie. "I think I was flirting with her. I never flirt with anyone and certainly never with another woman. What's come over me?" She laughed. "At least she didn't run for the hills. Maybe I wasn't flirting after all."

Once she had the lunches packed away in keep cool containers along with bottles of water, she hurried and put on her bikini. A look in the mirror made her shake her head before putting a cover-up over her suit.

†

With lunch in hand, Helen approached the part of the beach where she saw Katie stretched out on a blanket with her stylish wraparound sunglasses covering her eyes. She had her teal bikini on and that made Helen pause for a moment as she took in the sight of Katie's ginger-colored ponytail circling one side of her freckled face. Helen's eyes moved down her body and she gulped in a breath. *Definitely a runner's body.*

Katie lifted her sunglasses off her nose and looked at Helen. "Are you going to stand there and gawk or are you going to feed me?"

Helen couldn't stop the blush creeping up her face. "I wasn't gawking. I was trying to figure out if I should wake you."

"I wasn't sleeping." Katie's stomach rumbled.

Helen laughed. "Sounds like I got here just in time then."

Katie sat up and patted the bottom of the blanket. "The food goes here," then she touched the blanket next to her, "and you go here."

The blanket was not large therefore when Helen sat where Katie indicated their hips were touching.

Katie didn't move but rubbed her hands eagerly.

"What did you bring?"

Helen leaned down and pulled the cooler next to her. "Some very special bottled water that I'm sure came out of someone's tap."

"Ah, I've heard of that but never tasted it." Katie grinned. "What else?"

"Lettuce wraps of turkey and avocado, carrots, and grapes for dessert."

"Have you been snooping around my work?"

"No." Helen's eyebrows creased. "Why?"

"At the clinic where I work lunch is catered for the doctors and what you just described is exactly what I always have."

"Really? You have catered lunches?"

Katie laughed. "Yes, really. But we don't get the sumptuous feast the surgical staff gets."

The two women settled in to eat their lunch as the sun crept closer to their blanket.

"I am rather miffed with you, Helen."

"Me? Why?"

"You practically ordered me to wear my bikini and here you sit all covered up and that is not fair. Either you reveal your suit or I'm putting my shirt on."

"No, don't do that." Helen stood and unzipped her cover-up and let the garment fall onto the sand. "There you go."

Katie let out a wolf whistle.

Helen watched as Katie's eyes moved up her body, stopped at her breasts for a moment then continued their upward journey.

"Wow. You are absolutely gorgeous. I don't understand your husband and the neighbor. Like I said earlier, if I were a boy and had you in my life, I would never look at anyone else."

"She has big boobs." Helen felt a tingle when she sat down and the skin of her thigh touched Katie's thigh.

Katie looked at Helen's breasts. "Yours are perfect. Just the right size. Not too big or too small."

A silence ensued.

"It looks like the sun is reaching us," Katie said. "Would you please rub some of this sunscreen on my back?"

"Sure." Helen's hands were shaking as she squeezed the white cream on her palms and rubbed them together. She'd never been this personal with another woman—not even her sister. "Turn around." The first touch of her hand on Katie's soft, luxurious skin made Helen close her eyes as every nerve in her body came to attention.

"That feels so good," Katie whispered. "When you're done, I will do yours."

Helen's hands stopped—her center tightened. *Damn. Where's that coming from?*

Katie leaned into Helen's hands as they rubbed sunscreen on her back. *God, does that feel good.* She resisted the moan that wanted to escape and tried to keep her focus on the strong fingers massaging her skin, but her attention turned to the increasing tightness between her legs. *It's been a long time since I've felt that.* She squeezed her thighs together hard and went with the feeling.

"Okay, now it's my turn."

Katie heard the words but didn't react.

"Are you okay?" Helen asked in a shaky voice.

"Yes. Sorry." Katie looked at Helen. "I got lost in the moment."

Helen handed her the lotion.

24

When she reached for the sunscreen and her fingers touched Helen's, Katie gulped as she felt another release demanding attention.

"Let's see if I can get lost in the moment too," Helen whispered.

"I hope you do. There are no words to describe it. Well, maybe pleasurable is a good word."

With the flat of her hand, Katie began to rub Helen's back. It wasn't long before she once again became lost in her bourgeoning feelings for the woman. *Where is this coming from?*

Chapter Three

That evening was potluck with grilled chicken. Helen set her bowl of fruit salad on the food table and looked around at the people there. She was disappointed that she didn't see Katie and resigned herself to sitting with Bobby.

After the afternoon on the beach with Katie, she was both confused and elated. Her friend gave her a reason for feelings that she only thought of as myth. The way her body reacted to Katie's touch surprised her. It didn't repulse her at all. All she wanted was to be near her and bathe in the warmth that Katie created within her.

Helen sat and leaned away from Bobby. "Don't you even talk to me or try to touch me again."

"I told you I was sorry." Bobby glared at his wife. "We need to keep up appearances so don't you dare make a scene in front of my buddies."

"Or what? You'll hit me again?"

"How many times do I have to tell you I'm sorry?"

"You might as well stop now. There aren't enough I'm sorries to make up for what you did."

Helen saw Katie and Jack come into view and she smiled at Katie. Her reward was a brilliant smile.

Erica and Mike Ellison whisked Katie and Jack away to join them near the grills.

Disappointed and feeling sadness permeate her body, Helen let her mind wander to the afternoon picnic they had...

Helen liked the easy way about Katie and the repartee they shared as they lay side by side and the sun baked their skin.

"What are you going to do about your bruise?" Katie asked. "Makeup?"

"No makeup. To be honest I don't use any. Lipstick occasionally." Helen shrugged.

"You've got to be kidding me." Katie's eyes widened. "That's all natural?" She put her hand over her heart. "God, you are so beautiful."

Helen blushed.

"Sorry, did I embarrass you?"

Helen shook her head. "No, I'm just not used to hearing that."

"Then you need to start hanging around with someone who appreciates you."

"And that would be?"

"Why, me of course." Katie grinned. "When we go back I will get some makeup that will hide the bruise."

"Why should I?"

"Because everyone loves Bobby, no one will think he hit you least of all the wives. It would be your fault and they would make sure everyone knows that they think you are a crappy wife and he should have never left Karen for you."

"Obviously they already do. What more can they say?"

"Doesn't matter. Unfortunately, I know how they work. They are not very nice people. I heard them talking about Bobby's first wife and her hatred for you."

"But I never met him until after he was divorced."

"Again, the truth doesn't matter to them. They will spin the tale to put you in the poorest light possible. Trust me on this, Helen. They will be relentless in trying to get under your skin, just like they did last year."

"I remember I spent most of my time inside the RV until you came and sought me out." Helen smiled. "Too bad it was close to the end when you did."

"Yes, it was, and I regretted that. I knew they were lying but knowing what they are like I didn't want them to target me. Believe me, I called myself a wuss several times. Then I gave myself a swift kick in the butt and decided to speak to you." Katie smiled. "It was the best decision I had made in a long time."

"You are so good for my ego. Thank you."

"It's mutual."

Helen smiled and looked in Katie's direction and saw the woman smiling at her again. A shiver ran through her body and she looked away. The thought of her touch on her back made Helen close her eyes and dwell on the pleasurable feelings the touch elicited.

"Okay, the chicken is ready so soup's on, folks," Eddie Walton called out.

Bobby got up then looked at his wife. "You coming?"

"Not right now. I'm not hungry."

"Suit yourself."

Helen watched him walk away, grateful he didn't insist she join him. *Only a little while longer and I can give him the divorce papers.* She was so deep in thought she didn't notice the person standing in front of her until she caught a glimpse of a hand waving in front of her eyes.

"Oh, Katie, it's you. How long have you been there?"

Katie grinned. "Not long." She motioned toward the table and the people around it. "Aren't you hungry?"

"Not really."

"Why? What's wrong? Are you okay? He didn't hit you again did he? Those women haven't bothered you have they?"

Helen laughed. "So many questions. Are you sure you're not a lawyer? The answers to your questions are…not hungry, nothing, yes, no, and, they have left me alone."

Katie touched Helen's arm. "Tell me."

Helen felt Katie's eyes searching her face for an answer.

"Please trust me."

"I'm afraid to be alone with him."

"Did he hit you again? The truth."

"No. I told him he can sleep on the couch and not to try anything because I'd have one eye open and a weapon ready."

Katie scrubbed a hand over her face. "How did that go down?"

"As expected."

"Do you want Jack to speak to him?"

28

Helen patted Katie's arm. "No. I've got him under control. It's just unsettling since I know that if he hit me once he will do it again." Helen looked at the people standing around the food table. "Look at him over there, acting as if he's the best thing since chocolate."

Bobby was having an animated conversation with his golfing buddies—*the squad.*

"I agree he certainly hasn't shown me that he has a temper or abuses his wife."

"Is that how all wife beaters act?"

"That is what I've heard from some of my patients." Katie shrugged. "Sometimes they have no idea until one day he loses his temper and starts using her as a punching bag."

"If I can just get past the next few days and go home I will be okay. I've already spoken with my sister and she and her husband will be at the house when we get there. They are taking care of all the details so after I give him the divorce papers and make sure he is out of my house I can leave."

"Good thing you have satellite so you could speak with her. Did you use Skype?"

"Yes. She was appalled to say the least. Sally, that's my sister's name, is like a dog with a bone when she thinks someone she loves is wronged or falls into the hands of someone she deems unsuitable."

"Like Bobby?"

"Exactly."

"Is it his house?"

"No, I bought it years ago." Helen pictured her house. "It was built in 1938 and I had it renovated to its original glory." She smiled. "I love my house."

"Then why leave it?"

"It will be easier if I leave. That way he won't know where to find me. I'm having the locks changed so he can't become a squatter in *my* home."

"Good idea."

Helen nodded toward the four women looking in her direction. "Wonder what they will say when I divorce that son of a bitch."

Erin O'Reilly

"It's a given. It will be your fault. Who cares? You will never have to attend another squad event in your life." Katie patted Helen's hand. "It will take a lot of resolve to walk away from him. Most of my patients who are victims of abuse keep going back."

"I'm not most women. I could say the same about you?" Helen studied Katie. There was no denying that she was cute. Her wavy hair pulled back in a ponytail and her green eyes always glowed. The freckles on her nose filled out the cuteness factor to a T. But something else drew her to Katie like a moth to a flame.

"Hon," Jack interrupted, "me and the Ellisons all have our plates filled."

Katie looked at her husband. "Oh. Okay. Let me fill mine and I will join you in a few minutes."

"Okeydokey. Don't be long."

"I won't." Katie turned to Helen. "Sorry."

"Not a problem."

"Yes, it is." Katie blushed. "I'd rather stay here with you than suffer through a meal with the Ellisons. Erica is the most obnoxious one of the clique." Katie let out a long sigh. "I am sure she will try to strike up a conversation and get me to tell her what you and I were talking about just now."

"Nosy is she?"

Katie nodded. "That's her specialty."

Helen put her hand over Katie's. "For the record, I'd rather you stayed here with me."

Katie stood. "The sooner I get this over with the better. If I don't get to talk with you later, I want you to know that if Bobby does anything you can come to me and I will protect you."

"Thanks." Helen watched Katie as she walked away and a stirring of happiness bubbled up.

†

Just as Katie expected, Erica Ellison pumped her for information.

"Don't you think she is the most repulsive person you've ever met?" Erica asked. "Anyone who would sleep with a married man

30

and break up his marriage is the scum of the earth as far as I'm concerned."

"Exactly how do you know she slept with him while he was married? Isn't it possible that they met after the divorce? Seriously, Erica, I think if you'd try to get to know her you'd find out she isn't anything like you think she is."

"Don't tell me you are seriously trying to defend her. Bobby divorces Karen then shows up here six months later with her at his side. It doesn't take a genius to figure that one out, Katie. Besides Brandie said Karen told her."

Katie's smile didn't reach her eyes. She sucked in a deep breath, allowed her work persona to appear, and softened her voice. "Erica, I have spoken with her and she is a lovely woman. Just give her a chance."

"She's a wanton woman, what else is there that I need to know. Karen said she had a long line of men she manipulated into marrying her so she could get their money."

Katie stood and took a deep breath. "Don't believe everything a third party says, Erica, it can get you in a lot of trouble. I'm going to get dessert," she said to Jack. "Want me to bring you anything?"

"Yeah, that fruit salad looked great."

"Oh, no, don't get that," Erica said loudly. "*She* made it?"

Jack frowned at Erica. "What are you talking about? Who made it?"

"Helen," Erica spat.

Jack looked at his wife in question. "What's that all about?"

"Lies," Katie whispered before turning and leaving her dinner companions.

†

Helen watched the exchange between Katie and Erica Ellison with great interest. It was clear that Erica wasn't happy and for some reason Katie had a smile on her face. *What's that all about?* When she saw Katie at the food table she stood and made her way casually toward her.

31

Katie's eyes were narrow slits and her cheeks were tinged with red.

"I saw you and Erica having a conversation. Are you okay?" Helen asked.

"No."

"What did she say?"

"Lie upon lie."

Helen bit her lip. "About me?"

Katie sighed and turned to Helen. "Was it that obvious?"

"If you're asking if I could feel the heat of her anger, then the answer is yes. As for you, it looked like you were in control."

"I didn't feel that way. She is the most bullheaded woman I've ever met. Over the years, I've tried to be friendly despite the fact that I have never been able to tolerate her shrill voice or the words that come out of her mouth. I swear she must read every tabloid there is and then repeat it as fact."

"I'm sorry. Maybe I should let you be."

"No. Don't go. You are the only sane person here."

"If I'm making the time here uncomfortable for you it is only reasonable that I should keep my distance."

"Please don't do that, Helen." Katie's voice dropped an octave. "I would go mad without you in my world." She looked at her feet. "I mean here."

Helen closed her eyes, relishing Katie's words. No one had ever made her feel as special as her new friend did. "I would go mad too," she whispered. For a moment, it was as if Katie was the only one around her.

"I'm glad we settled that." Katie grinned then frowned. "Darn it, all your fruit salad is gone and that is what Jack wanted me to get for him."

"I saved some." Helen picked up a paper bowl. "I'll go get it then I will personally deliver it to him." She laughed. "I can't wait to see the look on Erica's face when I do."

†

Katie settled in her chair then smiled at Jack. "They were all out of the fruit salad. Helen said she had a bit more and went to get it for you."

Jack smiled. "I can't wait. It looked so good."

Inwardly, Katie smiled. What transcended between Helen and her all day long made her feel all tingly inside. She thought back to the last time she felt like that...

It had been during her first semester at the University of Texas in Austin. It was the first time she was on her own and although it was refreshing, there was a modicum of fear. Her roommate, Heather, made no excuses for her sexual preference and Katie had no problem with it either.

They had shared everything and were always there for each other. One night Heather came back to the dorm room, crying.

"Heather, what's wrong?"

"Everything."

"Tell me."

"Roxie dumped me for some chick with big tits."

Katie embraced her friend. "That's awful. What can I do to help you?"

"This." Heather kissed her.

The kiss was so soft and sensual and Katie could feel her body respond. She suddenly couldn't get enough and kissed Heather passionately.

"No, this isn't right." Heather pushed Katie away.

"It feels right to me."

"It feels like I'm taking advantage of you, Katie. I won't do that."

Katie watched the door close after Heather. A week later, Heather requested a new roommate and was gone.

Katie never saw Heather again but the memory of the kiss lingered on until other more pressing matters, like school, took the forefront—until that moment. The need to be with Helen again, if only to talk with her, was overwhelming.

Katie surreptitiously looked in Helen's direction and grinned when she saw her new friend beaming back at her. Helen was walking straight toward her with a bowl of fruit salad. The effect was warmth spreading through her body.

"Here you go, Jack. I heard that you wanted some of my fruit salad."

Katie watched her husband's reaction and was happy that he seemed pleased with Helen's gesture. When she turned toward Erica, the woman looked like she just sucked on a lemon. Katie could not suppress the chuckle when the word *sourpuss* came to mind.

Chapter Four

A tapping at the RV door had Katie scurrying to answer. "I was hoping it was you," she said, opening the door.

"You were, were you?"

Katie grinned. "Yep, my secret is out. I like being with you."

"The feeling is mutual. Do you want to go looking for shells again?" Helen held up her sack from the day before along with the stick. "Oh," she said, "I brought water too."

Helen's infectious smile filled Katie with a feeling of rightness and she smiled back.

"Have you had any breakfast? I've just heated up some sweet rolls."

Inside the RV, a timer was dinging.

"Did you just whip them up?"

"Hell no. They're out of one of those cans that you whack on the side of the counter."

"Ah, my kind of cook." Helen crooked her head. "They do smell awfully good."

"Then come on in and we can share a meal without four sets of eyes watching our every move." Katie moved back inside so she could turn off the timer and pull the rolls out of the oven. She looked over at Helen, who had moved inside the RV. "Take a seat."

"The table is set for two. Are you expecting someone?"

Katie winked. "Yes, as a matter of fact I was." She grinned as she spread frosting over the rolls. "Once these were done I was going to go over to your place and ask you to join me."

"Really?"

"Of course. Did you think I'd want to associate with the *squad's* wives? To tell you the truth, you are a breath of fresh air." Katie put the pan on the table. "Help yourself. I don't know about you, but my mouth is already watering."

Helen just stared at Katie.

"What?"

"All my life I've been about numbers and percentages. I have many associates but the only friend I have is my mentor, who is also my boss. I've never known anyone like you, Katie." She tapped her heart. "You make me feel warm here." She placed a fork in one of the rolls and put it on her plate. "Thank you."

"Hey, you haven't tasted them yet. You better save your thanks until you do. Be careful they're hot." Katie saw the blush climbing up Helen's neck to her face.

"I meant thank you for coming into my life and making it so much richer. Especially here."

Now it was Katie's turn to blush and she looked away. "We'd better eat up...low tide is in ten minutes."

†

"How was your night with Bobby?" Katie asked as they walked along the shoreline with the tide rolling in.

"He slept on the sleeper in the couch." Helen shrugged. "I heard him get up and leave to go golfing with the guys. He must have taken clean clothes with him last night for I found what he had on yesterday in the bathroom."

"Did he say anything?"

Helen shook her head. "Other than asking me if I would join the others for lunch today, he said nothing."

Katie grabbed Helen's arm and stopped her forward motion. "Wait. Did he really think you would join them?"

Helen nodded. "Yeah, he said if I was going he'd leave the truck for me."

"No way."

Helen closed her eyes for a moment reveling in Katie's touch before pulling her arm away. "Apparently he is living in an alternate universe."

Katie laughed. "Aren't all men?"

"You do have a point." Helen continued to walk along the beach with her head bent looking for shells—fighting with her mind that was filling fast with thoughts of Katie.

"Look what I found," Katie called from behind Helen.

Helen stopped walking, turned, and had to catch her breath. Katie was standing next to the water, with her shirt wrapped around her waist with only her sports bra showing, holding something up. *When did she do that?* Katie was running toward her.

"Look, it is a piece of a china cup."

Helen took the find and looked at it. There were barnacles on the curved edges. "I've seen lots of porcelain china in my line of work and I think this is the real deal."

"Yep, that is what I thought too. Even in this condition it is almost translucent."

"Did you see any more pieces?"

"No. The only reason I got this one is because it was lodged in that reef out there."

"Let's go back there and poke around and see what we can find."

Katie grinned. "Beat you there."

Helen laughed and easily caught up to Katie and touched her on the shoulder. "Tag, you're it."

Katie sped up and splashed into the water after Helen. "Yikes," she screamed.

Helen stopped and moved quickly to the fallen Katie. "Are you okay?"

Katie splashed water in Helen's direction. "Yes, I'm okay. Join me. The water is great."

"Hey." Helen sat down next to Katie and threw a handful of water in her direction. "There, now we are even…and for a good measure," she used the heel of her hand through the water, "one more."

Katie laughed and began slapping her hands on the water, spraying it toward Helen.

The water fight finally ended and both Katie and Helen were clinging to each other, sucking in breaths and trying to stop their onslaught of laughter.

"Thank you." Helen stood.

"No. No, thank you."

They both started laughing again.

"I can't remember the last time I had so much fun."

"Or got so drenched," Katie added.

"I guess we should get back and dry off." Helen shrugged. "Good thing the bitch posse went shopping. There's no telling what they'd think of us clowning around in this really cold water."

Katie hooked her arm in Helen's as they walked toward the shore. "Frankly, you are more important to me than anything any of them can say about what we do."

Helen stopped just as they reached the sandy shore. "You always know the right thing to say to make me feel important. Thank you." She moved in closer and pulled Katie to her and kissed her cheek. "You are very special to me."

A large white dog came barreling in their direction with a ball in its mouth. A young boy was chasing after the dog screaming, "Alaska stop! Someone stop her."

With a quick move, Helen reached out and caught the leash trailing behind the dog. Once the dog stopped, she waited for the boy to catch up.

"Got him. That's a really big dog for you to be handling all by yourself," Helen said.

"My dad and I were walking her when she took off after a ball someone threw for their dog," the small boy said.

"What's your name?"

"Nicholas."

Helen looked down the beach. "Is that your dad?"

"Yes."

"Thank you," the man gasped, coming to a stop in front of them. "She'd probably still be running if you hadn't stopped her."

"Not a big deal." Helen handed him the leash. "She's massive. What kind of dog is she?"

"She is a Great Pyrenees and believe it or not she is still just a puppy."

"Wow. Do you have a big yard for her?"

The man laughed. "I thought so but she just keeps growing."

Katie smiled. "Well, I hope the three of you have a nice walk. Take care."

"Thanks, you too."

Helen watched the man, his son, and their dog walk back the way they came from. "Did you see his eyes?"

Katie's forehead creased. "What do you mean?"

With a grin and a nod toward Katie's chest Helen waited for her friend to look down.

"Oh, my God. Was he ogling me?"

"I do believe so. Lucky for me, mine have never protruded much." Helen put her arm around Katie's shoulders. "Come on. You are obviously cold." She wiggled her eyebrows and laughed.

"I'm forty-four years old and a man ogled me." She shrugged. "Not bad for this old gal."

Helen smiled. He wasn't the only one.

"Once you get dry, come on over to my place and I will fix us lunch before we go have more fun in the sun while reading."

"Sounds good to me. What are you making?" Helen heard her stomach rumble and held a hand over it.

"From the sound your stomach is making it probably doesn't care." Katie laughed. "I thought I'd heat up some burritos that I brought with me."

"You made them?"

"No, silly. We are in a freakin' RV. It doesn't deserve anything homemade. I told Jack if he insists on going on trips in that thing he'd have to get used to heat and eat food."

"Burritos sound lovely." Helen chuckled. "You know, you are something else."

Katie raised an eyebrow. "Is that in a good way or a bad way?"

"Only in the most sincerely wonderful way. You have made an unbearable situation into something so special for me that in the years to come I will remember you with fondness." *Is it possible to fall for someone in only a few days?* Helen stared at Katie trying to discern if she too had the same feelings.

Katie turned away and started toward the campground. "Come on, I'm really getting cold and hungry."

†

After lunch, Katie and Helen carried their beach chairs down the boardwalk to a sandy area well above the incoming waves. They spent the time there in relative silence reading their books.

Letting out an audible sigh, Helen turned off her tablet.

"What's the matter?"

"This book has five stars and it ends with one of the main characters—actually the major one—dying." Helen shook her head. "I don't mind feeling all warm over something sweet and tender when I read but having someone you've invested time in getting to know and like only to have them die needlessly at the end isn't what I like to read."

Katie reached out and patted Helen's hand. "There is nothing bad about crying over a story. It means the author got it right."

Helen shrugged then closed her eyes, drinking in the warmth of Katie's hand on hers. "I wasn't crying." She grinned. "But I almost did."

"Ah, an oxymoron. Can there be such a thing as a compassionate banker?" Katie laughed and removed her hand.

Helen smiled, still relishing in the warmth of Katie's touch.

"Tonight we get to all go down to the *big* beach and eat sandy hot dogs and sausages," Katie said. "Now *that* should put a really big smile on your face."

Helen put her hand to her forehead. "Catch me before I swoon over that horrible news."

Katie chuckled. "What I don't get is why they think we need to pack everything up and go there for the sandy hot dogs when the sand right here is just as sandy." She looked around the area. "And it is closer to where we are staying."

"It must be one of those pilot things that involve some sort of tactical maneuver that only makes sense to them." Helen paused. "And probably to the four bitches."

"Sounds about right. If it helps, Jack told me it would be different this year." Katie looked at her watch. "In fact, the *squad* should be busy getting the fire pit ready by now."

"No offense to Jack but I don't think there's a way to avoid sand getting into your food when you eat it while sitting on a sandy beach."

"I agree. This is my least favorite night on this trip."

Helen let out a sigh. "I don't suppose there is any way I can get out of going is there?"

Katie's eyes opened wide. "And strand me with all those men and the four bitches. No way. You wouldn't be that cruel would you?"

"Not to worry. You are the only reason I would go." Helen surreptitiously looked at Katie as an electrifying shiver ran through her body. She could no longer deny the bourgeoning sexual feelings she was having toward Katie. *Where is this coming from?* She didn't know but she definitely liked how they made her feel. *I should stay far away from her before my libido kicks in and I do something reckless.* "There is no one else I'd rather share a sand-filled hot dog with."

"Thank, God. You had me worried for a minute."

"Really?" Helen crooked her head to one side.

Katie put her book down and turned toward Helen. "Don't you get it? Your being here and the time we've spent together have made me happier than I can remember ever being in a long time."

"For me too." Helen's heart soared.

Chapter Five

Katie sat in her sand chairs at the campfire next to Brandie. The woman plopped down beside her without even asking if it was okay. Jack and Bobby were busy helping the others roast their hot dogs and sausages over the fire pit the men had built earlier in the day.

Her gaze turned to Helen, who was sitting just on the other side of the fire with her eyes fixed on her husband; she was definitely scowling. Not that Katie blamed her. If she were married to such a blowhard who hit her, she too would look at him with distaste. The man always told the same story every time the group got together, embellishing his role a little more each time so he always came out the hero.

"So, Brandie, what news do you have about Karen? I understand you've spoken with her recently."

"Yes, I have. Thanks for asking. This is always a particularly hard time of the year for her—she so loved coming here with us."

"I understand. Everything happens for a reason they say."

"Harrumph. That reason is sitting right over there."

Katie bit into the hot dog Jack had brought her and gritted sand between her teeth. She shook her head and threw it back on the paper plate. She was glad she had eaten something substantial before attending the gathering.

"I don't think that is fair, Brandie, since Bobby had a big part to play in the divorce. You can't just blame one but not the other."

"I don't see it that way and neither does anyone else. She put him under her spell and made him do what he did."

Katie laughed. "Have it your way." Her eyes, as they had done continually since she first arrived, traveled back to Helen. Her friend was getting out of her seat and walking away.

"Good, she's leaving, I can't stand looking at her," Brandie said.

Katie looked at Brandie and shook her head before standing and walking quickly after Helen.

"Hey, Helen, wait up." Katie saw the woman's back stiffen slightly as she turned around. Katie's eyes met Helen's and she smiled. "Don't you know to take a buddy with you?"

"And why is that?"

"There are all kinds of wild animals out at night that could attack you."

Helen chuckled. "Really?"

"Oh, yes. All kinds of snakes, sand crabs, coyotes, and bobcats."

"Seriously? Sand crabs?"

"Just have one of their pinchers attach itself to your toe and you will know what I mean."

"I was just going to the bathroom. I hope I can make it unscathed to the concrete where I will be safe."

"You can't get away from me that easily. I will go with you."

Helen laughed then hooked her arm in Katie's. "Let's go then."

†

As with all bathrooms within the national park system, it was clean but cold. Katie didn't mind because being with Helen made her warm all over. She saw Helen staring at her. "What?"

"I was thinking about when we were on the beach, when you said if you were a boy you'd look at no one else."

"I meant that. What about it? Shouldn't I have said that? Did I offend you?" Katie could feel her insides shaking.

"No. Never. I'm glad you did." Helen paused and sucked in a deep breath of air. "If I were a boy, I'd only have eyes for you, Katie."

Katie was trembling when Helen moved and stood in front of her. When their lips brushed against each other, the long-forgotten feelings elicited by her roommate exploded inside her but this time they were for Helen.

The cackling of Brandie Markus's voice along with the voices of the others made Katie pull back.

Helen moved into a stall and locked the door.

Katie went to the sink, turned on the faucet, and plunged her hands under the cold water. She watched in the small mirror as the posse paraded inside the building with loud voices.

"Well, well, if it isn't Katie, best friend of the slut," Rachel said.

Katie smiled. "How were your hot dogs?"

There was a flushing sound, a stall door opened, and Helen exited. She stood by Katie and dipped her hands into the cold water. "Damn, that's really cold," she said under her breath.

"And look who we have here, the slut herself," Erica Ellison said with a sneer.

Helen let out a low growl and moved in a threatening manner in Erica's direction.

Katie lightly took Helen's arm and asked, "You ready?"

"Yep. Let's go, something really smells foul in here all of a sudden."

†

The night breeze hit Helen as she exited the bathroom. She looked at Katie, took her hand, and led her to the side of the building. Her fingers traced Katie's cheek before she leaned in and pressed her lips to Katie's. The kiss was sweet and tender, making Helen crave more. When Katie ran her tongue along Helen's lips she opened them willingly.

Katie moaned.

Helen wrapped her arms around Katie and held her closer. She pulled back slightly and looked at the woman in her arms. "It seems like I've wanted to kiss you forever."

Katie smiled. "I thought it was only me."

They kissed wantonly. Katie's hands tangled in Helen's hair and pulled her closer while Helen wrapped her arms around her waist.

Once again, the cackling of Brandie's voice had them breaking apart.

"Come on, we need to go before they get back and we're not there." Helen was breathing heavily.

Katie took Helen's hand and they began walking fast until they were halfway down the incline of the road.

"Look up there," Katie said. "That's the Southern Cross."

"Are you a stargazer too?"

"When I look at you I am." *I can't believe I said something that sappy. What a dork.* Katie was glad of the darkness—Helen couldn't see her blush.

A few seconds later, the four bitches were coming down the road with loud voices along with the annoying cackle of Brandie's laugh.

"How on earth do they stand that sound?" Helen asked.

"I never have."

Helen pointed to the sky. "Isn't that the Big Dipper?"

"Yep, it is." Katie said in a loud voice. "Do you see any other stars you recognize?"

The women passed them by with a noisy harrumph followed by loud audible whispering.

"Only nerds and freaks look at stars and know their names," Erica squawked.

"Guess they think that their words and actions are important." Helen chuckled.

"Just ignore them. We don't want to get into any sort of confrontation with them." Katie tried to stop shaking. "I want to kiss you again," she whispered.

Helen looked at the people sitting around the fire. "I can see them so I assume they can see us." Helen nodded in the direction of the water. "If we go down there and to the left I think we will be out of their line of sight." She took Katie's hand. "I want to kiss you too."

Deep in the blackness of the area, Helen and Katie stood face-to-face, holding each other and kissing passionately.

"God, I can't believe this," Katie whispered. "No one has ever made me feel so...so..."

"Turned on?"

"Yes." Katie pulled back a little. "You too?"

"Katie, I had no idea that the way my body is reacting right now ever existed. It's like you've burned a hole in my heart and crawled inside." Helen shook her head. "I'm a banker for God's sake. I don't *ever* throw caution to the wind. Everything is thought out and well planned yet with you I don't seem to be able to control my emotions."

"I like how that sounds. I want you," Katie said in a husky voice. "I have no idea of how but I want to make love with you."

"We may be fumbling our way through it but something tells me that it will be the most spectacular moment of my life." Helen leaned in, found Katie's lips, and began to devour them.

"Katie, where are you?"

The two women broke apart.

"Dammit, that's Jack." Katie cupped Helen's cheek. "We are far from being done."

"My sentiments exactly."

"I'm over here, Jack."

Until Jack became visible, Katie stood as close as she could to Helen, relishing in the feelings and emotions coursing through her mind and body.

"There you are," Jack said. "Why are you here in the dark?"

"I was showing Helen the stars and planets, and there was too much light back by the road to see them properly."

Jack put his arm around his wife's shoulders. "You're shivering." He took off his jacket. "Here put this on."

"I don't need your jacket," Katie said. "I was startled when you called my name. That's all."

Jack shrugged. "Okay, have it your way." He looked in Helen's direction. "You can't get a better teacher when it comes to stars or what's happening in the sky." He smiled. "She drags me out after midnight every August to see the Perseid meteor shower."

"She certainly has shown me a different side of her in her vast knowledge on the subject. I had no idea how fascinating stargazing could be." Helen laughed. "The other women said we were nerds and freaks for looking at the stars."

"Yes, Jack. Erica said that loud enough for us to hear. Didn't you hear her earlier when we were together? She wasn't nice."

"Harrumph, well, I tune out when you women gossip."

Katie narrowed her gaze. "Come on, they are about to serve dessert...homemade ice cream this year." Jack put his arm around Katie's shoulder. "Let's go get some before it is all gone."

"Lovely," Katie muttered. "Sandy ice cream. Yum."

Helen chuckled.

†

As hard as she tried, Helen couldn't stop gazing across the fire at the woman she'd held in her arms and kissed only moments before. A blaze was raging inside her that she knew only Katie could quench.

"Tomorrow we all go out deep-sea fishing."

Helen heard Bobby's words and rejoiced that they would be gone all day and she and Katie could have time alone. When her mind turned to being alone with Katie she tuned out everything else.

"Did you hear what I said?" Bobby asked.

Helen dragged her eyes off Katie and looked at her husband. "Yes, you're going deep-sea fishing tomorrow."

"Not just me. We paid for all of us to go together. They say the red snapper are bigger than ever."

"I don't like to fish and you know it," Helen spat. "You can count me out."

"I've already shelled out ninety-five bucks for you to be there and *you* will go."

Helen heard the tone of Bobby's voice and shivered. "Fine. I'll go. Don't expect me to fish. I don't like it and I'm not doing it."

"You can at least hold a pole. If you get a hit I will reel it in for you."

Bobby turned away to talk to one of his buddies.

Helen breathed a sigh of relief. Her attention turned to where Katie was sitting—she was gone.

Helen fervently looked all around but didn't see any sign of her. *Where did she go?* Helen could feel her heart deflate and tears threatened to fall.

"Hey."

Helen felt someone poke her in the back. When she heard the voice, she shivered before turning around to see Katie standing behind her. "Hey." She swiped at an errant tear that threatened.

"Are you okay?" Katie knelt next to Helen's chair.

Helen shook her head. "I'm fine." She looked into Katie's face and saw hope. "I looked over and you were gone," she whispered. "I'm not usually that emotional. It's just that..."

Katie smiled. "I know." She held out a bowl of ice cream. I got this myself, covered it with a napkin, and brought it to you so it should be free of sand."

"Until the napkin comes off." Helen smiled. "The wind will blow that sand right into the bowl."

"Then you better eat fast."

"Thank you. It was very kind of you to think of me."

"Always." Katie gently touched Helen's arm. "I need to get back."

"I know. Don't like it, but I understand."

Helen watched Katie walk away then looked down at the ice cream and grinned. The disillusionment that she was feeling only moments before turned into euphoria.

Katie returned to where she was sitting only to have Jack jump up.

"I'll be right back. I've got to make sure everything is ready for tomorrow. It is about a thirty-mile drive to Port Aransas and the Deep Sea Headquarters. We need to coordinate the time we leave."

Well, damn, I could have stayed where I was. She looked at Helen bathed in firelight. *My God, is she beautiful.* Katie could feel a tightening between her thighs when Helen looked at her. The look seared her soul, she was helpless to stop from closing her eyes, and going with the feelings that they invoked.

"What's going on between you two?" Rachel Matheson asked as she sat in Jack's seat.

Katie opened her eyes and looked at Rachel.

"I have no idea what you are talking about."

"Yeah, right." Katie shook her head. "What is it you want to know, Rachel? You haven't said more than two words to me since we got here."

"That's not true."

Katie raised her eyebrows. "Just ask your question then go away."

"We were wondering what is going on between you and that harlot, Helen."

"Hmm. This is a tough one. Would I rather hang out with someone who is kind and never bad-mouths anyone or with you and your three friends who love to tear others apart with your lies?" Katie winked at the woman. "Tell me, Rachel, who would you choose?"

"All I did was come over here to have a pleasant conversation with you and this is how you treat me. Well, if your tastes run toward someone like her then I'd say there is something very, very wrong with you."

"Contrary to your opinion, Rachel, I am very right in who I am and who I want to be friends with. You and *your* friends did nothing last year or this to get to know Helen. You make unfounded accusations without all the facts. At least you can try to be friendly toward her."

"Just what are the facts? Brandie says Karen told her that her heart was broken by not being here with us. And, it is all that woman's fault. She snared Bobby hook, line, and sinker."

Katie shook her head. "Brandie and Karen were bonded at the hip, Rachel. Brandie hung on every word Karen said and everything was gospel. Oh, forget it, this...is not my story to tell. If you want to know you'll have to ask Helen yourself."

"Well, I never."

"That is an understatement. Go back to your friends and tell them what I said."

Rachel stood.

"Oh, and try to keep the facts straight about what I said. I will know if you lie about me for one of your so-called friends tells me everything."

Katie watched as Rachel stormed off toward the other three and laughed. She observed that when Rachel sat down, the other three barraged her with questions. *Right about now she is wondering who it is that tells me what they say.* Katie laughed and looked at Helen, motioning for her to take the vacated seat.

"What's going on?"

"That's what she wanted to know."

"What is going on between you and me?"

"Yep."

Helen looked at the women who were all gaping at them. "What did you say?"

"I told them the truth."

Helen swallowed hard.

"I said I was mad about you and am trying to figure out a time when I can devour you," Katie whispered under her breath.

"Oh, you." Helen swatted Katie's shoulder. "What did you really say?"

"The usual. To paraphrase what I said...I told her that she and her friends are full of shit and one of them was telling me everything they say."

"Brilliant. Paranoia runs rampant amongst the bitches."

Helen held up her palm and Katie hit it.

"For the record, I meant what I first said." Katie held Helen's gaze. "The only problem is tomorrow is that damn fishing excursion. I don't know what they have planned for the next day. Hopefully they will all go golfing again. Other than that, I don't know what we are going to do but we will find a way to be together."

For a long moment, Helen looked at the burning fire. "Maybe we aren't meant to have a relationship."

"Is that what you believe, Helen?"

"No. No, I don't." Helen returned her gaze to the fire. "In three short days, I have found something I didn't even know I'd lost." Her gaze turned to Katie. "I want you more than I have ever wanted anyone," she whispered. "Let's see if we can come up with a plan tomorrow." Helen winked. "Unless you want to sneak out tonight."

"Don't tempt me."

"I guess I shouldn't. We already took a big chance out there on the beach. What if Jack hadn't called out to you and just happened upon us? What if someone discovers our attraction to each other? I'm afraid I'm not that good at subterfuge." She lifted a shoulder. "Do you think the men are speculating about us too?"

"Nope. Won't happen."

"Why?"

"They've got their heads so far up each other's ass that they can only see brown."

Helen laughed. "I hadn't thought of it that way. You, of course, are right."

"Tomorrow then."

"Definitely."

†

After stomping back to her chair, Rachel looked at the other three women and frowned.

"So what did you find out?" Erica Ellison asked.

"Nothing, other than one of you is telling her everything we say."

Brandie Markus's eyes widened. "You didn't believe her did you?"

Rachel shrugged.

"It's not me," said Cassie Walton. "I haven't said a word to the woman since that first day."

"Me either," Brandie added. "If you ask me, there is definitely something going on between those two. They are so buddy-buddy and have you noticed how much they touch each other?"

Rachel looked at Katie and Helen sitting next to each other. "Do you think that is how they see us?" *No way am I going to say anything bad about either of them.*

Brandie scowled. "Oh, come on now, you can't believe that."

51

"I don't know what to believe. Katie said we were spreading stories about Helen without knowing the facts." Rachel nodded in their direction. "Is that what we've done?"

"Rachel, Karen told me that Bobby was having an affair with Helen and that is why she divorced him." Brandie looked at the others. "Who do we believe? Our good friend Karen or that lying hussy who seems to have her clutches deep into Katie. We don't know what kind of bullshit she's feeding Katie."

"It must be something compelling for her to turn on us like she has," Cassie said.

"As for one of us telling her everything, that's a load of crap. She's just trying to make us distrust each other." Erica looked at the fire. "I hope none of you are going to take her remark seriously. I trust each of you. The one I don't trust is Helen."

"Do you think they are lesbians?" Brandie looked at each woman in the group.

"They certainly don't look the type," Cassie said. "Don't they have to look and dress like a man to be lesbians?"

"That's what I thought," Erica added. "Neither of them looks masculine. To be honest, they are both very pretty."

"That's true." Rachel scowled. "I've seen the men checking them out. Besides Jack wouldn't be married to someone like that. He's so masculine."

"Lust buzzards."

Everyone looked at Cassie and laughed.

"Where did you come up with *that* phrase?" Erica was grinning. "It is appropriate, though."

The others nodded.

Rachel, not knowing whom to trust, changed the subject. "That ice cream was good. I think I'll get some more."

Chapter Six

Helen pulled a pillow over her head.

"Get your ass out of bed. We need to be at the pier in an hour and a half," Bobby yelled.

She opened one eye. "It's still dark."

The hair in her face smelled of burned wood from the night before. *Last night.* Helen smiled. *Katie. If I hurry and get a shower, maybe I can maneuver it so we can sit next to each other while we drive there.* A vision of Katie came to mind—long ginger hair always in a ponytail, green eyes, freckles, and a figure that belied her age. *Exquisite. I can't wait to see her.* Helen's hand flew to her mouth. *What if she regrets kissing me?*

She rolled out of bed, pulled a pair of shorts, a short-sleeve shirt, and underwear from a drawer before heading for the shower. She growled when she heard the water running.

"Wouldn't you know it? That asshole is messing with my plans," she grumbled. Helen made her way to the coffeepot and poured herself a cup. The sound of the water stopped and with cup in hand and her clean clothes tucked under her arm, she went to the bathroom only to find the door closed.

"Come on, Bobby, I'd like to shower too."

The door opened and Bobby stood naked in front of her. "Plenty of time, babe, what do you think?"

"In your dreams." Helen pushed past him and closed the door. "Asshole. He probably used all the hot water." She stepped in the shower and ran her soapy hands over her body. Katie immediately came to mind. *I need to think of a way to be alone with her.*

†

Katie woke before the sun rose. The revelations of the night before played in her head like a short movie. She remembered every kiss, every touch and embrace. No one ever made her body hum the way Helen did. The fact that it was with a woman didn't bother her at all. All that mattered was her desperate need to see Helen again and touch her.

Katie sat in the sand with her arms wrapped around her knees and took in the beauty of the sky. The sun was rising over the Gulf and Katie wished Helen were there to share it with her. Threaded through the robin's egg-blue of the sky were purples and pinks before it turned white just as the sun began its ascent.

"Spectacular isn't it?"

Katie was sure her smile rivaled the spectacle of the sunrise. "I was just thinking that I wished you were here to share this with me."

"We must be on the same wavelength." Helen sat in the sand next to Katie. "How are you this morning?"

"Fantastic, and you?"

"Much better now."

Katie turned to look at Helen and frowned. "Did something happen with Bobby?"

Helen smiled and shook her head. "No. I woke up this morning and thought of you and wondered if you had any regrets," she said in a soft tone.

Not knowing if anyone else was around, Katie refrained from touching Helen even though she desperately wanted to. "Regrets? None at all. I dreamed about you, created fantasies of how I wanted to be with you." Katie looked over Helen's shoulder and saw Jack coming their way. "Crap," she whispered. "Why does he always feel compelled to track me down?"

"There you are. I figured you'd be up looking at the sunrise. We need to arrange who's going in what vehicle then head on out if we are going to be there on time."

"Jack," Helen said with a smile, "I was thinking that you and Bobby could sit in the front and Katie and I can ride in the back leaving room for two more of the guys in the middle. What do you think of that plan?"

"I think that is a great plan. I'll go make the arrangements. You two should go get your jackets and hats," Jack said over his shoulder as he walked away.

"You and me in the backseat huh?"

"Do you mind?"

"Heck no. Maybe we can put a small cooler on the seat so we will have to sit right next to each other." Katie shivered then laughed. "Wow, just the thought of that...wow."

Helen stood and held out her hand. "Come on. Let's go and get our things then climb into the backseat of your SUV."

Katie reached for Helen's hand and held it longer than necessary as another shiver coursed through her body.

"You felt it too?"

Katie nodded. "I'd rather spend the day with you than with the lot of them. Oh, God, I'm sounding like them aren't I?"

"No, I feel the same way." Helen kept hold of Katie's hand for part of the way as they walked away from the sunrise.

†

Katie put the small cooler on the seat, slid across it, and patted the seat next to her. "Sit here, Helen, that way you can rest your elbow on the cooler if you need to."

Helen grinned. "Thanks. I've got the drinks back here, guys. Just let me know if you need anything."

A series of four grunts was her reply.

"Not morning people are they?"

Katie shivered.

"Are you cold?" Helen asked.

"A little."

"Well, you're in luck, I packed a light blanket." Helen reached in the canvas bag by her legs. She pulled out a dark blue blanket, the size and kind the airlines used to use. She unfolded it and covered Katie's legs and shoulders. "Mind if I share?"

Katie nodded and watched as Helen covered her legs and shoulders too. The feel of Helen's bare leg touching hers made Katie suck in a deep breath. She rested her hand on Helen's thigh.

"Is that okay?"

Helen closed her eyes. "Perfect." She then placed her hand on Katie's thigh, looked at her friend and winked. "Getting warmer."

Katie squeezed Helen's thigh. "Almost."

"Too bad we are here with the others," Helen whispered.

Katie swallowed hard. "Yes, it is."

Helen's finger began to trace small circles on Katie's thigh.

With her eyes closed, Katie let her body melt into Helen. "Jack, the next place you see can we stop? I need to use the bathroom."

"Okay, but make it fast."

"I will."

Katie looked at Helen and saw a look that seared her soul. "Do you need to go too?"

Helen nodded.

"Looks like you're in luck. There is a gas station coming up," Jack said.

"Thank you. Does anyone else have to go?" asked Katie.

"I do," Helen said.

†

Helen and Katie climbed out of the SUV and walked quickly into the store.

Helen could feel the electricity between them as she asked for the key to the restroom. "Never in my life have I ever felt such intense emotion for anyone," she said in a low voice.

"Hmm. I feel it too."

"What are we going to do?"

Helen pushed open the door to the ladies' room. "It's a one-seater so you will have to wait in line." She grinned.

"I think not. We can go in there together."

With the door closed and locked, Helen pulled Katie to her. Her kisses were hungry and wanting and she could feel the tightening of her center when Katie answered her desire with a moan.

A knock on the door had Helen letting go of Katie. "Be out in a minute." She ran her fingers down Katie's cheek. "You are amazing."

Another insistent knock.

Katie flushed the toilet then ran water in the sink. "We'd better go," she said softly. "We need to stop meeting in bathrooms and find some place comfortable like a bed."

"I want you." Helen gave Katie one last kiss. "Forever."

†

The building for the deep-sea fishing excursion was the typical bait store—dark, dank, and smelly.

Helen and Katie walked quickly through the building to wait outside near the boat. They were standing together but not so close that they melded into each other. The next thing they knew the four bitches circled them, acting as if they were not there.

"Well, you know," Erica said, "I think it is just unnatural the way they are joined at the hip."

Brandie cackled.

"Well, I never would have believed someone like Katie is a homo. I bet that slut turned her just like she did Bobby," Cassie said.

"Excuse me," Helen said. "If Katie being friends with me makes you speculate that we are a couple then what does that make all of you? A four-way? From where I am standing, the four of you have been attached at the hip since you arrived—in fact, it's been that way for years from what Katie has said."

"Get real, bitch," Erica murmured. "Katie, do you really believe all the shit she spews?"

Katie raised an eyebrow. "It is a fact," she shrugged, "that you all are together all the time and are often nowhere to be found. Now I've heard of three-ways, but how does a four-way work?"

"Well, I never." Erica Ellison said.

"Haven't you heard about throwing stones in a glass house?" Katie raised an eyebrow. "Come on, Helen, I smell something most foul. Is it the same smell from the bathroom last night?" She sniffed in the air. "Nope, it isn't fish."

Helen laughed and began to walk away.

"You, ladies, and I use that term lightly, really ought to find out the facts and not be speculating by gossiping." Katie caught up with Helen.

"Are you okay?"

Katie let out the breath she was holding. "Yes. I've never been all that good at confrontation but damn that felt good."

"Sometimes getting in someone's face, especially if they are obnoxious, is freeing."

"I know one thing for sure."

"What's that?"

"There's no way we are sitting anywhere in their vicinity on the boat."

"I agree." Katie put her hand on Helen's shoulder and laughed. "If they only knew."

"They suspect."

"Yes, that is troublesome but not insurmountable. We just keep turning it back on them." Katie looked back at the foursome. "I've known them all for a long time and they are still the same bullies they have always been. My gran told me once that if they see you flinch they win."

"Then we won't flinch."

†

While everyone on board stood inside the cabin, the captain began his talk. He indicated where the life jackets were and what everyone should do and not do in case of an emergency. After introducing the crew and explaining how they'd assist everyone fishing, he cautioned that if anyone got seasick they should go outside and throw up over the rail on the leeward side.

"Lest you wanna have it come back in yer face," the captain said with a chuckle. "Now, let's get the boat started and find us some fish."

Although there were a few stragglers, most everyone in the cabin followed the captain out of the boat and found a place to sit and fish. Some who left the cabin went back in immediately and threw up in the waste can. A deckhand again made the announcement about throwing up over the rail, frowning as he changed the plastic liner.

†

"We're in luck," Helen said as she sat next to Katie. "The four of them are complaining about how cold it is so they are staying inside. I think I saw a couple of them throwing up."

"Really? I should go check on them."

"Why? I believe Jack told everyone to take something for seasickness before we left."

"I know, but doing what I do for a living makes me want to check on them."

"You're a good person, Katie. I'll save your seat."

"I take it they didn't have the foresight to pack a jacket or sweats."

"Katie, that would take planning and we know all they do is gossip."

"I will see how cold it is inside before I offer them our blanket."

Helen shook her head and smiled.

Five minutes later Katie returned. "Only Cassie and Brandie are throwing up and they are down to dry heaves now. I don't think they will be joining us any time soon."

"We can only hope the other two will stay inside with them," Helen said.

"Once the boat slows when we get to the fishing grounds they might venture out then."

"I hope not." Helen looked out at the water that surrounded the boat. "Look there!" She pointed to her left. "Dolphins. I count five of them...no six."

Katie scooted closer to Helen. "About on the way here..."

"You sitting so close to me now takes me back to being in the backseat with you." She looked around and saw they were alone. "No one has ever made me feel the way you do, Katie," Helen whispered.

"What's next?"

"You mean for today?"

"No." Katie's voice was just above a whisper, "Tomorrow...and after."

"I believe the squad is going golfing and the four of them," Helen nodded toward the interior of the boat, "are going along. Then that night we go to that fancy restaurant we went to last year."

"What about you and me? What are we doing?"

Helen leaned in. "I want to make love with you."

Katie closed her eyes and smiled. "Were you reading my mind?"

"Yes, along with your body language." Pleasure coursed through Helen's body and she let out a soft moan. "I haven't a clue on the how but I bet we won't have any problems in the doing." She moved close enough so that their bodies were touching.

"They will leave around eight." Katie looked at her wristwatch. "Twenty-one hours and counting." She grinned. "It can't come fast enough for me."

"Me either."

"Pardon me, ma'am. I have your poles," a deckhand named Sean said.

"For both of us?" Helen asked.

"Yes, ma'am. I will also bait your hooks for you."

Katie and Helen took their fishing poles and waited while Sean baited their hooks before throwing them out into the Gulf.

"What are we fishing for today?" Helen asked.

"Red snapper."

"Yum, one of my favorites."

Helen looked at Sean and smiled. "Thank you."

"Just let me know if you need anything."

Katie laughed when the twenty-something boy left. "Should I be jealous?"

"No, why should you?" Helen frowned.

"Did you see how he was carrying his knife?" Katie asked with a grin.

"You mean hanging down like a phallic symbol?"

Katie nodded. "Do you think it was advertising on his part? He certainly seemed taken with you."

"He was?"

"Yes, not that I blame him." Katie laughed. "He was practically drooling."

"You're joking right? He's young enough to be my son."

"No joke. Just wait until you catch a fish. I bet he will be here in a second."

"You're on." Helen thought for a moment. "What do I win when I'm right?"

Katie rubbed her chin before leaning in closer. "Me," she whispered. "And if I win—I get you."

"You already have me," Helen said. She felt a tug on the line. "Hey, I've got something already." She began reeling in the line.

Sean was there immediately. "As soon as you land it I will take it off the hook for you then bait your hook again."

Helen landed a red snapper and watched as Sean expertly removed the fish, baited her hook, and threw it back in the water, before picking up the fish.

"It's a nice size," Sean said before disappearing around the corner.

"Where's he taking it?"

"There is a gigantic cooler filled with ice where they put all the fish caught."

"Is my name on it?"

"No, I don't think so. Each person on the boat, fishing or not, has a limit of two fish. There are around fifty people on the boat so that means a maximum of one hundred fish for this boat. Once they reach that limit all fishing will stop and back we go to the marina."

"But what if mine is the biggest and someone else gets it?"

Katie laughed. "I'm sure Sean will make sure you get your fish." She winked. "By the way, I win."

With a serious look, Helen studied Katie's face. "There never was a contest. You'd always win, hands down."

"Hey, I got one." Katie, laughing, began reeling in the fish. "Get your pal Sean over here."

†

Back at the dock, Sean divvied the fish between the fifty people from the boat, who were now standing in a circle. Those who were just along for the ride each got two fish.

"That's not fair," said Helen as the four women from their group had fish dropped in front of them.

"That's how it is done. Besides, look at the sizes we got." Katie giggled. "Sean did right by you and obviously had a similar inclination about the squad wives. I wonder what they said to him. Did you see the size of their fish?"

Katie turned when an arm went around her shoulders. "Oh, Jack," she clutched at her shirt, "why do you always sneak up on me like that?"

"I wasn't sneaking up on you, sugar. I called out your name."

Katie furrowed her brow. "No, you didn't. I would have heard you."

"Tell her, Helen. You heard me didn't you?"

Helen smiled before tensing at Jack's arm wrapped possessively around Katie's shoulder. "Actually, I didn't hear you either. Katie was explaining to me why the other wives got fish even though they didn't catch any."

Jack looked over to the women. "They got the small ones. They won't get many meals outta 'em."

"Yes, that is what Katie said."

"Hey, we are gonna have them clean and wrap the fish for us while we get a bite to eat at the Fish House across the street."

Katie rolled her eyes. "Haven't we had enough to do with fish for one day? Can't we go somewhere else?"

"Not to worry. I checked the menu and they have a variety of items and not just fish."

"Are they all going along or is it just Helen, Bobby, you, and me?" Katie asked.

"Nope, the squad sticks together."

"Really? What's with you people that no one can have any time alone? Everyone always has their noses up in everyone else's business." Katie moved away from Jack's arm on her shoulder. "For the record, you should be applauding Helen. For the first time in years I'm actually enjoying this trip."

62

"Well, that's great, hon. Everyone in the squad—wives too—are all like family to me."

"I'm glad to hear that, Jack. As for their wives…well they are not on the top of my list right now."

Jack had a hurt look on his face. "They are my buddies' wives. Besides, you and Helen have had loads of time alone when we go to the golf course."

"Yes we have and that is what has made this time so special."

Helen knew Katie well enough to see she was beginning to get agitated. She grabbed Katie's arm but looked at Jack. "What time are we to meet at the Fish House?"

"'Bout, thirty minutes—once we get all the fish squared away." Jack's face softened. "We gotta get our pictures taken by our catch first."

"Do you think I can meet you there? I have a splitting headache and need to find a place to buy something for it."

"Helen, are you okay?" Katie asked. "Come with me. I think I saw some aspirin inside the bait shop."

"I don't think I could stand the smell of that place right now. I was just going to find a drugstore."

"I'll go with you." Katie turned to her husband. "We will meet you at the Fish House."

"Can you wait a minute, Helen, so we can get our picture with the fish? They are just hanging them up now."

"Of course we can, Jack. I would like to have proof for the guys at my firm that I actually did catch fish."

†

Helen saw an empty bench and walked to it. "Please, sit with me."

Katie shook her head. "Sorry. How is the head?"

Helen cocked her head to the side. "Sit. Please."

With a quick nod Katie sat.

"Thank you." Helen took Katie's hand in hers. "You know they are already speculating about us so we can't add fuel to the fire by going off to eat somewhere else. What do you want to do? Sit in the SUV and make out while they're having a meal?"

"It would be better than sitting with them, especially if we get to kiss." A small grin turned up her lips. "It is bad enough we have to endure eating in a restaurant with them tomorrow night. Can't we just have time to ourselves?"

"No, not this time."

Katie pouted.

"That's not going to work no matter how cute you are with you lip stuck out. We can suffer through a meal with them now. Tomorrow morning they will all leave for one last round of golf. We will have most of the day to ourselves."

Katie closed her eyes. "I'm sorry I think my hormones are on overload. Here you are with a headache and I'm bellyaching about where we're going to eat. I'm usually more sympathetic than this. It's just that I'm so frustrated being around them when all I want is to be with you." She stood. "Come on, let's find you a drugstore."

Helen gave Katie's hand a squeeze before letting go. "I really don't have a headache."

Katie's brow furrowed. "You lied?"

"I could see you were getting worked up, and I wanted to get you away so you could calm down."

"Thank you for watching out for me."

"You're welcome. We are here now and have to make the best of it." Helen lifted Katie's chin and turned her face to her. "What if we get there first and sit next to each other. If anyone tries to sit next to us we will say we are saving the seats for our husbands. Trust me, the last person I want beside me is Bobby, but he is better than any of those women."

"I guess this isn't the time or place to kiss you but that is exactly what I want to do right now."

Helen grinned. "I bet the Fish House has a bathroom with a lock on the door." She laughed. "Another bathroom."

Katie laughed too. "We seem to be using them a lot." She stood and held out her hand. "Come on, I really *do* need to pee."

†

A smiling Katie pushed open the door of the Fish House and stopped dead in her tracks.

Helen bumped into Katie's back. "What's the matter?"

"Freakin' unbelievable."

"What?" Helen peered over Katie's shoulder. "We just left the boat place ten minutes ago. What the hell are they doing here already? Didn't they have to wait for their pictures with their catch too?"

In the distance, Jack was waving.

Katie waved back and pointed toward the bathrooms.

Jack gave her a thumbs-up.

Helen knocked on the bathroom door and hearing no response opened the door.

"Thank God, it's another one-seater." Katie locked the door. "Did you see how the table was arranged?"

"Yeah, the four of them together with one chair empty on either side."

"It's like some evil plot they hatched in less than ten minutes." Katie turned to Helen. "How the hell did that happen?" She ran her fingers through her hair and held her head. "I can't believe it."

"Hey." Helen pulled Katie into her arms. "Do you trust me?"

Katie snorted. "What do you think?"

"I'll take that as a yes." Helen lifted Katie's chin before she kissed her. "The side of me I've allowed you to see is one no one else ever sees. In the real world, people consider me a bitch who is heads above than any of them. I didn't get to be in the position I'm in by being cuddly, sweet, and nice. I had to step on a lot of heads to get to where I am." She gestured at the door. "I would have had those four women for lunch and never flinched."

"Meaning?"

"It is the time to let that Helen out so she can take them down."

"That sounds ominous. If it were me...well, you know how that went, don't you? They blamed it all on your influence." Katie cupped Helen's cheek. "What will Bobby say when you put the *squad's* wives in their place?"

Helen raised an eyebrow. "Hey, he hit me, remember. He owes me."

"I'm sorry."

"Don't be. After being with you I know why men never interested me."

"I can say the same thing." Katie smiled. "What's next?"

"Our mission now is to take the bitches down."

"You can do that?"

"Watch me." Helen gave Katie a quick kiss and unlocked the door. "Just play along. Okay?"

"Yep, I've got your back."

†

"Hold your head up high. It will give us an edge," Helen said.

"Okay. I'm not sure I can sit by any of them throughout a whole meal."

"You'll be fine," Helen whispered as they approached the table.

Standing behind Erica and Cassie, who she considered the weakest women, wanting just to be part of the group, Helen grinned. "Excuse me, Cassie."

The woman looked up at Helen. "Do you mind sitting over there by Brandie? I'd really like to be in amongst you all since we haven't had much time together."

Cassie looked at the others before obediently standing and taking the empty chair.

Katie took a seat between Brandie and Erica.

"Great. Oh no. I see you all are still a bit green in the gills. You haven't recovered yet from vomiting all the time we were on the boat."

"We did not," Rachel proclaimed.

Helen fished out her phone. "Sure you did. I have pictures of the four of you around a big green trash can heaving your guts out." She turned on her phone. "Would you like to see?"

"No," Brandie barked.

"We were there to catch fish and all you caught was the whiff of each other's vomit." Helen grinned.

"Well, I never," Erica said.

"That's an understatement," Helen purred. "I understand that you often gossip that I was the cause of Karen and Bobby's marriage breaking up."

"We did not," Brandie said.

"Yes, you did," Katie interjected. "You trashed her the day we all arrived."

Helen stood. "Bobby, will you please come here and settle something for me."

Bobby looked at his wife in confusion and scraped back his chair.

Helen grinned when Bobby came to her side.

"Bobby, these ladies think that you and Karen divorced because you and I were having an affair," she said. "Is that true?"

Bobby looked bewildered. "No. Where the hell did they hear that? We met months after my divorce." He looked at the other women. "Who told you that?"

The bitches stayed silent.

Bobby shook his head and walked away.

"Hmm, it seems that you were all misled. Now, I'd like to sit next to my friend Katie. Rachel, you may take this seat."

Katie chuckled when the woman vacated her chair.

Helen took Rachel's place and patted Katie's thigh. "That, my dear, is how it is done."

"Remind me never to piss you off." Katie laughed. "Take a look at them. It's like they are afraid to look in our direction."

"Forget about them," Helen whispered. "What are you going to order?"

"Fish, of course."

"I'm not a big fan of fish."

They both laughed.

Chapter Seven

Katie woke before Jack and hurried into the kitchen to make coffee and start breakfast. There was no way she'd let her husband be late for his golf date. Her thoughts turned to Helen and her handling of the other women the night before. The four of them spent the whole dinner looking dour and appearing to be licking their wounds. They refused to look in her direction and left like a pod of whales.

"The woman certainly is a force to be reckoned with," she muttered.

"Who you talkin' about?" Jack entered the kitchen area.

Katie turned. "I didn't hear the shower run."

"I'll take one when I get back. I think we will only play nine holes today. The other guys' wives want to play too."

"But, Jack, this is the last chance you have to play with the squad. You should do eighteen and the women can stay in the clubhouse while you play the second nine."

Jack scratched his head. "Maybe. Hey, what was that all about down at your end of the table last night? You never did answer me when I asked. Bobby came back shaking his head saying *women.*"

"Nothing really. The other wives were speculating that the reason Karen and Bobby divorced was because Helen came on the scene."

"Was she?"

"No, and Bobby told them so."

"They really said that about Helen?"

"Yes. I've told you before they were vicious." Katie shrugged. "You never listen to me."

"That's not true."

68

Katie, not wanting a confrontation, just shook her head and handed him a large insulated cup of coffee. "Do you want something to eat? I've got bacon and eggs that I can make or are you all going to have breakfast on the way?"

Jack looked out the window. "Looks like they are almost ready to go." He grabbed a banana. "This will be enough." He gave Katie a quick kiss on the cheek.

"Please call me when you are on your way back so I can start getting ready for tonight."

"Will do, if I can get any reception. It's spotty at best."

†

Katie smiled as Jack went down the steps and exited the RV. She went to the window and watched as he and the others piled into cars. "Six men, four women." When the vehicles were out of sight, she hurried to the bathroom to take a shower and make sure her legs were silky smooth.

After her shower, Katie pulled on a robe, and hurried into the bedroom and removed the sheets from the bed. Once she changed the sheets, Katie put the dirty ones into the washing machine and started it. Then, she started pacing the length of the RV. Every so often, she would look out the window for any sign of Helen.

"Where is she?"

Katie recalled the drive back from dinner the night before when she and Helen were again sitting in the backseat.

Helen leaned into her and whispered, "Are you ready for tomorrow?"

"I feel like I've been ready all my life," Katie answered.

She looked out the window again. "Where can she be?"

When she heard a light tapping on the door, Katie had to stand still for a moment while a shiver coursed through her body. Once she gathered her composure, she went to the door and opened it. Helen was standing there dressed in a thin T-shirt and skimpy shorts. Her eyes immediately went to the protruding nipples and she gasped—Helen wasn't wearing a bra.

"You take my breath away," Katie whispered. "I thought you said your nipples never protruded?"

"Apparently all it took was the right person." Helen grinned. "May I come in?"

Katie took a step back. "I thought you weren't coming."

Helen climbed the two steps, closed the door, and locked it behind her.

"I came right after they all left but you didn't answer. I figured you were in the shower or maybe still sleeping."

Katie pulled Helen to her and kissed her lips.

"You shoulda let yourself in and joined me in the shower."

"Next time I will."

They kissed their way to the bedroom and stopped by the bed.

"This is a big step we're taking. Are you sure you still want this?" Helen asked.

"Yes." Katie put her hands under Helen's T-shirt and lifted it over her head. Next came the shorts and she giggled when she realized that Helen did not have any underwear on. She took a step back and admired Helen's body.

"You're magnificent. Absolutely magnificent," she whispered. "I want you more than I've ever wanted anyone or anything in my life."

Helen smiled as she untied the robe then ran her hands over Katie's shoulders lifting the robe so it slid off.

Katie suddenly became very self-conscious and looked at her feet. "My body is not...I haven't taken as good of care of it as I should have. Now, I wish I had. I can only imagine how disappointed you must be to see this." Katie waved a hand up and down her body.

Helen placed a finger over Katie's lips. "I love how you look." She smiled. "You have all the curves in the all right places."

"I do?"

"Yes." Helen wrapped her arms around Katie and their bodies melded together as if they were one. She tapped Katie's lips then let one finger trace down her chin, neck, chest, through the valley of her breasts, until she stopped at the navel. "Come lay with me and let me show you how you make me feel."

Katie pulled back the sheets and moved to the center of the bed.

Helen lay down beside Katie and gathered her in her arms. "Let me show you, Katie."

Helen had an idea of what she needed to do to pleasure Katie. She had only one experience before she met Bobby but knew what she liked. Bobby was the first one to have oral sex with her and she found it very pleasurable. Of course, once she refused to return his ministrations he never did it to her again. The night before, while Bobby slept, she went on the Internet and researched how to please a woman sexually. She would take her time, lavish Katie's body with her lips and hands, hoping it would bring her to an orgasm.

She began kissing Katie's lips then her cheeks and nose. She kissed down Katie's body until she reached her breasts then took a hardened nipple into her mouth and rolled her tongue around it. Her thumb and forefinger gently squeezed the other nipple.

Katie's hand holding fast to her hair encouraged Helen to linger and continue to pay homage to the perfectly shaped breast.

Eventually, Helen's lips continued down Katie's body, stopping at her navel where she tongued it, eliciting a moan from Katie.

She kissed her way down one leg, sucking on each toe, then made her way up Katie's other leg until she parted her legs and ran her tongue the full length of Katie's center.

"Oh, my God. Please don't stop," Katie cried. "I need you inside."

Helen sucked on the hardened nub, drawing it into her mouth. She heard Katie's continuing pleas, and easily slipped two fingers inside.

Katie began moving her hips immediately. "More, please, Helen, more."

With her free hand, Helen reached for a nipple and began rolling it between her fingers before she slipped one more finger into Katie's velvety insides. Her teeth were gently nipping at the swollen clitoris. It didn't take long for Helen's fingers and tongue to be in sync with Katie's thrusting hips. She could feel Katie tightening around her fingers just before her hips rose and her body arched. She cried out in ecstasy.

Helen kissed her way up to Katie's mouth and kissed her soundly.

With closed eyes and rapid breathing, Katie whimpered. When she opened her eyes, she grinned. "No one has ever made me feel the way you just did. No one. Never have I felt so adored." She ran her tongue over Helen's lips. "Is that how I taste?"

Helen nodded. "You are delicious. Did you like it?"

Katie wiggled her eyebrows. "Let me show you."

She flipped Helen on her back then lay on top of her. "I want you so much. I think I always have." Her kisses were gentle until Helen growled. Her mouth watered before she began her loving assault in earnest on Helen's body.

†

For the rest of the morning, Katie sought repeatedly to make love with Helen. At first she was awkward but as she learned more about how to pleasure Helen the more confident she became. When they both fell back, spent by the physicality and the emotions it evoked, Katie smiled.

"My God, Helen. I can't believe I've missed out on these emotions all my life. I feel even more like some teenager who just discovered sex and can't get enough."

Helen let out a satisfied sigh. "Deep down I knew something was missing from my life and here you are filling that need."

Katie lightly touched Helen's abdomen with her fingers then stopped at a small scar. "You have five of these scars. Did you have a hysterectomy?"

"Ah, the medical woman appears. Yes. I had one about three years ago."

"Why? Endometriosis?"

Helen shook her head. "No. Endometrial cancer."

Katie put her hand over Helen's heart. "Did you have chemo and radiation?"

"No." Helen put her hand over Katie's hand. "We caught it in the earliest of stages so all I had was a complete hysterectomy."

"Do you know how incredibly lucky you are?" Katie asked. "Most of the time when symptoms finally appear to where the patient notices bleeding or discharge, it has already metastasized."

"I had an incredible general practice doctor and the place she chose to biopsy in my uterus was exactly where it was." Helen leaned in and kissed her lover. "I believe things happen as they should even if we don't understand the whys. Obviously, I was destined to meet you and that meant I had to survive and live."

"I don't want to lose you," Katie whispered.

"You never will." Helen's eyebrow rose. "Why would you think that?"

"We leave tomorrow. You will go back to your life in Dallas and I will go back to mine in Austin."

"First of all, Dallas is only four hours away. Secondly, I have an apartment in Austin and once I sort things out with Bobby, I will move there."

"Just like that?"

"Yep, just like that."

"That's rather impulsive. I thought you money types tended to take the conservative approach."

Helen smiled. "Trust me. No one is more surprised by my actions than I am. For some reason, being with you feels so right that giving into my baser instincts are easy."

"You still plan on divorcing Bobby?"

"Yes. His hitting me made me realize even more what a mistake it was to marry him in the first place."

"Do you want me to go ahead and divorce Jack like I've wanted to for some time now?"

Helen shook her head. "I want you to do what feels right for you."

"But..."

From outside the sound of Brandie's obnoxious voice rang.

"Shit, they're back early. I told Jack to call me when he was on his way. He is usually reliable on that front."

Helen was out of the bed pulling on her shorts, shirt, and slipping her feet into her sandals. She sniffed. "Do you have any room spray?"

73

Katie reached for the nightstand next to her and flipped on the switch for a diffuser. Instantly the scent of lavender filled the room.

Helen ran into the bathroom and came back with a wet washcloth. "Here wipe your face and mouth then put it on your forehead."

With a quick motion Katie wiped down her face.

"Stay here. Put some clothes on then get back in the bed and take a nap. You have a splitting headache and we saw a vagrant. Oh, and don't forget the washcloth."

"Where will you be? They will see you leaving."

"Trust me."

"I do."

Katie watched as Helen left the room and closed the door behind her before scrambling to put her clothes on. She licked her lips and still tasted Helen then wiped her face again with the washcloth. She smiled before rubbing some hand cream on her hands and face.

†

Helen moved quickly to the door and unlocked it as silently as she could. Once done, she picked up a book from the couch, shook off her sandals, sat with her legs curled under her, and opened the book.

It seemed like a lifetime, but eventually she heard the door open and she surreptitiously watched as Jack entered the RV.

"Helen?" Jack glanced around the area with a concerned look on his face. "Where's Katie?"

"She had a headache and is lying down."

"Why are you here?"

"We are the only two in the camping area and I told her I'd stay out here to make sure no one tried to get in."

"That sort of thing never bothered her before," Jack said. His eyes looked at her with a hint of disbelief in them.

Helen heard suspicion in his voice. "When we came back from looking for shells Katie saw a man who looked like a derelict hanging around the bathroom area." Helen paused. If she was going to sell this story, she had to embellish it more. "Katie said he looked like a patient of hers when he was strung out on drugs." She shrugged. "She said he was really scary looking."

Jack frowned. "Did you alert the rangers?"

"How could we? All our vehicles were gone and we didn't have keys to those that were here." She shrugged. "I didn't want to leave her here alone while I walked to the visitor's center." She looked directly at Jack. "If he was still around I'd also be a prime target walking by myself."

"It never occurred to me that we were leaving you two here without transportation." He looked toward the closed bedroom door. "I'd better check on her."

"Okay, that's a good idea. I'm sure she will be reassured that you are here now." Helen stood. "I'd best get back to my own place and see what Bobby is up to."

Katie listened at the door and heard everything Helen said. When Jack indicated he was going to check on her, she hurried to the bed, got in, and pulled the sheet over her. She finally appreciated the smallness of the bedroom.

The door opened.

Katie held her breath commanding her racing heart to slow down. She closed her eyes, and rolled her pupils down below the lid. That way, she knew she wouldn't blink and give herself away.

Jack stroked Katie's hair. "Are you okay?" he whispered.

Katie didn't move.

"Katie," he said louder.

"Hmm," Katie moaned. "My head hurts."

"Can I get you something for it?"

"I already took something."

"Okay, I will be right outside if you need anything." He turned to go then stopped. "I'm sorry I left you here without an option for getting away. I'm going down to the ranger station and report a suspicious person lurking around the area. What did he look like?"

Katie yawned. "Tall, skinny, long greasy black hair and an unkempt beard."

"Okay, I will tell them that. Do you want me to ask Helen to come back and stay with you while I'm gone?"

Yes. "No, everyone is back so I should be safe. Just lock the door when you leave and let someone know where you are going and why."

"I'll go get Helen so she can go with me and help with the description."

Katie panicked. "No. Don't do that."

"Why not? Didn't she see the man too?"

"No. Her back was to him and I told her not to turn around since he might think we were alone. I was the only one that saw him clearly. By the time we got back here he was gone."

"Well, at least you saw him. I hope I don't have to come back and get you so you can talk to them yourself."

"Jack, please do not make this out to be more than it was. I saw a man. He frightened me. He's gone. End of story."

"Okay. I will alert the others to keep an eye out for him."

Katie listened as the door to the RV closed and she let out the breath she was holding. *When did I become such a good liar? I'm having an affair with Helen.* She smiled. *How long can I keep lying to him?* She pictured Helen and grinned broadly. *To keep Helen in my life I will do what I have to.*

Chapter Eight

The night air was warm and the six couples opted to sit outside for their evening meal at the restaurant. The four wives in a subdued, non-confrontational way were still chortling about Helen. They did not sit anywhere near her, leaving Helen and Katie to sit next to their husbands.

From her position on the other side of the table, Helen stole quick surreptitious glances at Katie, and her reward every time was a smile.

In a way, she was glad they weren't sitting next to each other. Helen didn't think she could keep from touching her. She looked around the table. *I wonder if any of the others can feel the sexual tension between us.* She only saw that each person, except Katie, was either stuffing their faces with the appetizers or talking with the person sitting next to them.

Helen's eyes tracked back to Katie and what she saw made her squeeze her thighs together. There was blatant need and desire on Katie's face. The look was undeniable; then she noticed Bobby was staring at Katie also.

"Is there something going on between you and Katie?" Helen asked.

Bobby's face flushed. "No."

"Then why is she looking at you?"

Bobby looked down at the table and began fidgeting with his eating utensils.

Helen grinned and winked in Katie's direction. "I don't think Madeline would be happy if she knew." Helen chuckled. "I might just have to tell her."

Bobby snarled, "I am not having an affair with Katie. She's my best friend's wife. I would never do such a thing," he said in a deep, angry voice. "If you know what's good for you," he whispered, "you'll keep your mouth shut."

Helen threw her napkin on the table and scraped her chair back. "Or what, Bobby," she whispered in his ear, "you'll hit me again?"

"God damn it, can't you let that go," he growled.

"No." Helen turned away and walked inside the restaurant and to the bathroom.

†

Helen entered the restroom and bent to look under the stall door to see if anyone was in there with her—she was alone. Several minutes later, two women Helen did not know entered the bathroom.

Disappointment and fear filled her soul as she entered the stall to settle her raging emotions and her trembling hands. *I wonder if he will hit me now or even rape me tonight.* All she needed to do was be safe one more day and then her sister and husband would keep her away from his rage. She heard the sound of the two women's laughter before the door opened and closed.

Resigned that Katie did not follow her into the bathroom she opened the stall door and stopped. Eyes filled with desire were staring at her.

"I didn't think you'd follow since it would be too obvious," Helen whispered.

"You are so beautiful." Katie took a step closer. "I need to touch you, feel you, and love you."

The door opened and a young girl entered the room.

"There's something to be said for a one-seater," Helen quipped. She reached out and gently stroked a finger down Katie's cheek. "Now that I know how much I feel for you I need the same thing."

The stall door opened and Katie took a step back.

The young twenty-something woman smiled at them, washed her hands, and left.

"I'd better get back to the table before Bobby puts two and two together."

"Why would he do that?"

"The look on your face was unmistakable. It was full of want and need and he saw that. I asked if there was something going on between the two of you."

Katie's eyes grew wide. "No. You didn't. Did you?"

"Like I said, I don't want him jumping to any conclusions. Either you were looking at him or me."

After giving Katie a light hug, Helen opened the door before looking back and blowing a kiss in Katie's direction.

†

Katie returned to the table just as the wait staff was serving the meal. She purposely did not look across the table—she couldn't trust her eyes not to betray her feelings. The server set a plate in front of her and she looked at it in confusion.

"I didn't order this," Katie said.

The man that served her meal was now putting a plate in front of Jack.

The waiter who took her order was immediately by the server's side. "Is there a problem?"

"I didn't order this," Katie repeated.

"You ordered a filet with mushroom sauce along with asparagus and a baked potato," the waiter said.

"No, I didn't. I don't like mushrooms or asparagus so I never would have ordered this."

The waiter turned to Jack. "Is that the meal you ordered, sir?"

"Yes."

The waiter then turned to Mike Ellison, who was sitting to Katie's left. "Is that what you ordered, sir?"

"Yes, it is."

Katie frowned when the waiter presented her with an order slip generated by the kitchen.

"You can clearly see the orders on either side of you are correct. Therefore, what I have for the person between them—that would be you—is exactly what you ordered."

79

Katie placed her napkin on the table, scooted her chair back, and stood. "Take me to the manager, please."

"I will gladly order you something else," the waiter said.

"What you don't seem to understand," Katie looked at his name tag, "Henry, is that I am the customer and the customer is always right. I told you I didn't order that meal and that should have been the end of it. Yet, you stuck your order sheet in my face trying to prove what I ordered is on the plate in front of me. Perhaps if you had written the orders down this mistake wouldn't have happened."

"Please sit down, Katie. You're making a scene. I will trade plates with you," Jack pleaded.

Katie looked down at her husband. "I don't want your food. I want what I ordered and that," she pointed at her plate, "isn't it."

The manager arrived at the table. "Is something wrong?"

"Yes, there is." Katie pointed to the waiter. "Henry here is trying to prove to me that what is on that plate is what I ordered." She glared at the waiter. "It isn't what I ordered."

"Of course, ma'am. Tell me what you'd like and I will see that it is made for you."

"And do what? Sit here and watch while everyone else eats? They will all be eating their dessert when I *finally* get my meal. I think not."

"Please, miss, tell me what I can do to make this right."

"Nothing." Katie was shaking with anger toward the man. That, along with her desperate need for Helen, made her turn and walk away.

†

Jack looked around the table at the others. "I'm sorry. She hasn't had a good day and is plagued with a migraine. The medication she took for it always puts her on edge."

Everyone around the table nodded in what looked, to Jack, like sympathy.

He turned to the waiter and manager who were still standing there. "I apologize for my wife's behavior but that is not the meal she ordered. This man," he pointed at the waiter, "should never have insisted that it was. She asked for a medium-rare New York strip steak, with a baked potato and a small green salad. That is what she always orders and you can clearly see that is not what is on her plate."

"Please accept my apologies for this problem occurring in the first place." The manager glared at his waiter. "I will make sure her meal is deducted from the bill and offer a free dessert for everyone here. Again, I am sorry for the mix-up, sir. Would you like me to get her the meal you described?"

"No, I don't think she would eat it. Thanks anyway."

Jack was digging into his meal when he heard his name.

"What's wrong with you, Jack," Helen said from across the table. "If you knew that wasn't what she ordered why the hell didn't you tell the waiter that in the first place? Why did you have to wait for it to all blow up before you acted like a man and spoke up for her?"

"Helen, watch your tongue," Bobby advised.

Jack held up his hand. "No, Bobby, she's right. I should have stuck up for my wife. I'll go find her."

Helen's feet pressed against the floor as she scooted her chair back. "Let me go. It's obvious she is very angry about what happened. I'll see if I can find her and unruffle her feathers before you speak with her."

"Thank you," Jack said gratefully. "I was such a jerk."

"Yes, you were. Let me go find her." Helen began to walk away before turning back. "You should have insisted he comp everyone's meal," she said before leaving.

Helen walked past Rachel and Brandie and overheard them saying, "she must be menopausal." She glared at them and they immediately looked away. *Bitches.* The other two women were giggling but when Helen passed them, they also stopped what they were doing.

†

Katie was sitting on a concrete wall in a dark corner of the patio where no diners sat. She suddenly felt chilled and didn't know whether it was from the night air or the emotions raging inside her. She was always the peacemaker who was never confrontational yet now in the course of several days she felt the need to attack and defend. *My hormones are raging and Helen's the reason. She is all I think about. I need to get hold of myself before everything implodes around me.* After their morning tryst, sitting across from Helen and not having contact was maddening. Her rampant feelings for Helen were making her crazy.

"Hey, are you okay?"

Katie looked up and saw Helen and it ignited an unquenchable fire inside her. "I knew you'd come."

"I did what my heart told me to do." Helen smiled. "It led me to you." She sat next to Katie. "What's going on?"

"I'm desperate to make love with you again. It is so frustrating to sit across from you and not be able to touch you."

Katie leaned in to Helen and kissed her.

"Not here," Helen whispered. "We are taking too many chances. They almost caught us earlier."

"Where?" Katie asked. "You've unleashed something in me that is unquenchable."

Helen took Katie's hand and led her to the darkest corner. Surrounding her lover with her arms she kissed Katie deeply.

"I need to touch you." Katie slid her hand down the front of Helen's slacks and under her silk panties.

Helen let out a moan. "Someone will see us."

"No, they won't." Katie easily inserted three fingers inside Helen. "You're so wet."

"God, Katie, what you are doing to me. We can't do this here." Feelings of need filled her body and she moaned.

"Want me to stop?"

"No never." It was only a matter of minutes before Helen felt her orgasm begin to erupt. She held Katie tight until the sensation slowed before passing.

Katie slowly removed her fingers before withdrawing her hand. She grinned before sucking on her fingers. "You taste delightful and very needy."

Helen rested her forehead on Katie's and sighed. "What are we going to do? This is so risky."

"We will work it out. There is no way I am going to let you go."

"I can't believe how much I need you, Katie," Helen whispered.

"Katie? Where are you?" Jack's voice cut through the darkness.

Both women moved apart.

"Damn it." Katie ran a finger down Helen's cheek. "Over here, Jack."

"Wow, could you have found a darker corner?" Jack moved to his wife and held her in his arms. "I'm sorry I didn't tell that nincompoop of a waiter that you only ever order a New York strip steak."

"I'll leave you two alone," Helen said.

"No. I'll go back with you. It's too dark for you to walk alone."

Helen looked at Jack then at Katie. "I will be okay. I'm sure you and Jack need to talk without me listening."

Katie took Helen's hand. "Come on, we will all go back together. I'm sure both your dinners are getting cold."

Chapter Nine

The drive back to the RV park was intolerably long for Helen. Instead of sitting in the back as she had previously with Katie, she was stuck sitting next to Bobby, who was driving. Jack and Katie went in their vehicle and Helen was dealing with a sense of acute loss. She kept recalling the brief moments that they had together when Katie pleasured her. Each thought made her squeeze her thighs together as the now familiar sensations Katie evoked in her threatened to erupt once again.

"Are we all going to sit outside tonight?" Helen asked her husband.

"I don't know," Bobby replied. "Why are you asking? You usually don't want to do that."

"It's the last night and I recall that after dinner last year everyone sat out on the beach around a fire. That's all. There's nothing nefarious about my question."

"After the fiasco Katie put on at dinner I don't know if Jack will be comfortable around us."

Mindful of the others in the vehicle, Helen kept her voice low. "*Fiasco*? You can't be serious. They brought her the wrong dinner and that arrogant waiter tried to put his mistake off on her."

"I could tell Jack was embarrassed by the whole thing. Why couldn't she just eat what she got?"

"Would you?" What an egotistical ass he is.

Bobby remained silent.

"No, you wouldn't," she growled.

"Hey, can you turn the radio down, I can't hear what you're saying up there," Rachel said.

Helen reached out and turned up the radio to spite the hateful woman. The subject of what happened at the restaurant ended.

†

All the vehicles arrived back at the camping area within minutes of each other.

From the SUV Katie saw everyone standing around and tried to filter through them all to find the one ray of sunshine—Helen.

As if her new lover knew she was looking for her, Helen appeared and a smile formed on her face.

"Are we all going down to the beach tonight and relax as usual?" Katie asked.

"If you'd like to, sugar." Jack smiled. "I'll fix you something to eat?"

"No." She continued to look at the group. "I imagine all your *squad* friends must think I'm crazy." She shrugged. "Maybe I am. I really don't care what they think about me."

"No, they don't and you shouldn't care about what others think." Jack pulled the car to a stop. "My opinion is all that should matter to you."

"Really? FYI, Jack, caring about what another thinks is only for those that matter."

"I hope that includes me." Jack looked at his wife. "Look, I should have stood up for you and I didn't. To be honest, when the server put your meal in front of you I wondered why you'd gotten that. I knew you didn't particularly care for mushrooms or asparagus but thought maybe you'd had a change of heart and decided to order something different."

"Yes, you should have. Look, I don't want to get into this with you. I'm sorry if I embarrassed you." Katie shook her head and turned to look out the window at Helen before opening the vehicle's door. "I'm going to change my clothes, get a bottle of wine, two glasses, and take them down to the beach."

"I'll be right there with you after I speak with the guys."

"The guys, it's always about the damn guys, Jack. You made it abundantly clear at dinner how much regard you hold me in." Katie couldn't believe she was confronting her husband. Normally she would walk away and ignore him but since Helen, she felt far out of who she thought she was.

"No, that isn't true. I was just so surprised that I didn't know what to say."

Katie lifted an eyebrow. "You really expect me to believe that?"

Jack hung his head.

"Exactly my point." Katie got out and walked directly to Helen.

"Hey, what's going on?"

"Wanna come with me down to the beach and share a bottle of wine and look at the stars?"

"I'd be delighted."

"Wonderful. I'll be right back after I change and get the wine."

Katie started for the RV and saw Jack looking at her with his mouth open. He walked toward her.

"Hey, Katie, I should be the one looking at the stars with you and not Helen."

Katie could hear the confusion in his voice and she felt herself soften toward him a little. "Jack, what you did hurt me deeply, and I need some time to work it all out in my head."

"I was caught off guard," Jack blurted.

"Caught off guard?" Katie felt her anger return. "Please, give me a break. You are the lofty Colonel McGuire who led his squad of fighter pilots into battle. Isn't that why we are all here? Do you really expect me to believe that you were simply caught off guard? Please, give me a break." She turned away then turned back. "It's more like I was someone you didn't want to defend because I was embarrassing you in front of your squad. That's what hurts the most, Jack. You put them in front of me."

"Keep your voice down. Everyone will hear you."

Katie shook her head. "The defense rests." With that said, she walked toward the RV.

†

Helen and Katie sat on a blanket drinking wine and talking softly. The others were huddled around a fire about twenty-five yards away and that was fine with them.

Katie pointed up. "Do you see that star that looks like it is moving across the sky?"

Helen looked. "No, I don't see it."

With her head next to Helen's, Katie took her finger and pointed to the area of the sky she was describing.

"See it now?"

"Wow, yes. Is it a comet or something like that?"

"No. It's a satellite. If you keep watching, you'll see a lot more."

Helen screwed her cup into the sand and laid back. "I've never noticed how many stars there are." She looked at Katie. "I was too busy climbing the financial corporate ladder."

"Now that you know about them maybe you will make time to look more often. You know there are apps for your phone so you can hold it up and find the stars easily. Unfortunately, we have no service here so I can't show you now." She grinned. "But I will later."

"I'll count on it."

Katie squeezed Helen's arm.

"I will miss you," Helen said. "I already do." She reached out and took Katie's hand.

Katie leaned back and lay beside Helen. "You know what scares me the most?"

"That the others will find out about us?"

"No." Katie bit her lip. "I don't care what they think. I'm afraid that when we say goodbye tomorrow we will become strangers again."

"I won't let that happen. I promise you it won't happen...ever."

"Helen, in less than twelve hours you and I will be heading away from here and from each other." Katie forced a smile. "I've seen it happen before." She shrugged. "Being married to someone in the military means you move a lot. That means you leave people behind that you promise to keep in touch with, but you never do."

"I thought you stayed in Austin when Jack was stationed elsewhere."

"Most of the time I did. Occasionally I'd join him when I thought the place, like England, was somewhere I'd like to see. But I never stayed long. I wanted to go back to my home and my job."

"Why didn't you leave him back then? It sounds to me that you didn't have much in common with him or even like being with him."

Katie shrugged. "You don't understand. I left because he was gone all the time. I didn't have a job there and was stuck alone most of the time." She laughed. "There's just so much Wives' Club bridge and mahjongg one can play."

"That sounds awful."

"Oh, it was. I had to deal with women like those four all the time." Katie sighed. "That was where I met Rachel and Brandie."

"Did you like them?"

"Hell, no." She turned her head and grinned. "Once a bitch always a bitch."

Helen laughed. "Good to know that my instincts about them were right." Silence ensued until Helen squeezed Katie's hand. "Tell me what's going on in that pretty head of yours."

"I don't know how I can go back to who I was. In five short days my life has profoundly changed and it is all because of you."

"Are you sorry, Katie?"

"No. I embrace the new me and rejoice in your coming into my life." She turned her head and gently kissed Helen's cheek. "I will never forget you."

"I will see to that since I plan on being in your life forever."

"I hope that's true." Katie straightened her back. "I remember last year when I first saw you and wondered why you let them force you to stay inside during the day. I wanted to know you better but didn't know if you'd let me in."

"You were the only one who accepted me and welcomed me." Helen sat up too. "I wanted to speak to you more too but I was afraid."

"Why? I only treated you with kindness."

"I know, but you'd be around them and I feared they would give you the cold shoulder if I tried to get to know you."

"I wouldn't have cared."

Helen smiled. "I know that now."

"You know, in all the years I've been coming to this gathering I never shared the stars with anyone else. Many a night I'd be out here just like this watching for satellites and shooting stars alone."

"Jack didn't stay with you?"

"No. He was more interested in drinking beer with the guys. Watching stars with me was beneath him."

Helen ran a finger down Katie's cheek. "Thank you for sharing this with me. I will treasure the memory always." She looked at the star-filled sky. "Look," she pointed to the left, "a shooting star. Make a wish."

Katie closed her eyes to make a wish when a voice startled her out of her reverie.

"Everyone is leaving," Jack said. "Time to go."

"You go ahead. We will leave in a little while," Katie responded.

"Then I'll stay with you two. After the vagrant you saw this morning around the camping area I'm not going to leave you here by yourselves."

Oh what a tangled web I've woven. "We will be fine," countered Katie. "I won't let you two be targets."

"This is our sixth year coming here. In all that time, I've always come out here at night and watched the stars. Alone, I might add. Helen is here with me so if someone comes along we can handle them."

"Hey, all I want to do is make sure you are safe. Is there something wrong in that? Come on now, let's go."

"You're right, of course. Thank you for thinking of our safety." She turned to Helen and shrugged. "I guess we should be mindful of the vagrant and go back to the safe haven of our RVs."

"It's true, that guy might be still lurking around." Helen stood and held her hand out for Katie to take. "Come on, let's get going."

Once Katie was standing she muttered, "He has some really bad timing."

Helen touched Katie's arm. "It's okay. He just wants to protect you from that vagrant we supposedly saw."

Katie stopped walking. "No, it's not okay. If I could I would spend the night with you on the beach."

"That sounds delightful." Helen smiled. "I wished on a star and I found you." She leaned in as if she were going to kiss Katie but stopped.

"Why did you stop?"

Helen pointed her chin at Jack who was a few yards ahead of them. "We've taken too many chances already."

Katie nodded.

"Meet me first thing in the morning right here and we can walk way down the beach," Helen whispered. "We can be together again. I'll bring a blanket."

The words were like a shot of adrenaline for her. "I will." Katie looked down the beach. "How far do you think we will need to go?"

"Not far but far enough that we will have our privacy."

"I'll be here before the sun rises."

†

Katie walked into the RV, saw Jack, and went immediately to the bathroom. She wasn't ready to look at Jack or answer the questions she suspected were lurking in his mind. What she wanted was to be back on the beach with Helen in her arms. She knew she'd have to hurry. If she didn't, Jack would be knocking on the door asking, in his at times irritatingly concerned voice, if she were okay.

Unable to deal with anything other than her own confusion, Katie came out of the bathroom and hurried to the bedroom.

"What gives," Jack asked.

"I'm exhausted," she said. "I'm going to bed." She stopped then turned around. "And for the record...I don't know if I can ever forgive you for your behavior at dinner."

"Sugar, what's gotten into you? I know I should have said something and I'm sorry I didn't. I know you were perturbed with

90

me when I said I'd stay with you on the beach but I just wanted to keep you safe, that's all. I am responsible for your safety."

"I don't need you to keep me safe, Jack. I'm forty-four years old and I can take care of myself. I don't need you following me around and sneaking up on me all the time."

"You still have that migraine, don't you? Want me to get you something for it?"

Katie, steadying her emotions, sucked in a breath. She could see the puzzled look on Jack's face and just wanted to look away but she couldn't. "Thank you for your concern but I don't have a migraine and I don't need anything. As I said, I'm very tired and just want to get some sleep." Katie shook her head and closed her eyes.

"Okay. I'm going to take a shower and then read some."

Katie rolled her eyes. She crawled into bed and turned on her side so her back was facing the middle. Once she had the sheets pulled up around her, she closed her eyes and saw Helen. She was almost asleep when Jack came into the room.

"I'm sorry about tonight. Will you forgive me?"

Katie counted to ten for he was never this conciliatory—he was always the one in charge. "It's been a long, emotional day and I just haven't anything to spare right now. If it is forgiveness you want you've got it."

"Okay. Thank you."

"Can we just drop it so I can get some sleep?"

"Sure."

"Good night." Katie closed her eyes and it wasn't long before sleep overtook her.

Chapter Ten

Katie stretched and yawned. The sky showed the pale light of early dawn, which meant that she could watch the sunrise with Helen. She slipped off the bed and crept out of the room gathering her shorts, T-shirt, hoodie, and sandals as she went. After going to the bathroom and brushing her teeth, Katie crept down the length of the RV. With a deftness she did not know she possessed, she left the RV so quietly that the only sound she heard was her own breathing.

†

Helen felt her heart skip a beat when she saw Katie standing on the beach. "Hey there, stranger. You out here to watch the sunrise?"

"No, I'm out here hoping to find someplace private so I can ravish you."

"I like the sound of that. Shall we explore farther down the beach?"

Katie grabbed Helen's hand and began running down the beach turning up a side path that led away from the beach area. "Here. Now."

Desperation and want made Helen pull Katie to her with kisses that begged for more. Fingers took purchase on bare skin, paying homage to the body she urgently wanted to own. She wasted no time in divesting Katie of her clothes. She smiled when she realized that, like herself, her lover wore no undergarments.

Helen spread the blanket on the sand and lowered their bodies on to it. Lying together naked in the early morning dawn, oblivious to the surroundings, they made love. Helen, on her knees, lavished Katie with her tongue, tasting the sweetness she knew she would always crave. It was a need borne out of deep desire and longing. All her life, Helen had the nagging feeling that she was missing something important. In that instant knew she had found what that was.

Just as the sun began its ascent, Helen lay on the blanket clinging to Katie, her back arched as deft fingers brought her to an all-consuming orgasm. "Wow. That was amazing." She pulled Katie to her and kissed her deeply.

"Mhmm, I think I could stay right here all day with you." Katie placed a chaste kiss on Helen's cheek. "Unfortunately we need to get back before..."

"They notice we are gone?"

"Yeah." Katie said. She grinned. "But it is tempting to just say the hell with it and stay right where we are."

"We can't, it's just too risky. We've been lucky so far so let's not press it."

Katie sighed. "I know you're right but I just wish things were different."

"They will be. I promise." Helen smiled. "Trust me when I say whatever it takes I will find you and be with you. There is nowhere you can go that I won't find you."

"Promise?"

"Yes, I promise."

Dressed, Helen took Katie's hand and they walked back up the beach toward the camping area. Only when they were close enough for others to see did she release Katie's hand.

"Thank you," Katie whispered.

Helen smiled. "My life has always been about control. I've never felt so utterly free as when we make love. I can't believe that of me. The self-assured financial whiz was just naked out on the beach, making love to you. I had no idea how freeing that could be."

Katie ran a hand down Helen's arm. "Neither did I."

"I guess we'd better get back before Jack sends out a search party."

"What about Bobby? Won't he wonder where you are?"

"Bobby only thinks about Bobby."

After a brief hug, they entered the camping area.

†

The RV was quiet when Katie stepped softly inside. Jack was still asleep, which was unusual but she was grateful she didn't have to explain where she was. She made her way into the bedroom, took her clothes off, and pulled her nightgown back on. It wasn't long before a sleep borne out of complete satisfaction overtook her.

Later, hearing Jack rummaging around in the kitchen, Katie's eyes opened. She lifted her head slightly and saw Jack heading down the hallway to the bathroom. Immediately she lowered her head and closed her eyes. Once she heard the door to the bathroom open and close, she took in the smell of brewing coffee and opened her eyes. She saw her T-shirt and shorts still lying on the floor and, remembering Helen's touch, she smiled.

Jack exited the bathroom and walked toward the front of the RV before he disappeared out the door.

Katie stretched and grinned when she felt sand in the sheet under her. After rolling out of bed, she walked to the kitchen area and poured coffee into her insulated coffee mug.

Her shoulders relaxed when she opened one side of the curtain that covered the front windshield. All the squad members were standing in a group chatting as they did every morning. Then her eyes rested on the lone figure standing near the RV.

Helen turned and grinned.

Katie waved for her to come inside.

"Good morning," Helen said as she climbed inside. "Jack said you were fast asleep."

"Obviously I'm not." Katie took Helen's hand and led her further into the living space. "Do you have any idea how turned on I am at this moment?" Katie could feel her cheeks heat up. "This morning was the best one of my life." She shook her head and laughed. "Here I go again sounding like a sex-starved teenager."

Helen put her arms around Katie's waist. "You're not the only one. I want you again, and after that again."

The sound of the door had Helen moving toward the coffeemaker and Katie into the bathroom.

Katie flushed the toilet, washed her hands, and exited the small area.

"Did you find the cups?" She saw Jack standing next to Helen.

"Jack helped me."

"Good." Katie gave Jack a questioning look.

"We are all going up to the diner for breakfast. You want to come along?"

"After last night's fiasco I think not."

"Come on. Last night is forgotten."

"I said, *no.*"

"Okay then. Helen, you want to come along?"

"Thanks for the invite but I've already had something and I need to straighten up the RV. You know...take the sheets off the bed and all the fun stuff of getting ready to leave."

Jack turned to his wife. "Want me to bring you anything back?"

Katie shook her head. "I've got all I want right here."

Helen turned her back to Jack.

"Okay. We should all be back in an hour or so."

"Enjoy yourself." Katie watched Jack disappear out the door.

The door opened again. "I'll leave the SUV here for you, just in case you need it."

"Thank you," Katie said. "On second thought, I will take a breakfast sandwich with egg and sausage, no cheese. Please don't order it until you're about to leave so it won't be cold when you get here."

Jack smiled. "You got it."

Katie stood next to Helen at the window. They watched the caravan of cars head down the roadway and grinned.

"That was some blush." Katie pulled Helen into her arms.

"I had to turn away. I'm glad you didn't add eat to your words."

"Now that sounds like a very tasty breakfast." She kissed Helen. "We have an hour. What do you suggest we do with that time?"

95

"Well." Helen snaked her hand under Katie's nightgown and tweaked an engorged nipple. "I think we should take full advantage of the fact that we are alone again."

Katie took Helen's hand. "I agree."

Their lovemaking this time was slow and deliberate yet with a sense of urgency that enveloped them in their own world.

"Please, Katie, I need to come."

"Not yet." She took Helen's hand and moved it where she wanted it to be. "We come together."

"Katie," Helen cried out moments later.

Katie collapsed on top of Helen. "I always knew I was looking for more but I never knew what that was," she whispered. She wiped at a tear that was brimming in her eye, threatening to roll down her cheek. "You make me feel things that in my wildest dreams I never thought I could feel."

Helen reached out and touched the tear. "Why are you crying?"

"I don't know what to do."

"What do you want to do?"

"Spend every day of my life with you."

"You know it will be messy."

Katie smiled. "Messy I can live with—you I cannot live without."

"I want you in my life forever."

†

Katie was folding the last towel when Jack entered their RV.

"Shoulda come with us. The pancakes at that place were the best I ever had." He looked around the interior of the RV. Looks like you've got everything in order so we can go home." Jack handed her a paper sack. "I checked and it is still hot."

"Thanks." Katie took the towel and put it in a laundry basket before pulling the breakfast sandwich out of the bag. "When do you think we will get home?"

"Don't know." He shrugged and looked at his wristwatch. "It's nine fifteen and it is about a five-hour drive. We should be home around midafternoon."

Katie bit into her sandwich. "This is good. Thanks. Listen, I almost have everything ready in here so I'm going to walk on the beach one more time while you do all the other stuff."

"Don't forget to take your buddy."

"What do you mean?"

"That stick you are always carrying down to the beach."

"Oh, yeah, right."

Jack paused and looked out the window. "Will you wait here for a minute? I'll be right back. There's something I need to do." Jack rushed past his wife, ran down the steps, and was gone.

Katie looked out the window to see what made Jack take off like that. No one was in sight. "Guess I'll finish up here until he comes back. I hope Helen doesn't give up on me while she waits on the beach." Katie finished taking the sheets off the bed. Looking around the area she decided there was nothing she needed to do that couldn't wait. She had waited long enough and seeing Helen was far more important—Katie left the RV for the beach.

†

Helen stepped out of the RV and looked around, hoping to see Katie. One last walk on the beach together is what they planned. *I wonder if she's already down at the beach.* She shook her head and walked toward the boardwalk and the beach.

"Wait up, Helen."

Helen closed her eyes and took a deep breath that let her business persona come to the forefront. She didn't need to turn around to know who it was but did anyway. "Jack, I didn't know you liked to walk on the beach."

"I don't usually, but I saw you headed this way and I wanted to speak with you."

Shit. She eyed the man and didn't detect any malevolence in his demeanor. "Okay."

Jack kicked at a small pebble before he raised his head and his eyes met Helen's. "It's Katie. I don't know what's happening with her. For the last year or so she's been more distant and argumentative. She never used to be that way."

97

Helen began walking again. "It sounds to me like you should be speaking with Katie and not me."

Jack shrugged. "I ask her but she doesn't answer or tells me nothing is wrong."

"Exactly what it is it you want from me, Jack?"

"I know you two are friends and I thought she may have said something to you."

Helen stopped walking. "Jack, Katie is my friend and I wouldn't betray her trust by repeating what we speak about."

"So she has spoken to you about whatever is going on with her?"

"I didn't say that. If you want to know if she said anything to me in private, you need to ask her. As I said, I will not break that trust."

Jack scrubbed his face with his hand. "I don't know what to do. She never wants to go anywhere or do anything with me anymore. I was surprised when she didn't give me any grief about this trip."

Helen garnered two things from what Jack said. First, Katie had been distant with Jack before she arrived there which squared with what Katie told her. Secondly, she wanted to come to the squad get-together this time.

"Jack, you know people change. I'm sure you are not the same man now that you were twenty years ago, or even two years ago. We all grow and change…it is the nature of life."

"I know all that and if that was all it was I'd…"

"Here you are. I wondered where you had gotten to. I've got all my chores done in the RV, now it is your turn."

Jack looked around at Helen then at his wife. "I thought I'd take a stroll down the beach and clear my head."

"Oh. Then why are you walking with Helen?"

"I joined her when I saw her."

"Well, unless you go back to the RV and do your part we won't leave until noon and that means we will hit the traffic around Austin."

Jack looked at Helen. "I guess duty calls. It was nice talking with you, Helen, see you later," Jack said before he turned and walked away.

Katie's eyes widened. "I can't believe he was here with you. It is where I wanted to be."

"Were you jealous?"

"No. Yes. I don't want to share you with anyone else. You are mine."

Helen ran a finger down Katie's nose. "Don't you know that I am yours and only yours?"

Katie smiled. "Yes, I do know that. Just as I know you are mine and only mine."

"Jack asked me if I knew what was going on with you."

Katie's eyes narrowed. "Like between us?"

"No, between the two of you. He said you'd become distant and he wanted to know if you'd said anything to me."

"What did you tell him?"

"If he wanted to know he should ask you." Helen regarded her friend. "He said this was the first year you wanted to actually come here."

Katie smiled. "That is true, and you know why."

Helen nodded. "Yes, I do. It is the same reason I wanted to come."

Holding Helen's gaze, Katie touched her hand. "I believe everything happens as it should and our being here together like this was meant to be."

"Shall we take one more stroll along our beach before we have to go?"

"Yes, I'd like that."

†

Once all the RVs were ready for the trip home the members of the squad and their wives met one last time.

"Guys, once again we had a terrific time but it is now time to return to our homes. Are we all on for next year?" Jack asked.

"You can count me in," was the chorus that answered.

"Great." Jack smiled as he went to each of the men he served with, giving them a salute and a firm handshake. "You guys are the best."

The four wives hugged each other and loudly affirmed that they too would be there supporting their husbands the next year.

Helen and Katie stood on the fringes watching the proceedings.

"I guess this is it," Helen said.

"There will never be an *it* where we are concerned." Katie moved closer and took Helen in her arms. "You have profoundly changed my life in the past few days by showing me a side of myself I had no idea existed."

Helen's arms tightened around Katie. "As soon as I get things straightened out with Bobby I will be on your doorstep. You can count on that," she whispered. "I've got you under my skin and I don't want to let you go."

Katie closed her eyes and sucked in a deep breath. "I hope that is what happens." She let go of Helen and gazed into her blue eyes. "I don't know what I'll do if I never see you again."

Helen smiled. "You will. Count on it."

"I will." Katie saw Jack coming in their direction. "Will you call or text me when you get home and let me know how things go?"

"I've got you on speed dial."

"Time to load up and get on the road," Jack said.

Katie gave Helen one last quick hug. "Take care of yourself."

"You do the same. Goodbye, Jack." Helen gave him a brief hug then nodded. "Have a safe trip and let me know when you get home."

Chapter Eleven

"Did you enjoy yourself?" Jack asked as the RV cruised down the road.

Katie looked over to the man she had spent more years with than anyone else in her life, except her gran. He was steady and supportive most of the time but he wasn't who she wanted in her life anymore. From experience she knew he wasn't always faithful but that had never really bothered her. Inwardly she laughed. *Strange how life works. Now I've turned those tables on him.*

"Yes. It was good getting to know Helen better." She shrugged. "As for the others, they were the same as always—gossip mavens."

"You didn't give them a chance, Katie. You and Helen were thick as thieves, ignoring them altogether."

With a shake of her head, Katie looked away. "For years I've been telling you how mean-spirited they are and you saw it firsthand yet you still defend them." She looked at her husband. "Just why is that, Jack? Does it put you in an unflattering light with the *squad*? Each and every one of them is a bitch and I for one have no use for any of them."

Jack kept his eyes on the road. "I think you are wrong. You haven't liked them from the very first time you met them and there is no changing your mind, is there?"

Katie undid her seat belt. "I'm going to take a nap."

"Are you running away again, Katie?"

"No. I'm fed up to here," she put her hand to her forehead, "with your stupid *squad*." Katie looked away.

†

The drive back to the outskirts of Dallas and Helen's home in Highland Park seemed like it took forever. Bobby opted not to take Highway 35 so they'd avoid the traffic in and around Austin along with the never-ending road construction. Instead, they took Highway 11. Helen always liked the city of Victoria since it had a multitude of restored older homes from the early 1900s.

"Can we go through Victoria instead of going around it this time," Helen asked.

"That's plain crazy talk. Why the hell would you want to do that? We'd have to stop for all the stop signs and lights."

"I'd like to see the homes."

"Not this time," Bobby grumbled.

Helen turned away and looked out the window as the landscape whizzed by.

Just as they approached the cutoff for College Station, Helen saw a car and truck involved in an accident ahead. Since there were no emergency vehicles, she surmised that it must have just happened. "Look, there's an accident. Stop to see if we can help."

"Not my problem, it's theirs."

Out her window, Helen saw a woman sitting on the ground, sobbing while holding another woman who was bleeding.

"Stop! They are injured!"

"You know about emergency first aid? I sure don't. All we'd do is be in the way with this rig."

"I know enough to help stop that woman from bleeding to death."

"Don't be so dramatic. We are not going to be their saviors. They got into the accident by themselves they can suffer the consequences."

"You are such a shit, Bobby. Where is your humanity? Isn't that what that *squad* of yours is all about?"

"Shut your fuckin' mouth or I'll shut it for you," Bobby screamed, grabbing her wrist. "This has nothing to do with the squad," he snarled. "Don't think I didn't notice how you treated the other wives. When we get home I'll make sure you understand not to act that way toward them ever again."

Helen pulled out the knife she'd stored in the side pocket of the door and poked the back of Bobby's hand with it. "Get your hand off me."

He didn't let go.

Putting pressure on the knife she let it prick his skin—blood trickled out. "I said, let go."

Bobby pulled his hand away and raised his lip in a snarl. "You'll pay for that big-time."

A police car with lights flashing came at them from the opposite direction. Helen was relieved that there would be help for the accident victims. *I just hope I'm not going to be a victim when I get to my house.*

The closer they got to her house the more dread she felt. She texted her sister three times to make sure they were at the house and ready for whatever retaliation Bobby would try dealing her when she gave him the divorce papers. In the days that they were gone, Fred, her sister's husband and a lawyer, had all the locks and security codes changed. In addition, there was a new security system installed, including protection for all the windows.

Thank God, Sally and Fred were able to expedite everything. Helen glanced out the window, seeing familiar landmarks that now for some reason appeared ominous. She was almost home but it didn't feel like home. Glancing at Bobby, she took a deep breath. *Now to deal with getting him out of my house.*

†

When the RV turned onto her street, Helen felt her heart sink only to have it relax when she saw her sister's SUV.

"Why the hell are they here and why is my truck in the driveway?"

"I invited them," Helen said, ignoring the question about Bobby's vehicle. She took a deep breath, hoping her casual answer would allow her to get out of the vehicle unharmed.

"Why did you do that? I don't want to come home to those people after a vacation."

"Those people? Really? It is my sister and her husband." *To hell with him.*

Bobby made a sharp turn into their driveway and eased the RV into its overhead enclosure.

"I want them gone."

"You surprise me. I'd think you'd want someone here so you can race next door and be up close and personal with Madeline." Helen knew she was baiting him but she didn't care. All she wanted was him to be gone from her life. *The sooner I get out of town the safer I'll be.*

"You don't know a damn thing. When they leave I will give you exactly what you've had coming to you ever since we left this house last week."

Helen schooled her features, not letting Bobby know how scared she was. "I'd recommend against that." She tapped her chest. "I can protect myself as I showed you in that damned RV and earlier on the road." Helen reached in the pocket next to the door, pulled out a knife again, and flashed it at Bobby. "Remember what happened the last time you gave me exactly what I deserved?"

"You haven't the stones to do that." Bobby turned off the motor.

"Go ahead and try. But I *am* warning you now that I am not bluffing." She put the knife back.

The door next to Helen opened.

"You're back. Did you have a good time?" Sally asked.

Helen stepped outside and hugged her sister close. "I'm terrified," she whispered.

"We won't let anything happen to you. Everything is in place and Fred drew up the divorce papers. Once we get you out of here he will help you with the restraining order in the morning." Sally took Helen's arm and led her toward the house.

"All the way here he's been hinting that I was going to get what was coming to me."

"Don't worry. Fred has it under control. He towers over Bobby and won't let him cause any trouble."

"I don't have a good feeling about this."

Sally patted her sister's arm. "How was the trip? As miserable as it was last year?"

Helen could feel the heat rise from her neck to her face. "It was an eye-opening experience."

"Do tell."

"Katie, the woman I told you about last year, the only one who was nice to me..."

Sally nodded. "I remember you mentioning something like that."

"We spent a lot of time together and really got to know each other."

"Why are you blushing? I don't think I've ever seen you blush before."

"Not blushing. I took one last stroll along the beach and the wind was so strong that sand blasted my face. I had to walk backward."

"That story may fly with some but not with your big sister."

Helen opened the front door, walked into the kitchen, and looked around. "I'm going to miss this place," she whispered.

"Don't think I forgot that you didn't answer my question."

"There's nothing to tell."

"So you say." Sally looked around the area. "I don't think he will notice the new security system. Fred made sure the sensors weren't obvious." Sally laughed. "On each window is a warning label indicating that the windows are linked to a security system and the police will be called if the alarms go off."

"He is too full of himself to think any warning applies to him."

"Are you still going to sell the house?"

Helen nodded. "If I stay here and he is next door with his floozy I'd be putting myself at risk." She shook her head. "I don't trust him. I'd rather have a fresh start." Helen looked around the room again. "Did you get all my important things?"

"Yes. They are all in storage. Once we get him out of the house I will arrange for movers to come and take all your furniture."

Helen accepted a reassuring shoulder squeeze.

"When we get back to my place I will give you all the particulars about the storage place and what is there." She handed her sister an envelope. "Here are the papers. Do you want to give them to him or have Fred do it?"

"It's only right that I give them to him. I will need you both by my side when I do, though."

Sally put her arm around her sister's waist and pulled her close. "We won't leave your side."

"Well, you're gonna have to leave soon because this is my house and I don't want you here," Bobby bellowed.

Helen spun around. "I invited them so they will go when I say and not before. Unless you've forgotten, the deed to this house and the property it is on is in my name not yours. I paid for it all so don't you dare think of it as yours—it isn't. Every piece of furniture, every nut and bolt is mine and mine alone." She held out the envelope. "This is for you."

Bobby ripped the envelope open and looked at the papers. "What the fuck is this?" He threw the papers toward his wife.

"I told you from the start, if you ever hurt me it was over."

"I told you I was sorry. How many times do I have to say that?" Bobby screamed.

Helen watched Bobby's hands ball into fists and knew what was coming next.

"Listen, Bobby, settle down." Fred moved so he was toe to toe with Bobby. "You crossed a line and no matter how many times you say I'm sorry it won't change what you did."

"You don't know jack shit," Bobby growled. "There's no way I'm letting that frigid bitch embarrass me like this."

"Not your choice." Fred was almost on top of the man. "Now go away and let your lover next door soothe you. You can tell her how terrible Helen is and maybe hit her too."

"Or what?"

"Or, I will call the police and tell them that you are violating the restraining order Helen has against you."

"Dickhead." Bobby pushed by Fred and went out the door slamming it behind him.

"Well, that went well," Helen said. "I thought we were getting the restraining order tomorrow."

"He doesn't know that." Fred shrugged. "I needed to de-escalate the situation. He was close to being out of control."

"Let's get out of here before he has time to become angrier and tries to come back," Sally said.

"Not before we make sure every door and window is secure. I will not have him come back in here and destroy what I've put into this house." Helen turned to Fred. "Did you change the garage door code?"

"Yes, and it has the same security as the house."

"Good. Did you sync my car to the opener?"

"Yep. We didn't leave any stone unturned. Bobby will not step foot in this house again without an escort." Fred smiled at his sister-in-law. "He will need to get his belongings. I will make sure I am with him along with an armed detective I employ when that happens."

"Okay, just as long as he is gone for good." Helen took one last look around the home that she loved. "Are you ready to go?"

Fred and Sally both nodded.

"I'll back my car out of the garage then shut it. Will you please be nearby until I am in the street?"

"Of course we will." Sally hooked her arm into Helen's. "Come on, let's get out of here."

The three turned and headed for the door.

"Stop right there."

Helen felt her body go rigid. She slowly turned to face her husband. *Where did he come from? Shit, we didn't check the locks.*

Bobby had an evil look on his face. "You will not embarrass me by walking out on me. I will not let that happen. It was bad enough that you were cavorting around with only Katie and ignoring the other wives. Do you have any idea how embarrassing that was to me?"

Helen shook her head. "Don't really care."

"I will *not* let you go."

"You have no choice. When you look at the divorce papers you will see that you get nothing—it all belongs to me." Helen grinned. "Remember the prenup you signed?"

"No one walks out on me." He moved quickly, grabbed Helen's arm, and twisted it.

Fred moved behind Bobby and put him in a choke hold. "Let her go."

Bobby twisted his wife's arm harder.

Fred applied more pressure.

Bobby began to sputter and finally let go.

"Go on and get out of here you two. I will be along in a moment."

†

After Helen pulled her Mercedes out of the garage she got out of the vehicle. "We didn't lock the front door after we went inside."

"No, I don't think we did. Don't you worry, Fred will take care of it." Sally pulled her sister into a strong hug. "I've got you and will not let him hurt you."

"Did you see the look in his eyes? I think he would have killed me if you and Fred weren't there."

"Tomorrow we will get that restraining order and find a safe place for you to stay."

"Did you get all my clothes and my gun?"

"Yes. Along with your jewelry and all the things you had from Mom and Dad."

"I'm glad Daddy isn't here to see what a mess I've made of my life. I should have listened to you and Mom when you warned me not to marry him." *I never would have met Katie if I hadn't.* "At least something good has come out of this sham of a marriage."

"What was that?"

"Huh?"

"You said, at least something good has come out of this sham of a marriage."

"I said that?" *Shit.*

"Yes."

"For the life of me I can't think of what that would be. It's been an utter failure from the start. What an idiot I was to think being married was better than all those blind dates."

Sally let go of her sister. "We all have those moments when clarity abandons us."

"I've had a doozy, but now I know what my path is and I am looking forward to a new chapter in my life."

"Like what?"

"I'm moving to my place in Austin."

"You have a place in Austin? I didn't know that."

"Yes. I use it when I need to work there. He won't find me since he doesn't even know it exists. The place is very secure and I will be safe there."

"I will miss you and so will everyone you know."

"I'll only be four hours away."

"And you will be safe there. Right?"

"That I will." Helen felt her phone vibrate and opened the text message. "I need to answer this."

How did it go?

Worse than I expected. Glad my sister and her husband were here. I think he would have killed me.

Are you safe now? Do I need to come up there?

It is all good. Fred had a choke hold on him.

Thank God.

Tomorrow I get a restraining order, speak with the people at work, and sort out a few other things. I will be heading for Austin on Friday.

Can you imagine what those words just did to me?

Yes.

I can't wait.

Me either. I will call you later.

K

Helen ended the conversation and turned to her sister. "Fred's been in there a long time. We should go check on him. There's no telling what Bobby might do."

"We will not go back in that house. Fred can handle himself." Sally looked at her sister. "Who were you texting? You looked so serious."

"Look, here comes Fred now."

Fred had Bobby by the scruff of his neck, dragging him out of the garage.

"Helen, close the garage door," Fred yelled.

Leaning into her car, Helen pushed the button and watched the door slide down. She watched as Fred gave Bobby what she thought were the keys to his truck before speaking to him. She couldn't make out the words but the obstinate look on Bobby's face was unmistakable.

"Guess this is it," Helen said. "You want to ride with me?"

Sally nodded.

†

Once Fred was back at his home he looked at Helen and smiled. "It took a bit of persuasion but I convinced him that if he continued he would go to jail and that was not someplace he wanted to be."

"Where is he now?"

"Don't know. I gave him the keys to his vehicle and told him that I would set the alarm system remotely and that all the doors and windows were armed. There's no way he could get back inside so he shouldn't try."

Helen looked at him. "What about the garage door? He can't use the old code to get in can he?"

"No. I made sure that I deactivated the code in his truck. When you are ready to look at them I have all the pertinent information and codes for you."

"Thanks." Helen let out a sigh. "You know he'll still come after me. I could see it in his eyes."

Fred had a sympathetic look on his face. "That is why we are getting a restraining order tomorrow."

"A lot of good they do."

"It will be better than nothing. At least if he does try something he will be arrested," Fred said.

"If he doesn't kick the shit out of me first."

"She's going to live in Austin," Sally said. "Is it a permanent move or just until this is over, sis?"

Helen looked out the kitchen window and thought about the neighborhood she loved and had lived in for fifteen years. It had been her dream home. She was meticulous in restoring the eighty-year-old home to its original state and the idea of selling it broke her heart. But, it was time for her to seize her life and live it in the happiness she now realized she never had. "It will be a permanent move."

"The kids will miss you."

"And I will miss them. Like I said, it's only four hours away. Less if there's no construction."

Fred laughed. "Highway Thirty-five without construction? In your dreams, Helen."

Helen was glad for Fred's comment for it helped lessen the tension in the room. She could tell that Sally wasn't finished interrogating her. It seemed that her sister always tuned in to whatever was going on in her day-to-day life but never on a personal level. What she had with Katie was very personal and Sally did not belong there. Helen was positive that Sally picked up on the change in her. How could she not—it was life-altering,

"Want me to get takeout or do you want to go somewhere to eat?" Fred asked.

Helen shook her head. "I don't want to go out. It will be dangerous for everyone around me. It is probably best if I go to a hotel. I don't want either of you or the kids to be his victims too."

Fred turned and looked at his sister-in-law, who was now sitting at the kitchen table. "Family takes care of family, Helen. You are *not* staying in a hotel. Is that clear?"

"Crystal." Helen brushed a tear from her eye. "Thanks for letting me park in your garage."

"We cleared it out for you." Sally hugged her sister. "No matter what, there will always be a place for you here."

Helen smiled. "Thanks. It's comforting to know." Holding her head in her hands, she let her tears fall. "I love my house. I love my job. This is the price I am paying for my stupidity in marrying that asshole when all the red lights were flashing not to."

Sally pulled out a chair and sat next to her sister. "I know all those blind dates that everyone was setting up for you were annoying. I'm sorry for my part in that."

After shaking her head, Helen looked into eyes that mirrored hers. "It was my choice and I ignored what was right in front of my face. I thought he was a fun guy—I was wrong."

"At least you found out."

"I should have known." Helen sighed. "What's done is done. Let's talk about something else."

"Sure what do you want to talk about? Your trip?"

"No. That will only remind me of what happened. Why don't you tell me about your catering? Any new jobs?"

"Yes, my schedule is so full that it is almost more than I can handle."

"Really? Why? Is there a problem?"

"You know I have ten employees, right?"

Helen nodded.

"Well, two of them, Rosa and Margaret, keep bringing me business. Every time I turn around I'm catering some kind of gay or lesbian wedding."

"Is that a problem?" Helen asked cautiously.

Sally shrugged. "Not my cup of tea but they keep me in business so I do what I must."

"What does that mean? If they weren't bringing you all that business you'd fire them?"

Sally didn't answer.

"Surely you don't mean that. Do you, Sally?"

"No. No, that's not what I mean."

Helen eyed her sister and wondered if it was deception she saw there or sincerity. She heard her name and smiled.

"Aunt Helen," Gracie, her niece, yelled as she came in the door.

"Hey, kiddo, where have you been?"

"I was over at my friend Julie's house." The girl wrapped her arms around her aunt's neck. "Did you have fun on your vacation?"

"Yes, I did."

Gracie looked around the kitchen. "Where's Uncle Bobby?"

"Not here, kiddo."

"Good. I don't like it when he is here."

"Why?"

"He's always so loud."

"That he is." Helen looked at Sally.

Sally shook her head.

"So where's your brother?"

"Probably out somewhere mooning over Janie Morgan." Gracie scrunched her face. "He is such a dork when it comes to girls."

Helen thought of Katie and smiled. "Yeah, that's how you act when you get around someone you like. When you least expect it the same thing will happen to you."

Gracie made a face and turned to her mother. "What's for supper? I'm hungry."

Sally hugged her daughter. "Haven't decided that yet. Dad said something about takeout."

"Rudy's barbeque?"

"Sounds good to me. What about you, Helen? Does barbeque interest you?"

Helen nodded. "Can't think of anything I'd like better."

†

For the three hours after Katie and Jack returned home, he asked her what was wrong twenty times and it was driving her crazy. In the past she just ignored questions like that but now the constant barrage was grating on her last nerve.

"Sugar, how about we go out for dinner." Jack pulled Katie to him.

Katie pushed away. "How about we don't. We have all that food left you insisted we take in case the others ran out. It will go to waste if we don't use it."

"Can't we freeze it?"

"Sure. All I want is a spinach and kale salad along with a piece of chicken and for you to stop following me around like a wounded puppy."

Jack threw his hands up in the air. "Fine. I just don't get you sometimes."

"It works two ways. I'll start making something for you to eat. What do you want? We have some of those frozen burritos left that you like."

"Sure, that sounds good. Whatever you make will be okay with me."

Katie saw her husband's hangdog look before he walked away and wished she could be nicer to him. "Why am I such a bitch around him?" She knew the answer—had for many years. She'd acted that way when she learned how irresponsible he was in regard to his affairs. Shaking the memory away, Katie pulled her phone out of her pocket and dialed a number she had memorized.

"Hi, can you talk?"

"We just arrived at my sister's house about an hour ago. Once I get everything settled I will call you back?"

"Are you okay?"

"I am now."

"Good. I'm glad to hear it. I miss you."

"Me too. Listen I need to go but I will call you later okay?"

"I hope you do."

"Count on it. Goodbye."

"Bye."

†

Katie and Jack sat eating their dinner, neither talking, just as they had so often before. Katie looked at the man across from her and sighed. For the most part he was a good guy and probably deserved more than what she could give him. Her heart ached for how badly she had treated him over the years never forgiving him for what he did. She wasn't happy and hadn't been for so long she'd forgotten the last time she felt any sort of joy with Jack. *Maybe from the beginning I wasn't happy.*

"I'm sorry for being harsh with you earlier, Jack." She closed her eyes. "You haven't done anything to justify my being so mean and nasty."

"I'm not complaining."

"You should." She looked him in the eye. "You deserve someone better than me. You need someone who is more compatible with you and will make you happy."

Jack shrugged. "Like I said, I'm not complaining. I know you are always preoccupied with your patients. It must be hard listening to other people's problems every day." He lifted one eyebrow. "Maybe you should think about lightening your load and only work part-time."

Katie sighed heavily. "Don't you get it? I'm not talking about my job. I do what I do because I care about people and want to help them."

"At what expense?"

"I don't know how to answer that, Jack. I truly don't."

"Therein lies the problem. Your answer should have been easy."

"You don't get it. My job is not the problem. Most of the time I am pissed off at you, Jack."

"Me? What have I done? I'm always pleasant and kind to you."

"You stood by and defended those women who you know are horrible because anything to do with your precious *squad* is sacrosanct. The way they treated Helen was a travesty but you did nothing. They had no consequences for their actions because you kept your mouth shut. On top of that, I dared embarrass you for objecting when my meal wasn't what I ordered, and you knew it wasn't but said nothing." Katie pounded the table. "Why are they so important that you compromise your wife to defend them? Tell me that, Jack, for therein lies the real problem."

Jack looked down at his plate and moved the burrito around with his fork before he put it down and shoved his plate away. "I've got to get the plane ready for this weekend."

"This weekend? Are you going somewhere?"

"I told you weeks ago. There's an air show at Tinker Air Force Base that my buddy, Mack Gillespie, and I are going to."

"Oh, yeah. I remember now. I didn't realize it would be right after we got back."

Katie watched as her husband got up from the table. Once he'd left the room she began to cry.

"Steady and reliable that's what I told Helen. All I feel for him is resentment and anger." She knew in her heart that even if Helen was not in the picture she was going to leave him—it was time. "I should have divorced him years ago."

Chapter Twelve

Katie walked into work Thursday morning feeling happier than she had in a long time. Helen had called her late the night before and the instant she heard her voice her body tingled all over. Helen's words still ran through her mind...

"Hey, I'm not calling too late am I?"

"No. I'm up hoping you'd call."

"I'm glad I didn't disappoint you then."

"Never. So tell me what happened."

Helen explained the whole debacle and how terrified confronting Bobby made her feel. She also told Katie about the accident on the road and his refusal to stop and help. "That's when I lost any respect I had left for him."

"I would have too."

"It doesn't matter now, since he is in my past. It's one, I might add, I'm not particularly proud of."

"Don't beat yourself up over that, Helen. Had you not married him we never would have met, and I for one, knowing what I do now, would be devastated."

"Me too," Helen whispered. "Tomorrow morning, Fred will help me file a restraining order. After that I will go to my office and let them know I'm taking a leave of absence."

"What do you think they will say to that?"

"It really doesn't matter because that is what I'm going to do."

Katie could hear the sorrow in Helen's voice.

"I don't have a choice."

"You always have a choice, Helen. If you want to stay there and do the job you love then stay."

"That's just it. I no longer have any interest in my job. The only thing on my mind is moving to Austin and having you in my life."

"Well, even if you lived in Dallas you couldn't get rid of me that easily. I will always be in your life no matter what."

"Ah, my stalker."

"You better believe that." Katie smiled. "Good news, Jack will be leaving for Oklahoma on Friday and won't be back till Sunday."

"Now that is good news."

Katie heard Helen yawn. "It's been a long day for both of us. You do know that this morning with you was my highlight."

"Mine too. We better stop talking about that or neither of us will sleep tonight."

"You're right. Good night, Helen. Sweet dreams."

"I will dream only of you. Good night. I will call you tomorrow."

†

"Hi, Katie, good to have you back," Gretchen, her triage nurse, said. "Looks like you got some sun. Did you have a good time?"

Katie shook herself out of her reverie and looked at the woman speaking to her. "It was interesting." Katie began walking toward her office with Gretchen at her side.

"Was it interesting good or interesting bad?"

Katie grinned. "Most definitely in a good way." Eager to change the topic, Katie asked, "Any problems while I was gone?"

"Nothing significant. Mrs. Alderman came in complaining about a sprained ankle and saw Dr. Williams."

"Was it broken?"

"No. He had PT wrap it for her and gave her crutches."

"Did she schedule a follow-up?"

"Yes. She has an appointment with you next Tuesday."

Katie unlocked her office door, walked in, and sat behind her desk. "What does the schedule look like for today?"

Gretchen held out a piece of paper. "Here you go...only fifteen for today."

"Thanks." Katie looked at the schedule. "Okay, let me get myself organized and we will start the day out on time for a change."

Watching Gretchen walk away, Katie's thoughts returned to Helen. *Will she really be here tomorrow?* Her head was at war with her heart. There was no doubt in her heart that Helen would be there and they would be together. The devil that was invading her head told her no way.

There was a soft rap on the open door and Gretchen popped her head inside. "First one's up."

"Thanks." Katie pushed away from her desk and stood. "No way am I going to listen to the devil," she mumbled. With a spring in her step, she started her day.

†

Helen was grateful for Fred organizing the restraining order and making the process easy for her. Now, she had to meet with the managing director in her firm to advise him of her situation and tell him about her move. She suspected that he wouldn't take the news well since they had worked together for years and in her current position he relied on her heavily. Not only were they co-workers but he was one of her only true friends.

Roger White was a bear of a man who had been Helen's mentor ever since she joined the firm. He was responsible for her being named a director when she was thirty-seven and Helen always looked up to him. Through the glass door, she could see Roger sitting at his desk. She tapped on the glass and saw him motion for her to come inside.

"Good morning." Helen walked toward Roger.

"Helen, how was the trip?"

"It was good. Well, good for the most part." Her eyes darted around the room for a moment before they rested on Roger's face.

"There is a situation that I need to speak with you about." She motioned at the door. "Do you mind if I close the door?"

"No, my dear. Tell me what is going on."

Helen sat in a chair opposite Roger. "My husband hit me and I've filed for divorce." She saw her boss about to speak and held up her hand. "He has not taken the news well and I am afraid he will come after me."

"Are you okay?"

"Not really. I'm terrified that he will harm me, or anyone around me. That's why I'm here."

"What can I do for you?"

"I need to take a leave of absence. I am moving to another city where I don't think he will find me."

Roger frowned. "Do you think he so deranged that he'd come after you?"

"I never thought he was, but had you seen the look on his face it would have scared even you." Helen shrugged. "At this point I don't think I should discount anything he might do. I heard on the radio this morning about a workplace shooting. I couldn't bear it if that happened here."

"Where are you moving to?"

"It's best if you don't know."

"I won't tell anyone if you are worried about that."

Helen smiled and shook her head. "That I know. I just think it's best if no one knows where I am for the time being."

"Are you leaving us permanently?"

"For now, no. It all depends on how my situation works out. I will know more once the divorce is over. I need to get my life in order and make some tough decisions about where I want my life to go."

"That sounds ominous. Is there something else going on that has you reflecting on your life?"

His soft brown eyes focused on what Helen thought were her eyes. She held his gaze.

"In all my years in finance I have never encountered another mind as agile as yours when it comes to the bottom line." Roger looked away. "I will be lost without your counsel and friendship."

Helen sucked in a breath. "This whole business with my husband has me reevaluating the choices I've made in my life." A slim smile crossed her lips. "My life, for as long as I can remember, has focused on work and only work. I never really took any time to enjoy anything else. I now see that the marriage was my biggest mistake."

"And working here?"

"My greatest accomplishment. I don't want to leave, Roger, but right now I must." Regarding the man, Helen let her expression become firm. "No one can know why I'm taking a leave of absence. I need our discussion to be between just us—confidential."

"I will keep everything we say between us, as I always have."

"Thank you." Helen scratched her face as a thought occurred to her. "Do you know anyone at the *Dallas Morning News* that owes you a favor?"

"Yes. Several."

"How about on the local TV channels?"

"Yes. I know that look on your face. What plan are you devising, Helen?"

"Oh, just a story about the sudden departure of someone key to this firm. Front page above the fold, lead-in news story that kind of thing."

Roger grinned. "Excellent diversionary tactic. Not sure we can get above the fold or even the first page but certainly on the first page of the financial section. Does he read the paper?"

"Surprisingly, yes. He reads it from the front to the back religiously."

"Then he won't miss it, will he."

"No, he won't. This way it will ensure that even if he has the notion to come here to find me he'd know I wasn't here."

"That would do it but what will we tell everyone here?"

"The same thing. If I tell them the truth there will be the chance of a leak. Oh, they'll try not to tell anyone but let's be honest here. Eventually someone will tell a spouse or a friend." Helen tilted her head to the left, "Fortunately for me, he has never had any interest in what I do for a living so I doubt that he'd find out from anyone here but I think to be on the safe side they don't need to know the particulars."

"As much as I don't like deceiving everyone, I agree it is the best course to take."

"If you want my input, I think Mike Lockhart will make an excellent interim director." She nodded. "He is next in line and has an incredible knack for the job."

Roger got out of his chair and came around the desk, stood next to Helen, and placed his hand on her shoulder. "The real reason you're leaving will go no further," he reassured her again. "As for Mike, I think he is the logical choice."

"I agree."

Roger pursed his lips and knit his eyebrows. "Are you sure your husband is that much of a loose cannon? The few times I've met him he never struck me as the murderous type."

Helen stood. "At this point, I truly feel that Bobby is capable of anything. I know he only hit me once but the look in his eyes when I gave him the divorce papers told me I shouldn't underestimate him."

"I've never seen this side of you, Helen. Usually you are resolute about your work ethic." Roger gave her a hug. "You have always been the glue that has kept me and this company going. Now it is my turn to return the favor."

"Thank you. You've always been my rock." Helen looked at her boss. "I appreciate your support."

"You will always have it." Roger let go of her. "I will call a meeting of all the staff for ten. Will that give you enough time to collect everything you'll need from your office?"

Helen nodded. "I want to speak with Becky myself. She has been a loyal PA and deserves to hear from me personally that I am leaving."

"But just for a time then you'll be back. Right?"

Helen shrugged. "I don't know. I have some other matters that need my attention before..." She let out a breath. "That is for another time. I'll go collect my things."

"You do that and I will make sure everyone is in the meeting room in half an hour."

Helen relaxed for the first time since arriving at the office. "Thank you, Roger. Your support means everything to me." She reached up and put her hand over his that was resting on her shoulder. "You have always been there for me from the start. I value your friendship and mentoring."

"I will be but a phone call away."

"Thank you." She grinned. "Any tips on buying a new car? Mine is too distinctive for me to drive right now."

"I agree. It's hard not to notice your vehicle. It depends on whether you want to stand out from the crowd or blend in," Roger said. "I'd advise buying a blend-in car that is used."

"That'll be a change." Helen laughed for the first time since she last saw Katie. "Low-keyed it is. I guess that means no leather seats that are heated and cooled, and I will have to buy one of those little portable GPS units."

†

Katie turned her attention from the television to Jack. "When are you leaving tomorrow?"

"I need to check out the plane in the morning so I guess I'll leave around noon." He looked at his wife. "Why did you ask? Do you want to go?"

"You know how I feel about being in small planes. They scare me. No, I don't want to go, I was just asking that's all."

"Full day tomorrow?"

"Yes, I looked at my schedule and I'm booked solid."

"Why didn't you just take Thursday and Friday off after our trip?"

Katie could feel herself bristle inside. Being retired meant he had way too much time on his hands. *No wonder he annoys me so much.* "Because I have a responsibility to my patients."

Jack shrugged. "Again I'll ask at what expense?"

"I have the same sense of duty to my patients as you do to your *squad*. You of all people should understand that."

"You're right. I'm sorry. You've seemed so preoccupied since we returned that I thought a few days off to yourself would do you some good."

"Thank you for the thought." Katie forced a smile. "I'm going to the gym after work tomorrow then out to dinner with a friend."

"That sounds fun. Which friend?"

"Don't think you know her. CH Dunham is her name." Katie prayed he didn't know the name Helen used for work.

Jack shook his head. "Nope, don't know the name. You should go to Bess Bistro. I hear it is excellent."

"I'll think about it." Katie stood. "Now that I think of it, I should get a gym bag together with a change of clothes and toiletries. I haven't worked out in a week. I need to get back to it."

"Good plan. I already packed my rucksack. Do you need any help?"

Katie shook her head. "No, I won't need much."

✝

Once in the bedroom, Katie shut the door and leaned against it. Technically, she hadn't lied to Jack. She told him the name of the person she would be with but it still edged on a lie. *Or is it a betrayal? How can I betray someone I've wanted to leave for years?*

Her thoughts turned to her beloved gran who always guided her when she was growing up. *It's a slippery road you're travelin' on, Mary Kate. Best think about what yer doin' before you slide off the edge into the mud.*

"I wish you were here with me now." She smiled. "You'd like her, Gran. She reminds me of you. Stalwart with a heart of gold."

Jack came into the bedroom and sat on the bed. "What's going on?"

"What do you mean?"

"With you. With us."

Katie sucked in a deep breath. "I didn't want to have this conversation with you now, but since you brought it up I guess now is as good a time as ever."

"What's going on?"

"I want a divorce."

"A divorce?"

"Yes. I fell out of love with you years ago when you came back from Japan with an STD and tried to hide it from me. You actually slept with me knowing what you had. The only saving grace was you were already on antibiotics. If you remember, I told you then it was over and told you to sleep in another bedroom."

"I told you I was sorry."

Katie shook her head. "Are you really that dense? It wasn't the first or last time you cheated on me, was it?"

Jack looked dumbfounded.

"Did you think I was that stupid, Jack?"

He said nothing, just looked down at his feet resting on the floor.

Katie looked at Jack. "Look, it hasn't been good between us for years. You deserve someone who will love you."

"And that's not you?"

"No, it isn't."

"Before you make a final decision, can we talk about it when I get back from the air show?"

"Sure, Jack, we can talk about it."

"Just give me a chance."

Katie sighed, finished packing the clothes she wanted, and zipped the small suitcase closed.

Chapter Thirteen

Just before entering the exam room of her last patient of the day, Katie felt the vibration of the phone in her pocket. She smiled reading the text message—*I'm in Austin*. She felt her body react in the same way it always did when her thoughts turned to Helen. Knowing they would be together soon made her feelings intensify.

With a hand on the doorknob, Katie schooled her features and entered the exam room. The elderly woman smiling at her was Esther Browning. Esther was Katie's very first patient when she joined the clinic ten years earlier.

"Hello, Mrs. Browning." Katie opened her laptop and found Esther's file. "What's on your mind today?"

"I needed to speak with you last Tuesday but you were not here. Now whatever is on my leg is worse."

Katie ignored the sharp words. "Why don't you sit up on the exam table and I'll take a look at it." She held out her arm to help the woman climb up the step and sit on the white paper that crinkled as Esther sat. "Which leg?"

"The left one."

While checking the woman's leg, Katie could feel eyes on her.

"Something is different about you," Mrs. Browning said.

Katie looked at the woman with a puzzled expression. "It looks like contact dermatitis. Have you used any new lotions, soaps, or sprays lately? Or have you been outside in your yard working in the garden?"

"I did buy some spray to remove the hair from my legs. I get this really sharp pain in my back when I try to bend down and use a shaver."

"Don't use it again. I will give you a prescription for the rash. It should be gone in a day or two." Katie felt the woman's back. "Where is the pain?"

"Could have been gone by now if you'd been here when I needed you." Esther wound her arm around to her back and touched where it hurt. "Right there."

Katie palpated the area gently. "Does it hurt any other time than when you bend?"

"No."

"I'd like to get an x-ray so we can see what's going on. It's probably nothing but I'd rather be safe than sorry." After filling out the necessary form for the x-ray, Katie looked at her watch then helped Esther off the table. "Take this to x-ray and they will set you up with an appointment for next week some time. Once I get the results I will let you know what, if anything, we will do. Here is the prescription for the rash on your leg. If that hasn't cleared up by Monday, call for another appointment."

"Should I be worried?"

"No. This is just precautionary." Katie smiled. "How are you doing since your husband had his heart surgery?"

"He's being a pain in the ass. Wants to go everywhere and drive by himself too. Do you have anything for that?"

"Unfortunately not. He probably is acting like that because he is feeling better and that is a good sign."

Esther eyed Katie. "There's something different about you," she said again, leaning her head to the left. "You look radiant and happy. That must have been some vacation you and your husband had."

"How do you know that?"

"That's what they told me when I called on Tuesday. They said you were taking a few days off with your husband."

Katie raised her eyebrows. "To answer your question, I did have a very good time."

"You should take trips more often." Esther winked. "Except when I need you that is."

With a laugh, Katie took her patient's arm and helped her to the door. "Make sure you remember to call and make an appointment if the rash doesn't go away."

"Are you going to be here?"

"Yes, and I will be sure to tell the schedulers to work you in if my day is full."

"Very well then." Esther reached for the door before turning to face Katie. "That glow on your face looks good on you."

†

It had been ten minutes since Helen spoke with Katie, who was only a few blocks away. She'd be arriving any minute and it was all Helen could do to hold it together. Everything was happening so fast that she was sure she was freefalling into an abyss. The one thing she knew beyond a doubt was the connection she had with Katie. That was real. That was what kept her going for the past two days.

Has it only been two days? She nodded. It seems like a lifetime ago.

Her mind turned to Bobby and she shivered. The look in his eyes still haunted her. All her life she had been self-sufficient with her eye set firmly on the prize. She had to step on many others to get to where she was but none of them ever frightened her. No one had until the man, who was her husband, glared at her with what she thought looked like deep-seated rage in his eyes.

A soft knock made her feel fleetingly afraid until she realized who was at the door. Katie.

Helen wrestled with the doorknob and managed to pull the door open. "Katie, you're here."

"For the whole weekend if that's okay."

"More than okay." Helen closed the door after Katie entered. She pulled Katie to her and hugged her. "I know it's only been a few days but it seems like forever since I held you last."

Katie buried herself further into Helen. "I thought I'd explode when you called. God, you have one sexy voice."

"I could say the same thing about you. Even when we texted I wanted you." Helen leaned in and kissed Katie's waiting lips. The kiss was passionate and full of promise.

Katie snaked her hand under Helen's T-shirt.

Helen froze and a chill ran down her spine.

127

"Hey, you're shaking. What's the matter?" Katie pulled away and took a step back.

"What if he finds out about us and he hurts you? I can't bear the thought of that happening to you."

"No one is going to hurt me or you."

"You don't know that."

"Yes, I do. I will protect you and not let that asshole hurt you ever again."

"How?"

"Who knows you're here?"

"In Austin or in this apartment?"

"Both."

"My sister knows I'm in Austin, and she knows I have a place here but she doesn't know the address. You are the only one who knows exactly where I am."

"That's good." Katie gave Helen a quick hug. "Do you have a weapon?"

"You mean like a gun?" Helen asked.

Katie nodded.

"Yes, and I have a permit to carry concealed in Texas."

"Great. Do you have ammunition or do we need to purchase it?" Katie tapped her fingers on her chin. "Maybe I should carry mine also. Once I was working late and some deranged drug addict came in demanding drugs."

Helen looked aghast and her heart sank at the thought of anyone assaulting Katie. "What happened?"

"The security guard saw him and had him in handcuffs in about two minutes. Anyway, after that I learned how to use a gun and obtained my concealed permit too." Katie lifted a shoulder. "The two of us together will be too much of a match for him."

Helen closed her eyes. "What if you're not here?"

"We will get you another deadbolt and maybe even a bar to go across the door."

"Deadbolt yes, bar across the door no. I'd feel like a prisoner."

"Okay. Then what about a chair under the doorknob?"

"That I can live with." Helen pulled Katie to her. "Can it be that simple?" She sucked in a breath. "This is such a nightmare. I

know that no one has seen this side of him
do anything crazy." She shrugged. "It is pr
paranoid but the look in his eyes terrified m
feeling that nothing will keep him away if he
are determined to get to me."

"I believe you. Tomorrow morning we v
added deadbolt to be installed on Monday. The
outlet mall near Round Rock and find you som
help you blend in with the *keep Austin weird* cro
fingers through Helen's light brown locks of h
haircut. Short I think."

"Is that really necessary?"

"Probably not, but on the off chance he finds
Austin it will be harder for him to recognize you."

"I won't wear flip-flops."

Katie laughed and pulled Helen closer. "Sorry, t
of the whole look."

"Ugh, my feet already hurt."

"Want me to kiss them and make it all better?" Ka
her eyebrows.

Helen caressed Katie's cheek and smiled. "You're
we don't have to worry about anyone interrupting us or
off to a bathroom."

"For the whole weekend."

"I want you." Helen's voice was full of desire.

†

Katie led Helen into the bedroom and put her finger ov
lover's lips when she attempted to speak. "Shh, let me take ca
you. Let me erase all that fear you've built up inside of you."

Helen closed her eyes. "I'd like that."

With deft fingers, Katie pulled the T-shirt over Helen's h
and lowered her shorts. She smiled—no bra or underwear. C
finger lightly pushed Helen's chest and she sat on the bed.

In a slow striptease, Katie began removing her own cloth
her eyes never breaking contact with Helen's. She removed her b
and pinched her nipples. "You like?"

len nodded.

ood." Katie removed her slacks and underwear. She slid
ger along her center and smiled before holding it out for
to taste.

he feel of Helen's lips and tongue sucking on her finger
Katie quiver with bottled-up desire. With tenderness grown
the deepest craving, she straddled Helen's lap before
ing them on the bed. "Never have I wanted anything as much
want you now," she whispered. The kisses that started as
e exploded into want and need.

Katie started her exploration of Helen's body at her lips,
n to the hollow of her neck, to the valley between her breasts
re taking a hard, swollen nipple in her mouth.

The hand on her head made Katie take long languished
athfuls, paying homage to each breast. Moving farther down,
put Helen's knees over her shoulders and her tongue made
g gentle laps along her folds of velvet.

"Oh, God, please," Helen moaned.

While her tongue kept stimulating Helen's sex, she inserted
o fingers and once Helen began to thrust harder she added one
ore. Katie could feel the tightness around her fingers and sensed
at it wouldn't be long so she nipped at Helen's clitoris.

Helen came immediately.

Afterward, Katie crawled back up Helen's body and held the
eautiful face in her hands before gently kissing her lips. "You are
nine. I won't allow anyone to hurt you. I will protect you always."

"How can you say that? We've only really known each other
a little over a week."

Katie placed Helen's hand over her heart. "It beats for you.
I've been waiting my whole life to find you."

"As I for you," Helen caressed Katie's face, "I am constantly
asking myself how I got so lucky in finding you."

"Not luck. We were predestined to be together. All our life
experiences led us to this point."

Helen grinned. "You mean the one guy in college, who was
my first, and Bobby, the only other man I was with sexually, were
part of this divine plan?"

"Yes. Don't you see how everything always works out as it should? Without those experiences we never would be where we are now."

Tears rolled down her cheeks. "With you it is so different. I can't get enough of you; but with Bobby I would lie there and pray for him to finish." Helen sighed. "I was so happy when he started up with the neighbor. It gave me a reason to not let him touch me again."

Katie smiled. "I've been with men other than Jack," she snorted and shook her head, "and I always wondered what the big deal was about sex too. I can't recall ever having an orgasm until you and I first made love."

Helen sighed. "Me either. Now if I watch a movie and they are making love I will know how it feels." She rolled on top of Katie and kissed her deeply. "My turn."

Chapter Fourteen

Helen looked down at a sleeping Katie and smiled. *My God, she is so beautiful. What she does to me is amazing.* She bent and lightly kissed her lover's lips. "Time to wake up, sleepyhead."

Katie smiled and stretched like a cat before she opened her eyes. "I can get used to waking up beside you." Her hand slipped around Helen's neck, pulled her close, and kissed her. "And this."

"Hmm, me too."

"What time is it?"

"Eleven."

"Eleven? I don't remember ever sleeping this late in my life."

"We were up most of the night doing this," Helen squeezed a nipple, "and this," she pulled the hardened nipple into her mouth, "and this," she ran her finger through the folds of liquid velvet. "On multiple occasions throughout the night."

Katie giggled. "That we did." She held up a finger. "Hold that thought for a minute while I go to the bathroom."

Helen stretched out on the bed and waited for Katie's return.

"We need to call a locksmith and we did plan on shopping today," Katie said from the bathroom. "Want to share a shower with me?"

"There's no one else I'd rather share a shower with." Helen shook her head. "Actually, I've never shared a shower with anyone. You will be my first."

"You are my first in so many ways, babe." Katie crooked her finger. "Come to me and let's make love again for the first time."

Helen wasted no time in going to the bathroom. She watched as Katie turned on the water, her eyes raking over the naked body she couldn't seem to get enough of. "I hope this is the first of many."

Katie stepped into the tub and held out her hand. "Count on it."

✝

"You've got to be kidding." Helen laughed. "I can't wear this." She looked in the mirror at the Daisy Dukes and the short-sleeved shirt. "I look like a teenager."

"Hmm. That you do." Katie let her eyes roam Helen's body. "No one would recognize you in that outfit. But, I must say I like how sexy you look in it."

"I will wear this at home only for you."

"Deal." Katie grinned. "Along with the flip-flops?"

"No flip-flops. The Toms I'll wear but not those things."

"I'll paint your toenails red." Katie wiggled her eyebrows. "You'll look really sexy in that outfit with your flip-flops as you do a striptease for me," Katie whispered.

"Okay, but I'll only wear them for you."

Katie rubbed her hand through Helen's hair. "I like your new haircut. Do you like it?"

"It will take some getting used to. I can't recall my hair ever being this short."

"You look sexy." Katie started to walk out of the changing room and took one last look at Helen. "Next we're getting you some of those skinny jeans."

Helen rolled her eyes. "Don't make me regret moving to weird Austin."

"Oh, I won't. After the next store I'll take you to one of my favorite restaurants."

"Well, in that case, I will reserve judgment until I see what kind of food you are serving me."

Katie gave Helen a quick kiss. "You'll like it and if you play your cards right I'll be your dessert."

✝

133

The moment Helen walked into the small cantina her stomach grumbled.

"Are you hungry?" Katie grinned then winked. "This place has the best Mexican food I've ever eaten. The *queso* is to die for."

"It smells wonderful." Helen looked around, noticing that the restaurant was not as small as she thought it was when she parked her car.

Katie took Helen's hand and guided her to a table in the farthest corner. "Is this okay with you?"

Helen smiled. "Perfect."

"Ah, *señorita*, it is good to see you again." Joe, a tall muscular man, stood next to the table smiling. "What would you and your friend like to drink?"

"They don't serve alcohol so a margarita is out," Katie told Helen. "I'll have water."

"That sounds good for me too." Helen nodded at the man before he left. "They know you here?"

"I come here every time I'm shopping near here."

"Is that often?"

"Yeah, I like to go to just peruse different stores and to see what the latest trends are. Since it is about a thirty- or forty-five-minute drive from my house to here on a light traffic day I sometimes stay overnight in a hotel. When I do, I come here for a meal."

"You and Jack?"

"No. You're the only one I've ever brought here." Katie shivered then shook her head. "I'd never take him shopping with me." She grinned. "You're the only one I've done that with."

Helen took Katie's hand. "Thank you. No one has ever made me feel as special as you do."

Joe put the drinks on the table. "Are you ready to order, *señoritas*?"

"I'll have the usual, Joe," Katie said.

"*Carnitas.* An excellent choice." He looked at Helen. "And you, *señorita*?"

"Why don't you choose for me, Joe."

"You won't be disappointed." Joe gave Helen a toothy grin and left.

"This is a family-run business. Joe works here only on the weekends. During the week he is a radiologist. "I've known him for years. In the early days we worked at the same hospital."

"Why don't you share this place with your husband?"

Katie shrugged. "Don't know. I guess I just wanted to keep it for myself," she smiled, "and now with you."

It wasn't long before Joe returned with their meals. "Be careful the plates are hot." He smiled. "Enjoy."

After taking a few bites, Katie looked up from her meal. "How do you like it?"

"It's delicious. Not sure what it is but I like it."

"That's the house special."

Helen ran her tongue around her mouth. "I can see why. It is very savory with just the right bite of hot."

"I'm glad you like it." Katie put her fork down. "I know you have a sister. What about the rest of your family? Any other siblings, a mother, a father, nieces, or nephews?"

Helen could feel her stomach roll and she looked over Katie's shoulder. *What do I tell her?*

"Sorry, I can see by the look on your face that I shouldn't have asked."

"No. It's okay. I just don't know what to say." Helen's eyes captured Katie's shimmering green eyes. *Is it possible? Can she truly be the unmet friend who I've always known would be my future?* "No other siblings. Just Sally and me. Sally has two kids...a boy and a girl." She pursed her lips. "Three years ago my dad was diagnosed with pancreatic cancer. My mom was by his side throughout all the treatments and through all the really bad days too. Both Sally and I put our lives on hold to be there to help her. Fortunately, they lived only forty-five minutes away. My mom was a dynamo in his care doing everything she could to make Dad as comfortable as possible. We were there to make sure they both ate and Mom got some sleep. I set up a portable office so I could do most of my work from there." Helen pushed her plate away. "It wasn't but three months before hospice started and he passed a week after that. We were all by his side.

"It was a life-altering experience for me. I realized just how important life is and to value each and every day along with the people in your life." Helen snorted. "I think that was part of the reason why I relented and married. I wanted what my folks had."

"What about your mom? Does she live close to you?"

"After a month of mourning she joined a support group and now travels all over the world with her new friends." Helen sighed. "I miss not seeing her as much. After losing my dad, I depended on her being there for me. I'm glad she is in England right now." She let out a long breath. "It's one less person to worry about getting hurt by that asshole." She shook her head. "She was totally against me marrying Bobby, telling me that he wasn't the one for me." She shrugged. "But I didn't listen and just went ahead even though I knew in my heart she was right."

Katie reached across the table and wiped a tear from Helen's cheek. Joe approached the table and Katie waved him off.

"You know, Helen," Katie said in a soft voice. "In my line of work I see all kinds of people and I've never found a way of predicting how anyone will react to different situations. Don't keep beating yourself up over someone you cannot control."

Helen nodded. "I know, but if anything happens to those I love, I don't know if I can ever forgive myself for putting them in danger."

"You've done everything you can to keep them safe. You're here now and I will do my level best to make sure no one harms you."

"How can you do that, Katie? Last I knew you still had a full-time job and a husband."

"Let me worry about that." Katie smiled. "Okay?"

"Okay," Helen said with reluctance. "Let's change the subject. Tell me about your family."

"Not much to tell really. My mother got pregnant at sixteen and as soon as she left the hospital she gave me to my grandmother saying she wasn't cut out to be a mother. I've never met her or seen her, except in a few pictures my gran had."

"She never came back? Even to see how you were doing?"

Katie shook her head. "No. My gran owned six Laundromats and that allowed her to take care of me when I was a baby. When I started school she took me to school and picked me up every day. There was a glass of milk and two cookies waiting for me when I got home. After we had dinner, she'd sit with me while I did my homework. Later on when I was older, she'd always say, *It's a slippery road you're travelin' on, Mary Kate. Best think about what yer doin' before you slide off that road into the mud.* She didn't want me following my mother's path."

"Mary Kate? Is that your given name?" Helen could see Katie's green eyes boring into her.

"I didn't mean to say that." Katie closed her eyes and red tinged her freckled cheeks. "It's a name my gran called me only when she wanted to get her point across. In return I'd call her *granny*." Katie smiled. "It was our gotcha kinda thing."

"That's cute. Is she still alive?"

"No. She died two years ago when she was eighty-four."

"I'm sorry. She sounds like a wonderful person."

"She was. I was at work and she called me and told me to come home. I asked if she called nine-one-one and she said, 'there's no need.'" Katie wiped a tear threatening to fall. "When I got there, Gran took my hand and said, 'it's time for me to go. My only regret is I can't help you with the sadness your marriage causes you.' Then she looked me straight in the eye and said the strangest thing."

"What was that?"

"'She's waiting for you. You'll recognize her right away.' After those words, Gran closed her eyes for the last time."

"Huh. What did you think she meant by that?"

"At the time, I was too shocked to give it much thought. Now, I believe she was talking about you."

"Really? Why? Other than the obvious."

"When we first met last year, I kept hearing her say, 'you'll recognize her.'" Katie shrugged. "I think I did when I saw you."

Helen smiled. "It is strange how life works isn't it. Last year when those other women made it clear I wasn't welcome I hid out in the RV most of the time." She frowned. "I don't know why I didn't see you then."

"I had horrible allergies the first few days and had to stay inside with the AC going full blast."

"I, of course, knew there was another wife and assumed that she had the same feelings as the others."

"I proved you wrong, didn't I?" Katie grinned. "In so many delicious ways."

Helen thought Joe looked tentative when he approached the table.

"Dessert?"

"Not this time, Joe. As always, the food was delicious. We still have shopping to do and I don't want to get a bigger size." Katie laughed and handed him a fifty.

"No, let me pay," Helen said.

"Next time. Right now, let's get out of here and back to our place," she whispered.

"Our place. I like the sound of that." Helen stood and put her hand on the back of Katie's chair and leaned in close. "Thank you. You've made me the happiest I've ever been."

"You keep whispering in my ear and I won't be responsible for what happens. I don't think Joe will appreciate me pushing all the dishes away and taking you on the table."

Helen laughed. "Well, by all means then, let's go."

Chapter Fifteen

Katie woke with a start but kept her eyes closed. She could feel legs and arms tangled as if they were one but it was something else that woke her. *There it is again.* It was a rumbling, similar to the sound of someone rolling a bowling ball on the floor. A chill washed over her. *Has he found her already?* She heard it again but this time it was clearer and louder and she relaxed. *It's only a thunderstorm.*

"Hey, what's wrong," Helen asked in a sleepy voice.

"Nothing. A thunderstorm is coming." Katie kissed Helen's cheek. "With the drought we are having I didn't realize what it was at first."

"Hmm." Helen pulled Katie close. "I'll keep you safe from the thunder and lightning." Helen pulled her closer.

"I knew I could count on you." Katie nuzzled Helen. "My gran used to tell me thunder was the angels bowling and the lightning came when they made a strike."

"It sounds like she was a wonderful person. I wish I'd had a chance to meet her."

Katie smiled. "She would have liked you and probably told me to dump Jack for you."

"I find that hard to believe."

"My gran was progressive and told it like she saw it."

"Hmm." Helen snuggled next to Katie and yawned. "She sounds like my kind of lady."

They both fell back to sleep as a storm raged outside of their snug world.

†

A loud clap of thunder that sounded like a bullwhip snapping made Helen sit straight up in bed. "That was close." She looked at the clock on the bed stand—it was black.

"Is it still raining?" Katie asked.

"Yeah, and now the electricity is out."

Katie wrapped Helen in her arms. "Guess we will just have to stay in bed until the lights come back on."

Just as their kisses intensified, Katie's cell phone rang.

Helen rolled on her back. "You better get that."

"Crap." Katie looked at her phone and shook her head. "I don't need this now." Nevertheless she held the phone to her ear and said, "Hello … Oh, Jack, why are you calling? … I'm in town. I came in yesterday and spent the night … Rain is coming down in torrents here and there are flood warnings, I'm sure. I think I'm going to spend another night and go to work from here tomorrow … How would I know what the weather forecast is, Jack? The electricity is out. I'm lucky to still have a cell connection … What do I think? With the way it is raining you should wait a day before flying back. If you're anxious to get back then maybe you should check the weather office there … No, I don't want you to come here. I'm perfectly capable of taking care of myself … Okay. See you then."

Helen moved away. "Are you leaving?"

Katie frowned. "Hell no. Why would you think that?"

"He calls, you go. Isn't that how it works?"

"Hey, that's just not fair. I've done nothing to make you think that." Katie sat up and wrapped her arms around her knees. "Did you listen to my side of the conversation? Did you hear what I said about spending another night?"

Helen could feel tears filling her eyes, and she looked away. "I'm being ridiculous, aren't I?"

"Pretty much." Katie reached out and touched Helen. "Tell me where this is all coming from."

Helen rubbed her face then took Katie's hand. "Everything is happening so fast. Two weeks ago I was an unfeeling woman who only cared about money and the bottom line. Now I'm a mess. I have you in my life, which is wonderful, and I think I have a psycho after me who might want to do me bodily harm." She shook her head. "I don't know what I'm going to do."

Katie scooted closer to her lover. "I promise it will all work out. You will be free of Bobby once the divorce is settled. You are the only one who has my heart and my body." She cupped Helen's cheeks. "I will be right here with you all day and through the night until I need to go to work."

"Then let's not lose this moment." Helen's lips moved over Katie's then her phone rang. "What the hell is going on? First your phone now it's mine." She grinned. "Hold that thought."

"Hello ... Oh, hi, Sally ... Yes, I was sleeping ... What time is it? ... Ten, really? ... The power went out so I went back to sleep ... Sure I can talk with Fred. Good morning, Fred. Did you tell Bobby's lawyer that the prenup is ironclad and we have video to prove he wasn't coerced into signing it? ... What? ... Really? Is he crazy? ... If you want to meet with me it will have to be in Temple ... Because if he follows you I don't want him to know where I am ... Okay, I will meet you at the Marriott at ten tomorrow morning ... Bye."

Helen turned her phone off and looked at Katie. "Can you believe he hasn't even hired a divorce lawyer yet? He told Fred I wasn't going to divorce him and he'd see to it that I changed my mind." Helen placed a hand over her mouth. "Now that he knows I've cut off his credit card I bet he wants me back as his meal ticket. Or, he thinks it will be easier for him to beat me up."

Katie gathered Helen in her arms. "Would you consider going back to him?"

Helen's eyes bulged. "Are you crazy?"

Katie laughed. "No. I knew you wouldn't go back to him. I was just yanking your chain. Once the electricity comes back on, we will work on a plan to keep him away on the off chance that he does find you."

"That won't stop him."

"Perhaps. It will give you time to call the police and arm yourself. Then if he does somehow manage to get in here you can shoot him before he gets to you."

†

Katie was working her way up Helen's body when the light from the clock radio began blinking.

"Impeccable timing. Although I must admit that you touching me in complete darkness was very erotic. I had to rely on all my other senses." Helen kissed Katie's lips gently. "You are something else, do you know that?"

"No, I'm not. I'm just Katie who has finally found herself."

Helen caressed Katie's cheek. "We found each other and it feels so right to me."

"Me too. Now, my dear, it is time that we see what we can do to strengthen your defense, just in case that horrible man finds where you live."

"Do we have to?"

"Yes, I insist. Your safety is paramount. So get your butt out of this bed and let's see what we can do." Katie saw the pout on Helen's face. "It won't take long and the faster we do it the sooner we can get back to more enjoyable pursuits."

"Okay, but I'm not getting dressed."

Katie wiggled her eyebrows. "Now that sounds so very indulgent and something I might think of as delightful."

Looking around the living area, Katie spied a chair tucked into a desk. "This looks like it is the right height and size." She took the chair to the door and tilted it so it was under the doorknob. "There you go your second line of defense after the door and your new deadbolt."

"I've seen that in movies but does it really work?" Helen stood next to Katie with her arm wrapped around her waist.

"Yes, I think it will work. I'd go outside and try to get in but..." she looked down her naked body. "Do you think your neighbors will care about what I'm wearing?"

Helen let out a deep belly laugh. "Their mouths would hang open at the beauty of your body." She hugged Katie. "We can try it out another time. Right now I don't want to share you with anyone."

Katie stepped back from the hug. "None of that body contact until we finish. We need to locate a convenient, easy-to-get-to place for your gun."

142

"This side table next to the couch has a drawer. I can put it in there."

"Good idea. It is easily accessible. Do you have that burner phone we bought yesterday?"

"I'll get it." Helen left the room for a minute, returning with the phone and the charging cord in her hand. "Here it is. I programmed in your number and Sally's number."

"Good idea. Let's put that on that same table with it plugged in so it will always have a charge." Katie looked around the room. "This is perfect. If you're in the bedroom or bathroom or kitchen you will have easy access to it."

"What if I don't hear him?"

"You will. There's no silent way for him to break down that door, especially with the chair there." Katie nodded. "You will have plenty of time to get to the phone and gun. Most likely the police will arrive before he can ever get inside."

"From your lips to God's ears."

"The only person who knows where you are is me and I'm not telling anyone."

"Are we done here?"

"Yes."

"Good, because watching you walk around naked is driving me crazy with want."

"Hmm, I can say the same. Let's find someplace more comfortable."

"Like the bed."

"My thoughts exactly."

†

"This is decadent." Katie put a forkful of chicken salad in her mouth. "Here we are at five in the afternoon, sitting at the table, eating while we are naked. Never in my life would I have imagined I would do something like this."

"We had to get out of bed at some point today. We must have burned up a million calories since this morning." Helen rested her elbows on the table. "Are you happy?"

"More than I ever thought possible." Katie put her fork down. "Are you?"

Helen smiled. "Yes. Ecstatic."

"Then why do your eyes look sad?"

"Not sad. I'm afraid I'll wake up and this will all be a dream. I'll have to go back to the life I knew without ever knowing the bliss of having you in my life."

Katie grinned, reached out, and pinched Helen.

"Ouch."

"It's not a dream. I am real and what we have no one can take away."

Chapter Sixteen

Katie woke at her usual six a.m. and gently rolled out of bed, careful not to disturb Helen. She stole a moment to look at the beautiful woman. *Gran, she is my dream come true.*

With a quick glance at her watch, Katie finished dressing. "If the traffic is bad I'll be late." She made her way to the bed, leaned down, and lightly kissed Helen's lips.

"Please don't go."

"I have to."

"Stay."

"Please don't ask me that, sweetheart. I'm not strong enough to deny you anything."

Helen opened her eyes and grinned. "I'm without a job or income so that leaves you to keep us in bacon."

"Bacon indeed." Katie leaned in again and kissed Helen passionately. "That is a promise of what's to come when I return after work."

"You're coming back?"

"Of course."

"What about Jack?"

"He pales in comparison to you. He is my past. You are my future. All I can think about is you and our life together, nothing else matters. So don't worry your pretty head about that. I have it all under control." She started for the door. "Let me know how it goes with Fred, please."

"Will do. Is it okay to text you at work?"

"If you don't I will be upset."

"Then I will." Helen blew Katie a kiss.

"I'll see you around five thirty."

†

To Katie's surprise, traffic was light and she arrived at the clinic in record time. She wanted to call Helen just to hear her voice but shook her head. "No, I need to take this time and figure out what I'm going to say to Jack."

She recalled what her Gran said when she told him she accepted Jack's proposal...

"Why are you going to marry someone so much older and that you can only see occasionally?"

Her curt answer was, "It's perfect. I'll have a ring and don't have to be with him all the time."

"That's a slippery road, Mary Kate," her gran replied.

"Yes, I've heard you tell me that since I was a teenager. It's the road I chose to travel, Granny. Besides, he seems good with the arrangement too."

"At the time I was comfortable with how the marriage worked. Now I feel trapped. How do I make this right and not hurt anyone?" Katie shook her head. "There is no other way then to just tell him outright that it is time that we divorce."

Her cell ringing startled her. She switched on the Bluetooth.

"Hello."

"Good morning, beautiful. Did you make it to work okay?"

Katie smiled. "Yes. Yes I did."

"Is this a bad time to call?"

"No. I arrived about five minutes ago and am still sitting in my car."

"Why?"

"I was thinking about you and didn't want the day to start just yet."

"I didn't want you to leave. I've gotten used to you being here with me."

"Trust me when I tell you that I didn't want to leave you either."

"You said you're coming back. Right?"

"As soon as I see my last patient I will be on my way. Are you getting ready for the drive to Temple?"

"Showered, dressed, and ready to go." Helen laughed. "I only have two hours before I leave and I am climbing the walls. I don't know what to do."

"Why not finish that book you started on vacation."

Helen laughed again. "Every time I look at it I'm reminded of you and then I'm totally lost in thoughts of you."

"Sweet talker."

"Truth teller." Katie sucked in a breath. "I've been thinking about what I'm going to say to Jack."

"What do you want to tell him?"

"I want a divorce."

"Are you sure that is what you want?"

"Helen, I've never been surer of anything in my life." Katie saw two other cars pull up and park. "Listen, my co-workers are beginning to arrive so I need to get inside. Can we discuss this along with your meeting with Fred when I get there later?"

"Absolutely. Have a wonderful day, Katie. I'll text you later."

"I'll look forward to it. Bye."

"Bye." Katie held the phone close to her heart and smiled. "Time for work." For the first time in her career, she wasn't looking forward to her job—thoughts of Helen consumed her.

†

Helen was ten minutes away from where she was to meet Fred when her cell rang. She pulled onto the shoulder and growled that the vehicle she was driving wasn't equipped with Bluetooth. The display on her phone read Fred.

"Good morning, Fred, please don't tell me you're canceling … He followed you. That's unbelievable. … What is he driving? The truck … A black Lexus? I didn't know he had that kind of money … Okay, I will watch for him, make sure he doesn't see me and meet you in the back … Please be there to let me in. I can't afford to hang around if he's there too … Okay, I'll see you in about ten minutes."

Helen merged into the traffic and took the next exit. In the distance she could see the Marriott. *How the hell am I going to drive into that parking lot without him seeing me?* She pulled off the road again, rummaged through her purse, pulled out her sunglasses before pulling a hat from the backseat over her now shortened hair. *It's the best I can do.*

The parking lot wasn't particularly crowded and Helen was able to see with ease the black vehicle parked facing the front door. She slid down lower in the seat, turned left, and went along the side of the building making a right when she reached the far end. As promised, Fred was standing at the door. Helen looked around before she parked her car, opened the door, and walked quickly to her waiting brother-in-law.

"Come on," Fred said. "The room is right inside the door."

"We need to check if he saw me and is out of his vehicle."

"Already taken care of. I anticipated he might do something like this so I had my detective follow me. She has an eye on Bobby and won't let him get anywhere near you."

†

Helen sat in a chair away from the window, wringing her hands. "What's going on, Fred?"

"Apparently Bobby thinks you owe him."

"That's absurd. He is the one who suggested the prenup. I'm glad you insisted on videoing that." Helen got up and paced the floor. "There's got to be something else you aren't telling me." She fixed Fred with a glare. "Out with it."

"He's claiming spousal support. He told me if you don't pay up he'll expose some shady dealings you did at your firm."

Helen slammed her hand on a table. "Who the hell does he think he is kidding? He hasn't a clue about what I do. He insisted on the prenup because he thought I was after his money."

"That's exactly what I told him. He also doesn't think you will go through with the divorce and told me that's why he didn't get an attorney."

"And?"

"He insists on going through with demanding spousal support unless you come back to him."

"That's blackmail. Tell me he can't do that?"

"He can't do that because the prenup is ironclad."

"What about his girlfriend? Can't we bring that to light?"

"She dumped him right after you did. She only liked all the things he bought her with your money."

Helen tapped her chin with her fingers. "What disturbs me the most is that he was brazen enough to follow you here." She looked at her lawyer. "I think he's hunting me."

"We have a restraining order."

"Oh, come on, Fred! You know as well as I do if he finds me that piece of paper won't matter. He'll beat me to a pulp if he gets the chance. I saw it in his eyes and I know you did too." Helen wrapped her arms around her waist. "He's trying to flush me out with all this crap about spousal support and about my job so he can get to me. He wants to teach me a lesson with his fists. I know that just as well as I know my name."

"We won't let that happen. Trust me."

Helen shrugged. "Trust has nothing to do with it, Fred. If he finds me it won't matter."

Fred took out his cell and did a quick text. "My detective is on her way here and she will make sure you get back to Austin safely."

"I can't believe this is happening to me." Helen looked at Fred. "This is so screwed up. Am I going to have to live the rest of my life hiding in the shadows?"

"No. He will relent. I've seen it happen repeatedly. Once we knock the wind out of him he will concede."

"Just how do we do that? We can't have him arrested. Other than that useless restraining order I am helpless where he is concerned. The only thing I have going for me is that he doesn't know where I am."

"Give me some time to work things out. I promise I will do everything possible to ensure that he will accept the divorce terms making you free of him." Fred shrugged. "It will just take some time."

Helen snorted. "By then I could be at his mercy."

There was a knock on the door and Helen froze.

Fred looked through the peephole before opening it.

"Helen, this is Cassie Grissom. She will make sure that if Bobby does see you he can't follow you."

"How?"

"Simple. I am going to park in front of him and have a chat with him. While you drive away I will make sure that I've obstructed his view of who is coming and going from the hotel. I will be there with Cassie and make sure he knows to back off or I will have him arrested."

"When he leaves I will follow him to make sure he doesn't follow you," Cassie added.

"Come on, Fred, he's not stupid. He'll know you can't just arbitrarily have him arrested."

"I know that. Just think how indignant he will be." He waited a beat. "He will be so angry that he won't notice a small, dirty, nondescript white car driving by." He smiled at her. "I like the haircut. It suits you."

"Thanks. Okay, let's get this over with."

†

Katie looked at her watch—it was past noon. *She should have called me by now.* Just as she knocked on the door of her last patient of the morning, her phone vibrated.

"Hey, how did it go ... He followed your lawyer ... Unbelievable ... Are you back home now? ... I have one more patient. Come to the clinic and have lunch with me ... Whatever you bring will be fine with me." Katie smiled. "Okay, I'll see you soon."

Katie knocked then opened the door. "Mr. Winton, I heard your cough in the hallway. Let's see what's going on."

†

"Here I am." Helen held up a paper bag. "I remembered you like wraps. Is black forest ham okay with you?"

150

"One of my favorites. After we hung up I realized I should have mentioned that I could get us something here."

"I liked doing this for you."

Katie smiled. "Take a seat."

Helen sat down in a visitor's chair in front of Katie's desk. She couldn't keep her hands from shaking as she unpacked lunch.

"He had the gall to follow your lawyer." Katie tilted her head and reached for Helen's hand. "He is seriously out of control but together we won't let him win."

"He terrifies me." Helen shook her head. "I can't believe I lived with him for almost two years and was so wrapped up in my own world that I didn't see this coming—I should have. Looking back on it, I knew he had a hair-trigger temper but I never imagined that he would make me feel so afraid."

"Become my patient and I can give you something to reduce some of your anxiety."

"Thanks, but no. I need to keep my wits about me just in case he finds me." Helen smiled. "Enough about that asshole. How has your day been so far?"

Katie shrugged. "It's all been routine, which is good since it keeps me on schedule. I was only fifteen minutes behind this morning."

"What do you want for dinner?"

There was a glint in Katie's eyes. "You."

"Don't you know that you've had me from the second I saw you last year?" She reached for Katie's hand. "You hijacked my heart."

A knock on the door had Helen pulling her hand back and leaning backward in her chair.

"Yes," Katie said.

The door opened and a tall Hispanic woman poked her head in the office.

"Your first patient of the afternoon is here. I'll need about ten minutes to get her vitals and all the other details."

"Okay. Thanks, Marta." Katie sighed. "As much as I'd rather stay here with you duty calls." She stood, walked around the desk, and held out her hand.

Helen readily took the offered hand and stood before wrapping her arms around her lover. "I'll surprise you for dinner."

"Really?" Katie lifted an eyebrow before leaning in and kissing Helen.

"I'd better go while I still can." Helen took a step back. "This was fun," she motioned to the empty sandwich bag on the desk. "I guess it would be too obvious if we did this every day."

"Probably, but I wouldn't care because not having you here would drive me crazy." Katie looked at her wristwatch. "Right, I'd better get going." She gave Helen a quick kiss. "Come on, I'll walk you out."

Helen walked down the corridor with Katie and had the feeling that everyone's eyes were on them. When they got to the exit she stopped. Reaching out she touched Katie's hand. "I'll see you later."

Katie leaned in and gave Helen a hug and one last chaste kiss on her cheek then stepped back. "Count on it."

†

Helen whistled as she put the finishing touches on the special meal she prepared for Katie. She heard a knock and lit the candles before rushing to the door, moving the chair, and opening it.

"Did you look to see who it was?" Katie asked as she hugged Helen close.

"No, I knew it was you."

Katie raised an eyebrow.

"I know. I should have looked but I knew. I don't know how I knew but I did. Besides no one else knows I'm here."

Katie raised both eyebrows.

"Okay, I should have looked and I'll never forget to do it again. I promise." Helen relaxed her shoulders. "I just was excited about showing you what I've done."

"Like what?"

Helen pulled the door closed, locked it, and snugged the back of the chair under the doorknob. She took Katie's hand and led her to the dining area.

Katie's hand flew to her mouth. "Oh, it's so romantic. Look at the flowers, the candles, and the good china."

"Wait till you taste what I've cooked."

"You cooked?"

"Of course." Helen schooled her features. "Tonight for your dining pleasure we have a cold kale and spinach salad with a smattering of spring mix. The dressing is an olive oil, balsamic vinegar, and garlic mix. For the main course we have fresh steamed carrots, a quinoa shallot pilaf, and cordon bleu. Lastly, I have fruit compote with vanilla sugar for a light dessert."

Katie's eyes widened. "You're a gourmet cook too?"

"No. Not really. Sally has a catering business. I helped her with investing and she taught me how to cook."

"What else do you make?"

Helen could feel her face heat up. "Well, actually, that menu is pretty much it."

Katie laughed.

"I can make a decent breakfast too." Helen pulled out a chair and waved her hand toward it. "Please sit. Everything is ready." She began to walk to the kitchen then turned back to Katie. "I also have a nice Bordeaux breathing to go with the meal."

Katie took a bite of the salad and closed her eyes. "Amazing. Tell me about your afternoon. You certainly were busy."

"After I left you I went to Whole Foods and bought groceries. I figured since I'm going to be living here I should stock the refrigerator, freezer, and cupboards with more than the few staples I brought with me." Helen lifted one shoulder. "Now you will never go hungry when you're here."

A lascivious grin curved Katie's lips. "I'll never go hungry as long as I have you."

"Will you stay for the night?"

"I still have the clothes I bought this weekend in my car."

"That means you will consider it?"

"Yes."

"What about Jack?"

"What about him?"

"Well, you saw him last Thursday and he came home today. Won't he wonder why you aren't home?"

For several minutes, Katie stared at the table while she took several bites of her meal.

Helen thought she wasn't going to answer and she began eating again.

With her head still down, Katie began to speak. "For many years now, I get up at five, dress in my workout clothes and go to the gym. When I'm done I shower and get dressed for work. When the workday is over I stay in my office going back through the files of the patients I had for the day." Katie looked up. "I don't get home until seven thirty. After I have something to eat I say goodnight, go to my room, sleep, and start again the next day."

"He says nothing? Why wouldn't he object?"

"Five years ago I told him I wanted a divorce. The compromise we worked out was that if I could do my thing without interference from him I'd stay." Her eyes met Helen's. "I am the dutiful wife for things like the squad's get-together or entertaining his friends for a meal in or out."

"You don't share a bed?"

"No."

"If you were to move in with me he'd say nothing?"

"I make sure I speak to him at least once a day." Katie's brow furrowed. "Would he say anything? I honestly don't know since I've never done that before. Shall I stay tonight and put it to the test?"

Helen smiled. "I'd like that."

"Done."

Chapter Seventeen

Just as dawn was breaking, Katie and Helen held each other, still basking in the glow of lovemaking.

"You are so incredible," Katie whispered. She kissed Helen's belly and looked up at her lover. "When we make love it is like I am lost and never want to be found. I only want to be with you."

"I know what you mean. When we are together it feels so natural. It's like breathing."

"After work I'm going back home so I can speak with Jack."

"Are you sure that is what you want to do?"

"Yes. He needs to hear that I'm divorcing him directly from me, face-to-face. It's the right thing to do." Katie ran her finger along the valley of Helen's breast. "After that—if the offer is still open—I'd like to live with you. Unless you think I'm rushing things."

"It'd be like heaven to wake up with you every morning forever."

"Now that we've settled that, I have an hour before I need to be at work. Whatever should we do in the meantime?"

"Come here." Helen embraced Katie and kissed her passionately. "I think we can fill the time by making each other scream the other's name."

†

Helen heard the knock on the door and smiled. "Katie's changed her mind and didn't go see Jack." She rushed for the door. About to open it she remembered Katie's admonition about not checking to see who it was. She could feel the chill run up her spine when she saw Bobby standing there.

"How the hell did he find me? I thought that detective was going to make sure he didn't," she whispered.

With an automatic move borne out of the practice Katie insisted upon, Helen touched the chair under the doorknob to make sure it was secure. While facing the door, she backed away until she reached the small end table that held her powerful snub-nosed revolver in the drawer. Her hand wrapped around the drawer pull and she eased the drawer open. For a moment she froze in horror as she heard what she was certain was a fist repeatedly hitting the door.

"Open the goddamned door! I know you're in there and I need to teach you a lesson on how to be a good wife!"

The sound of his voice made her skin crawl. For a moment she couldn't breathe and she began sucking in deep gulps of air.

"No. I won't let him hurt me." Helen grabbed the cell phone on the table and dialed 911 while she wrapped her hand around her revolver.

"Please help me! I have a restraining order against my husband and he is at my door … The Rutland Complex, building 5029, apartment 239 … Helen Dunham … Please hurry!"

Bobby was pounding on the door harder and Helen heard the unmistakable sound of a foot hitting the door. She could see the doorframe giving away more with each kick.

Her phone rang and after checking the readout, she answered. "Katie, he's here," she whispered. "Yes, I've done everything." Fear coursed through her body. "I'm terrified."

Just as she ended the conversation the door came crashing in.

"You bitch, I'm going to teach you a lesson you'll never forget."

Helen watched as Bobby advanced on her with a gun in his hand. She raised her gun and pulled the trigger just as a searing pain ripped through her body and she collapsed on the floor.

†

"Well, this is a surprise," Jack said.

Katie put her purse and keys on the kitchen countertop. She drew in a deep breath to calm her nerves. "We need to talk."

"Guess who I saw yesterday?"

Katie could feel her frown. *Didn't he hear me?* "Who?"

"Helen Swenson. I saw her coming out of Whole Foods. She'd cut her hair but I knew it was her."

Glad her back was still to Jack and she had the counter to steady herself, Katie's stomach roiled. "Really?"

"Yeah, I thought they were in town so I called Bobby to see if we could all get together."

Katie turned and glared at Jack. "You what?"

"Know what he told me? She left him the day they got back and filed for divorce. He asked me where she was and I told him I saw her coming out of Whole Foods." Jack looked at his wife. "He said he's been trying to find her so they could talk about counseling. Did you know that?"

"What else did you tell him?" The hands at her side balled.

"He wanted me to follow her and let him know where she lives but I couldn't do that since I had a dentist appointment. But I did watch where she went and told him the type of car she was driving and the license number. I must say that rust bucket she was driving surprised me."

"You stupid asshole. Do you have any idea what you've done?"

"I didn't do anything wrong. I saw Helen and thought Bobby was with her. I thought it was strange that he hadn't called me and figured they just got to town. I wanted us to get together with them. I thought you'd be glad since you and she have become friends."

"Did he tell you why?"

"Why what?"

"She's divorcing him, you idiot." Her jaw was clenching and she wanted to reach out and slap the man.

"Yeah. He said she found someone with more money."

"And you believed him?" Katie couldn't keep the incredulity out of her voice.

"Of course. He's one of my best friends. He wouldn't lie to me."

Katie moved until she was toe to toe with Jack. "He hit her," she yelled.

"Bobby wouldn't do something like that."

"I saw the mark on her face!" Katie pulled her cell out of her pocket. "If he hurts her again it's on you."

"What are you talking about? He wouldn't hurt her, that isn't who he is. I can't believe that he ever hit her. You must be mistaken."

"Are you really that clueless? Didn't you even wonder why Bobby wouldn't know where she was living?"

Katie shook her head. "Pick up, come on pick up." She glared at Jack. "Helen, are you okay?" She could hear the tremor in her lover's voice. "Did you put the chair under the handle like we practiced? ... You called nine-one-one and they are on their way ... That's good ... Keep the gun with you until they get there and if he gets in don't hesitate, just shoot him ... Okay ... I'll be there in fifteen minutes."

"Where are you going?"

"He's at her door, demanding she let him in so he can teach her a lesson." Katie snarled. "You son of a bitch, how could you do something so stupid!"

"What? I didn't do anything."

Katie didn't listen as she raced to the kitchen, picked up her keys and purse.

"You're in no shape to drive. I'll take you."

"No," Katie growled. "You've done enough damage already."

Jack grabbed Katie by the shoulder and pulled the keys from her hand. "I said, I'm driving."

†

Two police vehicles with lights flashing were parked in front of Helen's apartment building.

The moment Jack stopped the car, Katie jumped out with her medical bag in her hand. She raced full speed into the building and repeatedly punched the elevator's up button. Deciding it wasn't coming fast enough she ran to the stairs and took the steps two at a time until she reached the second floor. When she opened the door to the floor, she saw a policeman standing in front of Helen's door.

"Hold on there," said a tall, wavy-haired policeman.

"I need to get inside. She's my patient."

"It's an active crime scene, ma'am. No one goes in."

"Look, no one is here yet to help her and I can." Kate held up her black bag. "I can."

"Okay, go ahead."

Katie pushed past the man.

"How did you get in here?" a policewoman kneeling by Helen asked. "You're contaminating the crime scene."

"I don't give a damn about that. Can't you see she's bleeding out and there is no one else here to help her? I can." Katie's eyes only focused on Helen who was lying on the floor with red creeping up her white shirt. She immediately placed her fingers on the carotid artery and let out a relieved breath that Helen had a pulse. She continued her visual inspection of Helen and was glad when her eyes opened.

"Are you with me?" Katie asked.

"You came."

"Yes. I need to stop the bleeding."

Once she opened her bag, she took out all the gauze she had. *This isn't going to be enough. Shit.* After she identified where the gunshot wound was, her deft fingers pressed the gauze against the bleeding. Katie kept her eyes on Helen's chest as it rose and fell. Blood seeped through the gauze and bubbled up between Katie's fingers.

"I need to stop this bleeding." Katie looked at the policewoman. "Get some towels out of the bathroom will you."

"Ma'am, you can't be here," the tall, blond woman said.

"Are you or anyone else here going to save her life?" Katie glared at the woman.

"I'll get the towels."

Katie's head jerked up when she heard Helen's voice.

"My phone...call Sally."

"I will."

Helen gave a weak nod.

Katie looked around and spotted the phone next to Helen's left leg. She stuffed it in her bag while keeping pressure on the wound.

The officer returned with the towels. "Is this enough?"

"Yes. Thanks. Any ETA on the medics?"

"They're on their way up now."

Katie sent up a silent prayer and pressed a towel on the wound. Her shoulders relaxed some when she heard the clattering of a gurney.

"Gunshot to the left abdomen."

"Okay, Doc, we'll take it from here."

Katie looked up and saw Ben Nugent, whom she had many classes with in the early days of her career. "Glad to see it's you, Ben." She moved her hand to let Ben take over before moving to cradle Helen's head.

"You're in good hands now," Katie whispered. "Hang in there. Don't you dare leave me."

"Did I shoot him?" Helen managed to gasp.

For the first time, Katie took in the room. Her eyes tracked to Bobby who was lying on the floor by the shattered door. "Yes."

Helen closed her eyes. "I'm sorry. I don't want to leave you."

Katie's heart lurched and she sent up a silent prayer. *Please, God, don't let her die. I know I won't make it without her.*

"Katie, we need to move her now," Ben said. "We'll take good care of her. I'll see you at St. David's."

Katie looked at Ben. "Please don't let her die."

Dazed and terrified, Katie gathered her bag and walked past Bobby lying in his own pool of blood with another medic tending to him. She couldn't help snarling at him.

Jack was standing just outside the apartment door and began to ask questions as soon as she stepped into the hallway. Katie started to walk away but stopped. "That's your good buddy in there along with the woman he shot. Can you now see how much damage you've caused?"

Jack just looked at her dazedly. "Is he going to make it?"

Katie shook her head. "I don't know. You'll have to ask the medics when they come out," she said softly.

Outside, she got in her car only to realize Jack still had the keys. Rummaging inside her medical bag, she pulled out a spare set of keys and started the car.

The fifteen-minute drive to the hospital took an interminably long time and she blew out a breath of relief when she saw the sign for the ER.

†

Katie held her breath as she stood outside the cubicle where the ER doctors were working on Helen. She resisted the urge to pull back the curtain and go inside. She needed a definitive diagnosis so she'd know what to tell Helen's sister when she called her.

In her opinion, based on the location of the wound, Helen would be going to surgery within a short while. She speculated that depending on the damage the bullet did, the surgeons would remove at the least Helen's spleen. If there was more damage, there was the possibility of more extensive repairs.

"Please don't die on me. Gran keep her safe for me. She's the one."

"What's happening?" a low voice asked.

Katie knew the voice and looked up at her husband.

"I'm waiting to see if Helen is going to make it."

"Bobby is in serious condition."

Katie remained silent.

"I just can't get my head around him shooting Helen. I don't think he would do such a thing unless provoked."

"Didn't you notice the doorframe was in shambles?"

Jack just stared at her.

"Tell me exactly what she did to be responsible for him breaking down the door and shooting her."

Jack's face was somber with a look of dismay. "I know the man. I've been in battle with him. That isn't him."

"I don't know what to say to that. Do you agree with a man beating down a woman's door and threatening her within an inch or less of her life?"

"Don't you even care how Bobby is doing?"

"Frankly, at this moment, I don't give a damn."

Katie turned her back to Jack when the doctor came out of the exam room.

"We are sending her up to surgery," Dr. Connie Hardee, a short, dark-haired woman said.

"Her prognosis?"

"Good. She should make a full recovery unless we find more damage than the spleen."

"Thank God."

The doctor squeezed Katie's hand. "We will take good care of her. Why don't you use one of the doctor's rooms while you wait? I'll make sure they know where to find you."

"Thanks, Connie, I'll take you up on that. I have some calls to make and I need privacy." She turned to Jack. "Go home. There's nothing you can do here."

†

The doctor's room was small but it had a sink, a toilet, and a ready supply of scrubs. Before Katie did anything else she needed to get out of her bloody clothes. After washing the blood from her hands, she changed into scrubs before depositing her soiled clothes in a plastic hospital bag.

Do I call Sally now or wait until the surgery is over? If it were me, I'd want to know now. With Helen's phone in her hand she gently wiped off Helen's blood, turned it on, and then frowned.

Password? Her mind raced back to a conversation she had with her lover the week before. *My password is the date we met last year.* Katie ran her hand through her hair as she calculated what the date was. "That's it." After tapping in 0524 she smiled and stroked the screen that had the selfie of them.

"I remember when we took that. Can it only have been a short time ago?" She sighed. "What do I say to her sister? Hi, I'm Katie, your sister's lover. Oh, and by the way, her crazy husband just shot her."

With a resolve she knew she needed to have, she found Sally's number, pressed call, and then the speaker button.

"Hey, sis, I almost didn't recognize your new number. How are you doing?"

Katie called upon her professional persona and cleared her throat. "Hello, is this Sally?"

"Yes. Who is this?"

"I'm Katie, your sister Helen's friend."

"Katie? You were the one she talked about after that trip."

"Yes, that's me."

"Why are you on my sister's phone? What's wrong?"

Katie heard the worry in the voice. "Bobby found her."

"Oh my God, no," Sally sobbed. "Is she…"

"No. He did shoot her though. She's in surgery now. As long as the bullet didn't do extensive damage the doctor expects her to have a full recovery." Katie waited until she thought her words had sunk in. "She asked me to call you." Katie heard an audible gasp.

"Where?" Sally asked.

"Where was she was shot?"

"No. What's the name of the hospital."

"St. David's Medical Center on East Thirtieth in Austin."

"I'm on my way."

"Wait, don't hang up. I know you're concerned and want to see her but driving here now won't get you to see her any sooner. The surgery is still ongoing and once that is done she will be in recovery before they take her to a room."

"But at least I will get to see her," Sally countered.

"Probably not until midmorning tomorrow. Why not get some rest then leave early morning. By that time she will be lucid and you can see her then."

"I will not be dissuaded by you. I am leaving now."

"I understand, and that, of course, is your choice. If it were my sister I'd feel the same way. Just be prepared that they might not let you see her when you get here. It probably won't be until the morning."

"I appreciate what you're saying and thank you for your concern."

"I will be in the hospital in the morning. If you'd like to call me at this number I will find you and take you to her. Or you can ask when you get here for me and they will page me. Just ask for Katie McGuire."

"They know you?"

"Yes, I work for the St. David's system."

"My husband and I will be there as soon as we can. Thank you for calling me."

Katie held the phone to her breast and finally let her tears fall. She flopped down on a small bed and sobbed herself into a restless sleep.

†

Katie was holding Helen in her arms while blood streamed out of every orifice of her body. Try as she may, she didn't have enough hands to stop all the bleeding. Helen was moaning and crying for help but there was nothing Katie could do to save her. All she could do was hold her lover while she bled to death.

A knock on the door made Katie open her eyes immediately and sit straight up. The scrubs she wore were saturated with sweat and she shivered at the cool sensation. The knock came again and the realization made her shoot off the bed and open the door.

Her friend Connie stood at the door. "She's in recovery. I was with her while the surgeons did their thing."

"You did that for me? Didn't ER need you?"

"Yes and yes. I sensed how important she is to you and asked to be there. Except for the two shootings it was a slow night."

"Thank you. Yes, she is very important to me." Katie sucked in a breath, knowing she still had to ask the question. "Prognosis?"

"Excellent. There was a bit more damage, which is why surgery took longer than expected."

"But she's okay?"

"Yes."

"Thank, God. Is it okay to go to recovery?"

"Of course. You know the way."

Katie hugged Connie. "I am so glad it was you in the ER. Thank you for everything."

Connie patted Katie's shoulder. "Go on. She should be coming around about now."

"Thanks again." The dream forgotten, Katie hurried out of the room.

†

Helen opened her eyes and tried to focus as she looked around the room. Various curtained off areas held hospital beds, which, by her count, were all unoccupied. She closed her eyes trying to regain her brain function. Bobby had come crashing through the door and shot her—that was clear—but something else was lurking just outside of her memory. She closed her eyes.

A gentle hand ran across her forehead. Helen took in a deep breath and looked up. "I thought you were a dream."

"No. I'm real." Katie bent and kissed Helen's forehead. "How are you feeling? Drowsy?"

"Did I kill him?"

"No. It was touch and go for a while but the medics got him stabilized." Katie shrugged. "I think he might still be in surgery. Other than that, I know nothing about where the bullet penetrated his body or the seriousness of his wound. Would you like me to find out?"

Helen shook her head as a quiver ran through her body. "Does that mean he will come in here after his surgery is over?"

"Won't happen." Katie stroked her lover's face. "They will take him to a private room with a guard at the door. I am pretty sure they arrested him."

"How do you know that?"

"I have my sources."

Helen closed her eyes. "Does that mean it's over?"

"Yes, sweetheart, it is over."

"Sally?"

Katie looked at her watch. "I called her and she insisted on driving down here immediately. She should be here any time now."

"I don't want her to see me like this."

"She won't be able to come in here. She won't be able to see you until the morning when you're in your room all cleaned up and not so groggy. I told her that but she didn't listen."

"Yeah, that is how she is. Stubborn to the end whether she is right or wrong. Thank you for calling her," Helen mumbled. "I'm so tired."

"Get some sleep. I'll be back in the morning."

"What time is it?"

"Almost midnight."

"Don't leave me. I don't want to be here alone."

Katie bent and kissed Helen's lips.

Helen's eyes shot open. "Is anyone watching you?"

"Don't know. Don't care. I want you to know as long as I'm alive you will never be alone. I will stay with you until you fall asleep."

"Please don't leave me."

"I won't."

Helen's lips curled into a small smile before she closed her eyes and let the sleep of relief overtake her once again.

Chapter Eighteen

Early the next morning, after receiving a call from Helen's sister, Katie entered the lobby and looked around trying to find Sally. She spotted an anxious-looking woman with a tall, fit man, looking as if they were searching for someone. *That must be her.* Katie made her way to the couple.

"Hi. You must be Sally. I can see the Helen in you."

The woman blushed. "She's a bit taller and thinner than me."

"You have her eyes. She was moved to her room early this morning. I can take you to her if you'd like." Katie couldn't stop the butterflies that appeared in her stomach when she first spotted Sally. "She's still groggy from the surgery and on some strong pain meds. When I looked in on her ten minutes ago she was sleeping." Katie smiled. "I know she will be happy to see you."

Blue eyes appeared to focus on her and Katie could feel the butterflies flapping harder in her stomach. "I'm trying to prepare you for when you see her." Katie smiled. "She's not quite the dynamo she normally is."

"Yes, I understand that. Sorry, dear, this is just so overwhelming. My mind is a jumble from a lack of sleep. I'd like it very much if you could take us to her." Sally turned to her husband then back to Katie. "I'm sorry. This is my husband, Fred Jamison."

Katie held out her hand.

"It's a pleasure to meet you," he said, taking her hand.

"For me too. Sorry it isn't under better circumstances." The softness of the man's hand surprised Katie. "Okay then, let's go see Helen."

"This is her room." Katie stopped in front of a partially open door. "Let me check to see if they've finished with her vitals and drawn all the blood they'll need." She turned and smiled at the couple behind her. "I'll only be a minute."

A nurse was finishing her assessment when Katie walked into Helen's hospital room.

"How's she doing? Her sister is outside and anxious to see her."

A short, curly-haired woman smiled at Katie. "Her vitals look good. She manages to stay awake for a little while at a time. Please remind the family that they must limit their visit."

"I will. Thank you." Katie watched the woman leave then turned to the sound of Helen's low voice.

"You're here. Guess what, I feel nothing," Helen slurred. "All I need to do is push this little button and the world is wonderful."

Katie smiled and shook her head. "Morphine will do that to you." She moved to the bed and gave Helen a light hug along with a kiss on the cheek. "Are you ready for some visitors?"

"Is Sally here?" Helen seemed to be struggling to keep her eyes open.

"Yes, she and Fred are right outside the door." She patted Helen's hand. "I'll bring them in."

"Wait."

Katie tilted her head. "What?"

"Is all the blood gone?"

"Yes. They cleaned you up and you are still just as beautiful to me as ever."

"Hmm, you say the nicest things." Helen pushed the button again.

"I'll get them." Katie opened the door and motioned for Sally and Fred to come into the room.

Sally rushed to the bed and looked down at her sister lying there. "Oh, Helen, I was so scared."

"I'm good. No worries."

Katie touched Fred's arm. "I'll step out and give you some privacy. Right now you can't stay more than a few minutes. Try to make sure that she keeps calm so avoid any questions about the shooting."

"Will do. Thank you so much for taking such good care of her. I don't know how Sally would handle it if she..." he shrugged, "...you know."

"She's going to be fine." Katie took one last look at Helen and her sister before quietly moving out of the room.

Sally held Helen's hand as she wiped a tear away with the other one. "I can't believe he actually did it. You kept telling us but I really didn't believe he'd actually hunt you down much less shoot you. How did he find you?"

"We shouldn't be talking to her about that," Fred whispered. "They don't want her getting agitated."

Sally glared at her husband. "I'm her sister and I can ask her any damn thing I want," she whispered back.

"I know you're concerned but don't ask her about that now. She's just come out of surgery," Fred countered.

"Fine."

Helen, trying hard to focus, looked at her two visitors and shook her head. "Don't know how he found me. Katie, do you know?" She looked beyond Sally and Fred. "Where is she?"

Fred moved closer to the bed. "She stepped out to give us some privacy."

"No," Helen cried. "I need her in here."

Sally smiled and patted Helen's hand. "We are here and you have me to take care of you now."

"She told me she'd be back and we can only stay for a few minutes." Fred spoke in a soft manner.

Helen could feel her heart begin to race and her face break out into a sweat. "I need her in here now. She saved my life."

With a concerned look, Sally frowned. "I'm here now. You don't need to worry about your safety I will keep you safe."

Helen gasped for breath and clutched at the bed sheets.

"I'll go find her and have her back here in a jiffy." Fred patted his sister-in-law's hand. "Try to relax; it is not good to get yourself all worked up after your surgery."

"It's not necessary to find her. I'm here," Sally argued.

Fred took his wife's arm and led her away from the bed. "Can't you see that you are upsetting her? That's the last thing she needs after all she's been through."

"Fine. Go and find her but I'm not leaving."

Fred left the room.

Sally returned to her sister's bedside. "You need to get a hold of yourself and calm down."

Helen let out what sounded to her like a slow, drugged growl. "I just need Katie to be here. She saved my life, you know." She could feel her body begin to shake. "Something is wrong. I don't feel right."

"Hey, relax. I didn't mean to say anything to upset you. You need to stay calm. You've just had major surgery."

"Where's Katie?"

"Fred's gone to find her." Sally brushed the hair out of her sister's face. "Try to take some deep breaths to calm yourself down."

Helen could feel her chest tightening.

"Now that I am here, I'll help you get back on your feet so you can get back to your home where you belong."

Helen gulped in a breath. Her head was spinning and she closed her eyes trying to center herself. "Everything is too foggy and your words aren't making sense."

"It's probably your medication."

When the door opened and Helen saw Katie she let go of the breath she was holding.

Katie took one look at Helen then the monitors and rushed to her side. "You need to relax, Helen," she said softly. "Your blood pressure is up and so is your heart rate. Try to take slow deep breaths."

"I already told her that," Sally interjected.

"I don't feel so good."

Katie softly stroked Helen's forehead. "No wonder. It looks like you are having a panic attack. Slow down your breathing. You are safe. No one is going to hurt you."

Helen's breathing slowed and she closed her eyes.

"We should go and let her rest," Fred said.

"Helen asked me to book you a room at the Hilton. She said to make sure you knew it was on her since her apartment is still sealed."

"That's not necessary," Sally said. "The only important thing to me is that she is alive. I will stay by her side until she goes home with us."

Katie nodded. "You cannot do that. The hospital has rules and times for visiting."

Sally looked at her sister then glared at Katie. "Surely there is someplace here in the hospital like a waiting room that we can stay in?"

"Sure there is, but it isn't meant for extended stays and it isn't all that comfortable. The hotel is close by and you can get a nap and be refreshed when you visit her again. Right now, Helen needs to rest so she can recover enough to go home. She can't be upset again. It is critical she remain as calm as possible during the early stages of the healing process."

"I didn't mean to upset her."

"I know. It's hard to see someone you love like this. She's on morphine and it can do funny things to people. You have to understand she had a big surgery along with a traumatic event. She needs to be cared for with gentle hands and we must pick our words carefully."

Sally's head fell. "I'm sorry. I was just so worried with all these questions racing through my head while we were driving." She shrugged. "They just all came tumbling out at once."

"Next time think first then talk," Fred said.

Sally scowled at her husband.

"You know I'm right don't you?" Fred asked.

"Is it okay to come back and see her after we get settled?" Sally asked.

"Certainly. Why don't you wait until this afternoon so she can get some sleep? She will be more alert then."

Sally kissed her sister's cheek. "You get some rest and we will be back later." She caressed Helen's cheek. "I am so glad you are going to be okay."

Once the door closed behind Sally and Fred, Katie turned toward her patient.

"Are they gone?" Helen asked with her eyes still closed.

"Yes. Had I known they would upset you like that I never would have left the room."

Helen fidgeted with the sheet. "She means well. Sometimes she just gets carried away and doesn't stop to think. What I don't understand is when did she become so obnoxious?"

"She wasn't obnoxious. It was obvious she had good intentions and that she was very worried about you."

"I know she is." Helen let out a sigh. "It was just so overwhelming."

"Of course it is. A lot has happened to you and I doubt you've even had time to process it all."

"I can't seem to get my head around it all."

"Then just let it go and get some rest. You'll be surprised how much better you will feel once you get some decent sleep." Katie leaned in and kissed Helen's cheek. "Why don't you close your eyes and I will sit here next to your bed." Katie sat in the chair.

"I'd like that." Helen yawned. "I could sleep some."

"Then do. Just so you know I have filled out the necessary forms and you are now officially my patient."

"Hmm, I like being your patient."

Katie watched Helen struggle to keep her eyes open. "Before you fall asleep listen to me. I've taken the day off from work but I need to go to my house and get some clean clothes and take a shower." Katie tugged on the green material. "All I have to wear right now are these scrubs."

"You look cute in 'em," Helen slurred.

"I'll stay with you till you fall asleep then go."

"You'll come back won't you?"

"Try and stop me." Katie leaned in and kissed Helen's lips. "You get some rest now. I'll be back before you wake up."

"Okay." Helen closed her eyes and fell fast asleep.

†

Katie walked into the laundry room from the garage, dumped her bloody clothes in the washing machine, and started it before entering the kitchen. She looked around. She remembered that when she first saw the room before they bought the house she instantly liked it—always liked it—it was what drew her to agreeing to move there. Now, it seemed foreign to her.

"Oh, you're back," Jack said. "How is Helen?"

"She'll make a full recovery." Katie looked up and saw sadness in Jack's eyes.

"Did you hear the news?"

"What news?"

"Bobby died."

"Yes, I knew that. It will save the taxpayers from paying for a trial." As soon as the words came out Katie regretted them. "I'm sorry that was insensitive and uncalled for."

Jack swiped at his eyes. "They will probably arrest Helen for his murder."

"Are you serious?" Katie couldn't believe her ears. "She had a restraining order. He broke down her door and shot her." Her eyes fixed squarely on the man across from her. "Do you really think Helen had some culpability in what happened?"

Jack shook his head. "He was my friend."

"I'm sorry for your loss. I truly am. I know how much you regard all your squad." Katie patted her husband's arm as she passed him by. "I need to pack some things," Katie said over her shoulder as she walked out of the kitchen.

"Why? Are you going somewhere?"

Katie saw the sorrow on Jack's face and couldn't bring herself to tell him she was leaving him. "I need to stay in town for a few days."

"Why?" he asked.

Katie closed her eyes.

"Who is he?"

Katie chuckled. "*You* of all people are asking me that?" She shook her head.

He followed her into her bedroom. "You've told me before on more than one occasion that you wanted a divorce. I've thought about the why often and realized there must be someone else. It's the only reason that made sense. But you never went through with it so I figured your fling was over. This is the first time you are taking action. So who is he?"

"It doesn't matter if there is someone else or not. The problem lies between you and me and I don't see that ever getting better. I won't live like this anymore." She took a small suitcase out of the closet, unzipped it, and started putting clothes in it.

Jack grabbed her arm. "It matters to me."

"Let go of me." Katie's words were slow, deliberate, and held repressed anger. "Take your hand off me. Now."

Jack lessened his hold. "Why are you throwing away everything we have together?"

"You threw it away years ago, Jack." Katie wriggled out of his clutch. "You were too busy with your planes and squad to notice."

"Then why did you stay?" Tears were welling in his eyes.

"Because you were older and I thought being dependable was enough. You were unfaithful but I could always count on you in a clutch."

"I'll change. I'll do whatever you want me to. Please, Katie, don't leave me."

"I'm sorry." Katie looked him square in the eyes. "You're not who I want to be with anymore."

"But *he* is?"

Katie just looked at the man. "Once I find a lawyer I will have him contact you."

"Don't do this."

"It's already done." Katie turned and walked away.

†

When Sally and her husband visited again that afternoon, the nurse on duty advised them that Helen was still agitated and their visit could only last for ten minutes.

Sally wasn't happy but nodded in agreement.

"She needs her rest more than seeing us right now," Fred said. "Try to keep your comments general so she doesn't get upset again."

"I know I went overboard earlier and I won't do that again." Sally arrived at Helen's hospital room door. "It's just that she's my sister and my responsibility since Mom isn't here."

Fred spun around. "I understand that, darling, but if you truly want her to get better you need to be mindful of what you say. She doesn't need questions about what happened right now."

"I know. I will keep it simple."

†

Helen looked at who was entering her room and forced a smile.

"Hey, sis. Are you feeling better?" Sally asked.

"I slept for a few hours but I'm still incredibly tired." Helen held up the button for the morphine. "This keeps me really loopy."

"Sometimes loopy is a good thing, especially if it helps you get better." Sally soothed her fingers along her sister's cheek. "I was so worried about you and all I did was to make you feel worse earlier. I'm so sorry for that."

"So much has happened...it is overwhelming," Helen said tiredly.

"I know, and when you're ready we can talk about it all." Sally smiled. "Whenever either of us have a problem we've always been able to solve anything as long as we were honest with each other."

Helen closed her eyes and shook her head. "Not now."

"Later is good," Sally said.

"Keep it general." Fred looked at his watch. "The nurse said ten minutes and it's been twelve we need to go."

Sally waved him off. "Ten minutes is just an arbitrary number. We can stay as long as we want."

"No, you can't," the nurse said from the door. "Ten minutes is ten minutes and I gave you twelve. Now say your goodbyes and you can visit her tomorrow when she is stronger."

Sally kissed her sister's cheek. "I'll be back. Get some rest so you can get better and go back to your home."

Helen whispered, "See you later. I'm going to sleep now."

As the nurse fluffed up Helen's pillow Sally and Fred left.

"I wish they'd realize that I am really not up to visits just yet."

"It's hard for families sometimes to understand what it takes to heal," the nurse said.

175

"Yeah, I get that now. I guess you need to be in this bed to understand."

†

Helen was glad not to have the hassle of her sister for the rest of the day. The only one she wanted to see was Katie, who had spent the night before with her in a very uncomfortable recliner that was brought into the room.

Katie hadn't come back and that made her insides quiver with apprehension. Lying with her eyes closed she was trying to digest the idea of Katie actually leaving Jack and filing for a divorce. She couldn't complete one thought without her brain flying off somewhere else. Nevertheless she knew there would be time for the details later. All she could focus on now was the distinct possibility that she would spend the rest of her life with Katie. Her body trembled at the thought—it felt so right.

The door opened and Helen's heart leapt with joy at the sight of Katie. "You came back."

Katie grinned. "Just like a bad penny."

"Not even close." Helen held her arms open. "Come here and kiss me before I die of the starvation of your lips not being on mine."

"Wow, you are feeling better, I see. I thought I'd find you still sleeping."

"Sally and Fred were here a little while ago."

"They must have had a good effect on you. It's nice to see you smile again."

"This smile is for you only."

"The visit didn't go well then?" Concern covered Katie's face.

"No, it was okay. Sally tried her best not to be her usually overbearing self but she still managed to annoy me." Helen shook her head. "I guess it is a sibling thing."

Katie looked at the monitors. "Your vitals look good."

"I feel a lot better now that you are here." She paused for a moment. "The nurse told Sally and Fred to go home and not come back until tomorrow."

"And that is okay with you?"

"More than okay. The peace and quiet is wonderful."

"Do you want me to go?"

Helen's eyes bulged. "No. Why would you think that?"

Katie caressed Helen's cheek. "Because at this point in your recovery you need all the peace and quiet you can get."

"What I need is you." Helen crooked her finger. "Come here." When Katie got close she said, "Lean down." Katie's lips against hers made Helen tremble with desire. She pulled away. "Is it possible to lock the door?"

"No. I can't believe you are even considering such a thing. How many times have you pressed that button?"

"Whenever I hurt."

Katie's head shook. "Even if I could lock the door I wouldn't." Katie put her hand over the bandage covering the incision on Helen's abdomen. "You need to heal first."

Helen let a pout form on her lips. "I know, but it doesn't change what my body wants—it wants you."

"We will have plenty of time for that. Especially now that I've moved out."

"You did? Where are you staying?"

"At the moment, nowhere." Katie closed her eyes and shook her head. "I need to tell you something."

Helen could feel her body tense. *Here it comes. She's going to tell me she needs time before she commits to me fully.* "What?"

"They had to rush Bobby back to the operating room this morning. He died on the operating table."

"He's dead?" Stunned, Helen said, "I killed him."

"You were defending yourself. There is a big difference between that and outright killing someone."

"I wanted him dead. I wanted him out of my life."

"Sweetheart, that wasn't why you pointed your gun at him and pulled the trigger. It was either you or him."

"Or both of us." Helen looked into the green eyes and shed a tear.

"Tell me what you're feeling."

Helen shook her head. "Numb, I guess. Relieved. Sad. Happy. Guilty. All of those together. I don't know how I should feel."

Katie laid her head on Helen's shoulder. "Everything you are feeling is normal. Give it a few days and then maybe you will want to talk to someone about it in depth."

"I'm talking to you aren't I?"

"Yes. I was referring to someone who is trained in helping you with what you're feeling. I can listen and throw out suggestions but I'm not trained in how to support you with this."

"I understand. Let me think on it."

"Take all the time you need."

"Will you stay with me tonight?"

"Of course I will. Let me get a change of clothes from my car so I will have something to wear to work tomorrow."

"Do you have to work tomorrow?"

"Yes. I broke a lot of appointments today so I can't do that again." Katie shrugged. "I owe it to my patients."

"I know." Helen said with another pout. "I'm your patient too."

"You are my most important one but the others are counting on me too."

Helen smiled. "Go get your things and hurry back. Kissing isn't too strenuous is it?"

"No, it isn't, as long as that's all we do." Katie winked. "I'll be back before you know it. In the meantime try and get some rest."

Chapter Nineteen

"What a difference a good night's sleep makes," Helen said. "I can't believe how much better I feel."

"That's what you need to recover. Sleep gives your body a chance to heal." Katie eyed her. "Just don't think you are all better now and get yourself upset again."

"I won't." Helen watched as Katie finished dressing for work. "Do you really have to go?"

"Yes. Just because you're feeling better doesn't mean you don't need more time to rest."

"But I rest better with you here."

Katie shook her head. "Pouting isn't going to work."

"Can't blame a girl for trying."

"Will a kiss satisfy you until I get back?"

"No." Helen had a glint in her eyes. "But two will."

"You're being a goof so I know you are feeling better." Katie leaned in and gave Helen two kisses. "There, that should hold you till I get back."

The door opened and a man carrying Helen's breakfast entered. "Here you go," he said, placing a tray on the rolling table.

"Thanks." Helen looked at Katie. "You'll be back right?"

"Yes, as soon as I can," Katie promised. "Two of my patients are in the hospital and I need to check on them. Once I finish with them I will stop in to see you before I go to the clinic." Katie winked before she went out the door.

"Yum," Helen said sarcastically before moving the eggs around the plate. "I thought she said they had really good food here."

Helen had finished what she could of breakfast, had more blood tests, and was waiting on her morning assessments. She lay back and closed her eyes just as the door opened. She opened one eye and watched Sally saunter into the room.

"Did I wake you?"

"No, I was just closing my eyes." Helen yawned.

"Feeling better today?"

"Yeah, I slept most of the day yesterday and all last night. Didn't know how tired I was."

"Well, you look a lot better. You have some color back in your face."

"Bobby is dead."

Sally put her hand over her mouth. "You killed him?"

"He was trying to kill me, Sally."

"No. No, that's not what I meant." Sally bent and gently hugged her sister. "If anyone could have defended herself and won it is you. I've never known a stronger or more determined person in my life. That is what I've always admired about you, sis—your strength."

"Yeah, well the burden of taking someone's life, as horrible as Bobby was, is a heavy load to carry."

"Maybe if we talk about it then you will feel better."

Helen scrubbed her hand over her face then looked at her sister. "I wish it were that easy. Honestly, I do. I just don't have the energy right now for any sort of discussion."

"Did he rape you before he shot you?" Sally asked in a whisper.

Helen snorted then quivered. "No. He didn't get close enough for that."

"Then what has you looking so down?"

"I'm not depressed, if that is what you're thinking. It's the drugs mostly. This ordeal has shown me that I want, no need, to take a different direction for my life."

Sally's brow furrowed. "Like how?"

"I already told you that I really don't want to talk about this anymore. I can feel it in my chest and that is not good."

"You can trust me with anything," Sally persisted.

"I've met someone that matters and that terrifies me."

"Matters romantically?" Sally's tone was cautious.

"It's more than that." Helen looked into her sister's blue eyes. "It's like I've found someone who gets the real me."

"And why does that scare you? It seems to me that is exactly who we all hope to find. I know I've found it in Fred." Sally smiled. "All you have to do is give in to it."

"That's the problem. I have. Now I just want to chuck it all and spend the rest of my life just being happy." Helen eyed her sister, trying to judge whether to say more or just let it be. *My mind is too jumbled right now to say anything that will make sense.*

The door opened and Helen let out her breath.

"Time to take your vitals, Ms. Dunham, and get you cleaned up." The short, dark-haired nurse looked at Sally. "Will you please step out for a few moments?"

Sally nodded. "I'll go to the cafeteria for some coffee and a bagel then come back and we can finish our conversation. Want me to bring you anything?"

"Right now she needs to stay on the diet the doctor ordered," the nurse said.

"Okay. Be back in a little while."

A feeling of relief washed over Helen and she smiled at the nurse.

"Thanks for telling her that. I don't think I could stomach anything more." Helen scratched her head, puzzling over why she was so relieved when Sally left.

†

Helen heard a soft knocking on her door and sighed, certain Sally was back.

She was surprised when a woman dressed in street clothes came through the door.

"Can I help you?"

The woman smiled and held out her badge. "I am Detective Amanda Brewer, one of the detectives on your case. I asked at the nurses' station and they said I could come in. Are you feeling up to a few questions?"

"Sure. Take a seat."

Detective Brewer held up a recorder. "Is this okay?"

"Yes."

"Can you tell me in your own words what transpired at your apartment two nights ago?"

Helen explained how Bobby had hit her and she filed for divorce; how he threatened her and her lawyer helped get a restraining order before she moved to Austin. She related that he had somehow found where she was and began pounding on her door and the events subsequent to that.

"The next thing I knew I was waking up in the hospital."

"Do you have a license for your gun?"

"Yes, and I have a concealed handgun license."

"Do you know if your husband had a gun along with a license too?"

"No idea. He didn't share that much with me."

"To the best of your knowledge all that you've told me is accurate?"

Helen nodded. "Yes. I'm sure you saw the door and where he lay in relation to where I was."

"Yes, I did. It took a lot of anger to destroy that door."

"It was in self-defense that I shot him."

"Yes, that is obvious but we still need to investigate."

"That's all I know."

"Fair enough." The detective turned off the recorder, stood and, nodded. "I will transcribe this interview into a document. Then I'll call you in a few days to set up an appointment for you to come down to APD, after you've been released from here, to sign your statement."

"Okay. Thank you, Detective Brewer." Helen gave the woman a quizzical look. "May I ask if I'm going to be charged for his death?"

The detective smiled. "No, it was clearly self-defense. I know people don't think much of restraining orders but they do help. In your case it explains one of the reasons you had to shoot him."

"Thank you."

†

Once again her door opened. "What is this? Revolving door day?" She smiled when she saw Katie. "First Sally, then the nurse, then a detective, and now the only one I wanted to see."

"A detective?"

"Yes, she wanted my statement about what happened with Bobby." Helen frowned. "I asked if they were going to charge me."

"Surely they aren't, are they?"

"No."

"That's good news. How are you feeling?"

"Tired, but better now that you are here."

"I can't stay long. I'm ahead of schedule since I stayed here last night, but I had to see how my favorite patient was doing before I go to the clinic."

"I wanted to get some sleep but Sally said she'd be back so I will wait till she leaves."

Katie frowned and pulled her phone out of her pocket. "Hold that thought. I'll be back. The patient I just saw is in distress and the doctor needs me."

Helen watched Katie walk rapidly out the door and sighed.

†

When the door to her room opened again, Helen looked at it expectantly—horror filled her face. "Ingrid, what are you doing here?"

"You killed my brother, bitch. I told you if you ever hurt him you'd pay and I'm gonna make sure that happens."

"He attacked me." Helen's heart began to race as she realized she had no way of getting away. Her fingers felt for the call button but she couldn't locate it.

"You shot him dead and if it's the last thing I do I will make sure you pay." The tall blonde dashed for the bed and wrapped her hands around Helen's neck. "You whore. All he wanted to do is make up with you," Ingrid screamed. "And what did you do? You found yourself a rich old man then killed Bobby."

Helen grasped at the hands tightening around her neck. "No, that is not true," she choked out.

183

"Liar. I'll find the bastard and when I do he will pay too." Ingrid tightened her grip.

†

Katie was about to enter Helen's room again when she heard screams from a voice she didn't recognize. She grabbed a passing nurse. "Get security now."

Pushing the door open and seeing a large blond woman with her hands around Helen's neck, she moved quickly forward. "What's going on in here," Katie demanded, wasting no time in clutching at the stranger's hands. "Let her go."

The woman kicked back, catching Katie's knee.

Stumbling away, Katie stopped herself from falling by grabbing the arm of the nearby recliner. Once again, she came at the woman, jumping on her back and squeezing her wrists as hard as she could. "Let go!"

A hand released from Helen's neck long enough to strike Katie in the face, making her let go. She fell to the floor with a thud.

In a flurry of action a dark, muscular man came out of nowhere, grabbed the woman around her upper body, and yanked her away.

Rubbing her cheek, Katie stood. Immediately her eyes went to the bed where Helen was gasping for breath.

Katie rushed to Helen's side and let her fingers gently probe the rapidly bruising neck. All during the exam, she tried to tamp down the feelings of rage against the now struggling blond woman.

"Are you okay, Helen?" she asked.

Helen cleared her throat. "Yes," a scraggly voice replied.

Katie turned to the security guard. "Are you going to call the police and detain her until they get here? She needs to be arrested for attempted murder and assault."

"It is standard procedure, ma'am."

It wasn't long before another guard, who also took hold of the woman, joined the man.

"Let go, assholes! She's gonna pay for her sins!" Ingrid struggled to free herself then stomped on one guard's foot.

"You're not getting away so stop struggling," the newer guard said.

"Pigs."

The men, holding Ingrid by her arms, began dragging her out of the room.

"You won't get away with this, slut. I'll make sure you and whoever you're fuckin' pays," Ingrid screamed.

The door closed but Katie could still hear the woman's protests. Sitting on the side of the bed, Katie soothed her hand over Helen's hair. "Sure you're okay?" She inspected Helen's neck again. "It is already turning black and blue. I need to get a doctor in here to check you out."

Helen was trembling as a lone tear worked its way down her cheek. "Will this ever end?"

Katie furrowed her brow. "Who the hell was that?"

With her eyes closed Helen rubbed her neck. "His sister."

The door opened again and Katie protectively wrapped her arms around Helen. "I won't let anyone hurt you ever."

A nurse followed by a doctor came into the room.

"Is she the one that was attacked?" a tall, slender woman asked.

"Yes, Doctor Martinez."

"I'll check her out."

"Thanks. I'm glad you're the one doing it."

The doctor smiled and began palpitating Helen's neck. "Everything seems to be okay." The doctor turned to the nurse. "Check on her frequently to make sure she is breathing okay."

"Will do, Doctor."

The two women had been gone from the room for less than a minute when the door opened again.

"What happened?" Sally asked, walking quickly toward the bed. "I saw Ingrid being dragged down the hall screaming."

"Ingrid tried to kill me."

Sally's hand flew to her mouth as she pushed Katie aside. "Oh, my God. Are you okay?"

Katie took a step back and watched the scene unfold before her.

"Look at your neck," Sally cried. "I'll call Fred and he'll make sure they put that psycho bitch in jail. The whole lot of them are crazy. Remember how she acted at your wedding?" She took her phone out of her pocket. "Fred, there's been a situation with Bobby's crazy sister. Get here as fast as you can."

"She wanted to kill me," Helen sobbed.

Katie moved the other side of the hospital bed and took Helen's hand. "They've got her so you needn't worry about her. Listen, I need to get to the clinic. I'll be back later to check on you." Her eyes went to Sally. "Your sister will take good care of you in the meantime."

"Yes, I will."

"I'll go see if the police are here yet and give the two of you some privacy," Katie said.

Helen's eyes looked up. Katie could see them pleading for her to stay. She leaned in and kissed Helen's cheek. "I won't be long. Promise."

When she reached the door, Katie heard Sally ask, "Just what's going on?"

†

On his way down the crowded hallway, Fred stopped Katie. "What happened?"

"You'd best come with me."

"What did Ingrid do?"

"She's Bobby's sister, right?"

Fred nodded.

"She tried to kill Helen."

"Why?"

"Because Bobby died."

"Shit."

"Security has her. I think the police should be here by now."

Fred turned. "Lead the way."

†

An average-built police officer with dark skin, dressed in jeans, an open-collared shirt, and a sports jacket ushered Katie into a small room. One of the security guards was there.

Holding out a badge the man said, "I'm Detective Hardgrave. I'm one of the detectives involved in the Bobby Swenson shooting. Did you witness the attack, Ms...?"

"McGuire. Katie McGuire."

"Ms. McGuire," the man echoed. He jotted down something then shoved a notepad toward Katie. "I'll need a contact number so we can get in touch with you for your formal statement."

"Certainly, Detective." Katie saw her name on the notepad and jotted down her phone number.

"Tell me in your own words what you witnessed."

"I was about to enter my patient's room when I heard shouting coming from inside. I told the nurse closest to me to call security. When I opened the door I saw a woman strangling Helen...my patient, I mean."

"What happened next?"

"I tried twice to get her to let go. First time she kicked me, the second she slapped me hard enough that I fell to the floor." Katie conjured up the vision and shivered. "Next thing I knew security was there and they pulled her away."

The detective looked at the security guard. "Do you have anything to add?"

"She's one strong woman. It took both of us to get her under control. She was kicking, screaming, and struggling to get away all the way down here."

"Helen's lawyer is outside and would like to speak with you, if that's okay."

The detective nodded and opened the door. "Sir, will you join us?"

Fred entered the crowded room and cleared his throat. "I'm Fred Jamison, Ms. Dunham's attorney."

"Detective David Hardgrave."

The two men shook hands.

"I do not know if you are aware of it, Detective, but Ms. Dunham was shot by her husband recently."

"Yes, I am aware of that. I'm the lead detective in the case involving Bobby Swenson. My partner came to the hospital to question Ms. Dunham earlier. I arrived just as security was subduing the woman." He looked away. "Once I found out what was going on with security I put two and two together and told the guards I'd handle the situation."

"That woman was trying to murder my client."

"By all the accounts we have there is enough evidence to arrest her for attempted murder."

"Good," Fred replied.

"Is there anything more you need from me, Detective? I have patients I need to see," Katie said.

"I have all your particulars, Ms. McGuire, and we will be in touch for you to sign a formal statement later on today or tomorrow."

Katie scraped her seat back, stood, and closed her eyes. Reliving the deranged woman trying to kill her lover made her realize just how close she came to losing Helen—again. She looked at the detective. "It must run in the family."

Detective Hardgrave nodded. "It would seem that way."

"I have a few more things to discuss with the detective, Katie. I will catch up with you later."

Katie nodded and left the small room. She looked at her watch and realized she still had time to check on Helen once more.

†

"Time to spill the beans," Sally said.

"About what? Bobby or his lunatic sister who just tried to kill me too?" Helen rubbed a hand over her forehead before touching her neck. Letting her eyes gaze into the ones that reflected her own, she smiled. "I have a guardian angel. If it hadn't been for Katie I'd be dead by now."

"What's going on between the two of you?"

Helen shrugged. *We've never talked about anything this personal.* She didn't have a clue about what her sister thought about same-sex couples. She knew lesbians worked for her but didn't know what she really thought about them.

"I want answers, sis. It is obvious there is a special connection and I'm hoping you will be honest with me."

Helen had a bad feeling regarding what she was about to say. *She's my sister. She'll love me no matter what. Right?* Her stomach churned. "I love her. We are lovers."

Sally's face screwed up. "You're a lesbian? When? Have you always been? Is that why you never wanted to date any of the men I fixed you up with?" She frowned. "Why didn't you tell me?"

"How can I explain?" Helen pressed her fingers against her head, massaging at a threatening headache. "My work has always been my lover. I didn't date those men because I wasn't interested in them." She fixed her gaze at the window. "I never had a clue about love or sex for that matter. My experiences were limited even with Bobby. I was glad when he took a lover because I never was interested in having sex with him."

"And now you want to have sex with a woman?" Sally stood from her seated position on the bed. "I guess the signs were all there and I just didn't see them."

Helen's brow furrowed. "There were no signs to see. I didn't have a clue myself."

"Had I known you were into women I never would have kept setting you up on dates with men."

"Didn't you hear me? I didn't know myself until I met Katie. There's nothing wrong with loving her. Love is love." Helen could feel her heart begin to pound. "I had no idea until a few weeks ago that this is how I feel and neither did she. It is so new, weird, and strange, yet oh so right to me. With her I can breathe and be who I am and not worry that she will eventually hurt me like Bobby did." She shrugged. "She has shown me just how right life can be."

"And she makes you happy?"

"More than I ever thought possible."

Sally let out a loud sigh. "I can't tell you I am happy about this situation but if it is what you want then I will try to accept it." Her eyes turned to Helen. "Do me one favor."

"What's that?"

"Really think about this before you jump headlong into it."

Helen rubbed her head. "I already have." She wiped her nose with the back of her hand. "Ingrid is out to kill me and Katie."

"No, she won't."

"You're delusional if you think she won't get out on bail. Then, she will stalk me until she finds out who Katie is and she will kill her to punish me."

Sally handed her sister a tissue. "We won't let that happen," she whispered.

"I couldn't bear it if she hurt Katie."

Sally touched Helen's hand. "If you really care about her and what Ingrid will do, you need to think about letting her go."

Helen bowed her head. "I can't do that."

"I think that is a wise thing to do, sis. You need to get back to work, to your house, and forget about everything that's gone on."

Helen shook her head. "I'm not going back there."

"Why? That's your home. It's where you belong."

Helen closed her eyes. "I love Katie and want to make a life with her."

"You know it won't be easy. The practical thing to do when you leave the hospital is to move back to your home in Highland Park."

"I won't do that. Katie is who I want in my life."

"At what cost?"

Helen frowned. "You just don't get it do you? What we have together will never end. It runs that deep. I have no options where Katie is concerned, Sally. Katie gives me life and that is what is important to me."

Sally shrugged. "Is it okay if I pray for you?"

"Yes."

†

Helen watched her sister leave with tears tumbling down her cheeks. Never in her wildest dreams did she think her sister would react the way she did. Her support was lukewarm at best and it was clear that Sally did not approve.

"I don't know her at all. Is it possible that she's a homophobe? I wonder if her lesbian workers know that?"

Helen rested her head against the pillow, torn between her love for her sister and her deep feelings for Katie. Sally was the one person, other than her mother, who had known her from the time she was born. Behind her sister's veiled support, she could feel vehemence and dislike. The attitude coming from Sally not only shocked her but wounded her deeply. Looking at the clock on the wall, Helen tried to calculate what time it was in England. She had a deep need to speak with her mother and tell her everything that was now escalating out of control. She needed the guidance that only her mother could give.

Leslie, a very cute young woman who had been her day nurse since the day before came into the room. "You doin' okay?"

Helen shook her head.

"Got the blues. I've seen it lots of times. Being in here will do that to you." She looked at the chart. "You should be going home in a few days." Straightening the sheets, she smiled at her patient. "You sure are lucky to have Katie watching over you. I know she is not a doctor but if I needed urgent medical help she's the one I'd want to see first on the scene."

A smile curved Helen's lips. "I'm very fortunate to have her in my life as a very good friend too."

Leslie finished her assessment. "As far as I'm concerned she is the best."

"You're right. If I have to make a choice of who will be my main health care professional she's the one I'd choose hands down." Helen looked at Leslie and held up her cell phone. "It's okay to make a call from here right?"

"Yes. We have Internet too if you need it."

Helen smiled. "No, I just need to call my mom and tell her what is happening with me."

Leslie turned to leave.

"Oh, one more thing, Leslie. Can you have a sign put on my door that says something like no visitors, check with nurses' station? And tell them unless it is someone important, like the police or medical personnel, no one visits me."

Leslie looked puzzled.

"So much is happening that I need to get some sleep. I'm exhausted and it's been like a revolving door."

"Of course we have a sign for just that." Leslie smiled. "Leave it up to me."

"Thank you. I appreciate that."

†

The phone on the other end was ringing and Helen was glad she talked her mother into an international plan. She enabled the speaker and waited. *Come on, Mom, answer.*

"Well, isn't this a lovely surprise," Carolyn Dunham said.

"Hi, Mom." Helen's voice was trembling.

"Darling, what's the matter?"

"Everything. Everything is the matter."

"Tell me."

The words started tumbling out of Helen's mouth. "Bobby hit me and I told him I wanted a divorce. He didn't take it well. I moved to Austin so he wouldn't find me but he did and he knocked down the door and shot me."

"Oh, my God."

"I shot him too and he's dead. Then Ingrid, his sister, came after me and tried to strangle me."

"Slow down, sweetheart. Are you all right?"

"Yes, I'm in the hospital. I had my spleen removed."

"Is Sally with you?"

"Yes. My friend called her and she came to Austin."

"Thank goodness for that. Family is important at a time like this."

"There's more."

"Yes."

"I've met someone that matters. I'm pretty sure Sally is against it."

"Why on earth would she feel that way?"

"Because it's a woman."

"You're in a relationship with a woman? As in sexually?"

"Yes, Mom, I am."

"Does she make you happy?"

"More than I ever thought possible."

"Exactly what did your sister say?"

Helen was silent for a moment.

"Are you still there?" Carolyn asked.

"Yes. It wasn't so much what she said as her tone and words. She didn't hide her disappointment. It was obvious that she wasn't happy."

"Well, that sounds about right. Tolerance has never been one of her stronger points. In case you hadn't noticed, she can be very judgmental. Along with that, you know the weird church she belongs to teaches intolerance against anything they deem evil."

"Yes, I know that. Are you ashamed of me or want to disown me?"

"No. Never. What's her name?"

"Katie." Helen smiled. "She's a nurse practitioner and she's saved my life both literally and figuratively."

"I'd like to meet the woman who has made my little girl happy. I can hear the happiness in your voice when you said her name."

"I'd like that too, Mom."

"Good. I will make arrangements and be on the next flight I can get to Austin."

"Mom, you don't have to do that."

"My little girl is in trouble and that is where I need to be. There is nothing here in London that I haven't seen before or cannot see again."

Helen sniffled. "Thank you. That means more to me than I can say."

"I'll email you the details as soon as I get them. I'm certain you won't be able to drive yet so maybe your Katie can pick me up."

"Thanks, Mom." Helen began to sob. "I need you."

"Hang on, sweetheart. I'll be there as soon as I can. Take care, darling."

"I will. Bye."

Helen held the phone to her heart and closed her eyes before her shoulders relaxed in relief.

With the head and legs of the hospital bed raised, Helen wiggled her butt in the depression the movement created. It was thankfully quiet and she breathed in deeply. *Mom's coming.* She yawned and closed her eyes. *I'll just take a little nap.*

†

The elevator bell rang and Katie watched as the doors slid seamlessly open. To her surprise Sally was standing in the corridor glaring at her.

"Hello, Sally, how is your sister doing?"

Sally grabbed Katie's arm and dragged her away from the elevator.

Confused, Katie knitted her eyebrows. "What's going on?"

"I will not let you ruin my sister's life. You keep away from her, do you hear me? Leave her alone to live a normal life and not the perversion you've taught her."

Guess Helen told her and it didn't go well. "Unless she tells me to go I'm going nowhere," Katie growled. Turning away, she swung back around. "Don't you ever speak to me that way again."

"Or you'll what? You're an abomination and should be ashamed of yourself and begging God-fearing people for forgiveness and repent your abhorrent behavior, you pervert."

"My God is all about love." Katie shook her head before turning and walking away.

The cruel words had hurt her deeply but she refused to let the hateful woman know that. Yet, by the woman's stance it was obvious that Sally knew exactly how the words affected her. *I let her do that.* She knew she should have walked away the moment the woman started speaking her vile words. *God only knows how those cruel words hurt Helen.*

Katie looked down the hallway toward Helen's room. She debated whether to go to her or give her some space—space lost. She looked at her wristwatch and knew she needed to get to the clinic but she needed to see Helen and make sure she was okay.

When she pushed opened the door to Helen's room she saw she was sleeping and breathed a sigh of relief. It was obvious that Sally hadn't said the same things to her sister or she wouldn't be sleeping so soundly. With quiet steps she walked to the bed and gave Helen a soft kiss before leaving.

†

Katie whizzed past hospital personnel, other people, and medication carts at a fast clip. She was late but she was glad she took the time to check on Helen.

Once in her office with the door closed, Katie bent over the wastebasket and dry heaved. Her heart was racing and the tears that continually threatened to fall burned her eyes. "What a horrible woman."

A soft knock at the door was followed by Sari Mitchel entering the office.

"Oh, my God, are you okay?" Sari moved quickly to Katie's side.

"Something I ate didn't agree with me," Katie said. Standing, she looked at the woman who'd be her nurse for the day. "What's the schedule like?"

"In a word…packed."

Katie groaned and returned to the wastebasket.

"Do you want me to see if I can reschedule or at least get you something to settle your stomach?"

With one last retch, Katie stood again. "No, I'll be okay. I've got something to calm the spasms and once I take it I'll be as good as new. If it doesn't work I'll be so far behind I won't be able to see daylight."

Sari put a comforting hand on Katie's shoulder.

Katie forced a smile in the direction of the small, thin woman. "What did you eat?"

"Nothing yet this morning. It must be the residuals of a hastily eaten meal last night. I'll be good to go by the time you have my first patient assessed."

"Okay. I'll get," she looked at her list, "Mr. Ferguson's vitals and have him in the room and ready for you in about ten minutes."

Katie looked at the clock and shook her head. "Good, I'll start the day off only ten minutes late."

Just as she reached for the doorknob to the exam room, Katie's grandmother's voice sounded in her head. *It's a slippery road you're travelin' on, Mary Kate. Best think about what yer doin' before you slide off that road.* The familiar phrase gave her pause when she remembered her gran's words a few days before she passed. *Love is never lost unless you want it to be, Mary Kate.*

Even when I'm gone from this world, my love will be with you and sustain you through the most difficult of times. Just remember me and if you need me, all you have to do is ask.

"I need you now, Gran. I'm so confused. I can't believe I let that vile woman speak to me like that."

†

Sally, after ranting to her husband for thirty minutes about her sister and Katie, was still fuming when she arrived at Helen's room. She was ready to open the door but stopped when she saw the large printed sign on the door. "What the hell?" Her anger increased and she stomped off to the nurses' station where she tapped her fingers in irritation when no one looked up to acknowledge her.

"Excuse me. I want to know why I am not allowed to visit my sister."

A nurse with sandy-blond hair and wearing glasses looked up. "May I help you?"

"Why is there a sign on my sister's door that says No Visitors?"

The woman gave her a blank look.

"Helen Dunham's room," Sally said forcefully. "She's one of your patients."

"Please keep your voice down," the nurse said. "If there is a sign like that on her door then the doctor must have ordered it. I'd suggest you call the next time you want to visit to find out when is the appropriate time. Obviously now is not that time. We have specific visiting hours." The woman placed a card on the countertop. "Here they are and as you can see there is a twelve-hour window."

Sally couldn't believe her ears. "What kind of hospital is this that won't allow me to see my own sister?"

The nurse looked up. "Your sister underwent major surgery and has been through a very serious and traumatic ordeal today. Right now what she needs is peace and quiet and that is why the doctor ordered the No Visitors sign. I'm certain that you want your sister to recover. Don't you?"

Sally nodded. "Yes, more than anything." She blew out a breath. "I'm just so worried about her."

"I understand," the nurse said in a calm and quiet voice. "You need to let us do our job and get her better. Right now that means no visitors. If you will call this number," she handed Sally a sticky note with a phone number on it, "we will let you know when the doctor decides she can have visitors. It will save you a trip." The nurse smiled.

"Yes, of course, you're right." Sally scooped up the piece of paper. "Thank you." She looked at her husband. "Come on, let's go. I hope I don't find out that woman is responsible for that sign. I've got to get Helen away from her."

"Sally." Fred looked at her with concern. "Helen is a grown woman who is intelligent enough not to let anyone make her do something she doesn't want to do. You need to let it go and let her live the life she wants."

"The hell I will," growled Sally. "I will not allow that pervert to sully my sister any more than she already has."

Fred shook his head. "You're making a big mistake."

Sally shook her finger at him. "No, I am not."

†

The day was fraught with more emotions than Helen ever knew existed. Exhausted from the episode with Ingrid and the suspicion that her sister might be a homophobe, Helen closed her eyes in an effort to rest only to open them again as events repeatedly played in her head. It was past six and Katie still hadn't returned to visit. *Where can she be?*

Helen opened her cell phone and sent Katie a text.

I thought you were coming for lunch. What happened? I miss you. After pressing send she waited for a reply—none came.

Is something wrong? Are you okay? I'm worried about you. Helen let out a breath when she saw that Katie was answering.

You were sleeping when I came by earlier and I didn't want to disturb you. Right now I am playing catch-up since I was out yesterday. I should be there in about ten minutes.

Please hurry I need to see you and touch you. I need you.
I will be there as soon as I can.
Okay I can't wait.

†

Katie arrived at Helen's hospital room with a bright smile on her face. Seeing the sign on the door she made a mental note to find out why it was posted. She pushed the door open and caught her breath when she saw Helen. Katie had been on an emotional rollercoaster for the last two days and could only imagine what Helen was going through after being shot and nearly strangled.

"Hey, good looking, how are you feeling?"

"Like a million dollars now that you're here."

Katie looked at Helen's blue eyes that were focusing on her.

"What's with the sign on the door?"

"Sally was here and I just didn't want to hear anything she had to say. So when she left I asked the nurse to put a sign on the door for no visitors."

"Why?" If what Sally said to her earlier was any indication, Katie already knew the answer.

"I told her about us. I think she might be a homophobe," Helen softly said.

"I'm not surprised. I met her in the hall on my way back from speaking with the police and she read me the riot act about corrupting you."

"I'm sorry. Her thoughts are not mine. I want to be with you and if Sally doesn't like it then it is too bad for her."

Katie took a few steps toward the bed. "Really? The last thing I want is to come between you and your sister."

"The only one in the way is Sally."

Katie leaned in and kissed Helen. "I still feel guilty."

"You shouldn't. I called my mom and she is coming here."

"I thought she was in England."

"She is." Helen shrugged. "She said her little girl was more important." Tears filled her eyes, threatening to spill over.

Katie couldn't help the smile that curled her lips. "We all need someone like that."

"I have two someones who care about me that way."

"Yes, family is important in times like these."

Helen shook her head. "I didn't mean Sally. I meant you. I'm sorry she was hateful toward you."

"There is a saying that blood is thicker than water. I think it applies here. Sally is your sister and you have a history with her." Katie touched her chest. "We only have a brief history." She sat on the edge of the bed before kissing Helen gently on the cheek.

Helen pursed her lips. "I thought I knew her. But now I realize I never really did."

After taking Helen's hand, Katie gave it a gentle kiss. "She's your family. If there is one thing I know about you, it is that family is paramount. If you'd like me to leave I will. I won't like it. In fact, I'd hate it but I'd do it for you because it's the right thing to do."

"How can I choose? I don't want to lose you and I don't want to not have my sister in my life." An anguished look crossed Helen's face. "I don't know what to do. But know this, Katie. You are in my life for keeps. I think from the very first time I met you a year ago I knew that."

"I will not pressure you. Take your time and do what is best for you. Not what is best for me or your sister but for *you*."

Helen nodded. "You saw Jack yesterday. What did he have to say about Bobby dying?"

"He was upset. That didn't surprise me. What I found amazing was he thought they'd arrest you for his murder." Katie grimaced. "He saw what was left of the apartment door and you lying on the floor in a pool of blood. I think he is delusional or he just doesn't want to believe anything bad about one of his *squad* members."

Helen looked out the window. "I think they all live in a fantasy land where the others are concerned. When the detective spoke with me this morning I asked if she was going to arrest me. She said no, it was obviously self-defense."

"It is an absurd notion for anyone to think you'd be guilty of murder. He came after you." Katie couldn't stop the tears from coursing down her cheeks.

"Why the tears?" Helen wiped the tears away with her thumb.

"You came so close to dying twice now. I don't think I would survive if you weren't somewhere in the world." Katie looked away. "I think you should choose your family. I couldn't bear to see the pain in your eyes on holidays or birthdays if Sally wasn't there." She shrugged then turned to look at Helen. "In the end, it would break us apart for there would always be that between us. Even if you won't mean to, you will blame me."

"I'd never do that."

"Unfortunately you will."

"No, I won't. Besides, my mom is coming and she will straighten Sally out." Helen grinned. "She has a way of doing that with Sally."

"And you too?"

"No, not as much. I was a very focused child."

Katie smiled. "Yes, and you still are. I can tell that when we make love."

"Get used to it for I plan to be in your life for a very long time."

"I'll hold you to that."

Helen yawned and closed her eyes. "Sorry, I can't seem to keep my eyes open."

"Not surprising. You've had a long day fraught with too much drama. I need to get going anyway. My hotel room has a whirlpool bath that is calling my name. I'll check in on you tomorrow before I go to work." Katie leaned down and gave Helen a chaste kiss on her cheek.

"Can't you spend the night again?"

"No, I don't think my back will take another night in that chair." She smiled. "I will be back first thing in the morning."

"Will you call me when you get to the hotel so I can tell you goodnight?"

"Of course."

The pout on Helen's face was evident.

"Please stay and lay with me. I need to feel you by my side."

Katie shook her head then smiled. "You know I can't resist you. Let me go find some scrubs to wear then I will be back to lie down and hold you. At some point I will have to go to my hotel room so I can shower and change for work."

Helen grinned. "I can live with that."

Chapter Twenty

It was early in the morning and Katie was just parking her car at the hospital. She had left Helen sound asleep several hours earlier. A smile curled her lips recalling how right it felt to hold Helen while she slept. Yet the memory of Sally's words still invaded her thoughts. The ringing of her phone through the car's speaker brought her out of her feelings of dejection when she saw it was Helen.

"Good morning," she said.

"Hi."

Helen's voice sounded weary and Katie's heart clenched. "Are you okay?"

"Yes, I just woke up and missed you holding me."

"I was just sitting here in my car thinking about how I liked spending last night with you."

"Will you be in to see me later?"

"That I will have to play by ear. I'm still playing catch-up." Katie looked at the time glowing on the display in her car. "Who am I kidding?" She laughed. "I'll be there as soon as I put my things in my office."

"Fantastic. I have something to ask you when you get here. It's a special favor."

"Now I'm intrigued. Any hints as to what this special favor is?"

"Nope, not until you get here."

"Then I will bypass the office and be right there."

✝

Helen grinned when Katie walked into her room. "That was quick."

Katie went to the bed and kissed Helen soundly. "Now out with it, what is this special favor?"

"I need you to do something for me later today."

"Anything. What do you want me to do?" Katie gave Helen's body a once-over. "Besides the obvious."

Helen grinned. "Well, there is that but it is not what I'm talking about. I just got an email from my mom and her plane arrives at ABI at six fifteen. Do you think you could pick her up and bring her to the hospital for me?"

"You really want me to pick your mother up? Why not Sally or Fred?"

"They don't know she's coming and she asked specifically if you'd meet her and bring her to the hospital."

"Oh. Okay." Katie blinked. "I'm shocked."

"I told her all about you and she wants to get to know you."

"Really?"

"Yes, really. Will you do it for me? Please?"

"Of course I will. How will I know it's her?"

Helen laughed. "She asked the same thing. I told her to look for a cute freckle-faced woman with ginger hair tied back in a ponytail. Then I sent her your picture. I will send you hers."

Katie was speechless.

"Are you okay?"

"Yes. I'm just stunned that she is so accepting when your sister is totally the opposite."

"We need to make time to talk about us, Katie, and how to not let the chasm named Sally come between us," Helen said in a soft voice. "I won't lose you to the bigotry of my sister. You are far too important for me to allow that to happen."

"I'd like that." Katie sighed. "For the record, I have no intention of letting Sally come between us. I do, however, know how much family means to you and do not want to be a sticking point for you."

"It will never happen. Don't you know that?"

"In my heart I do, it's my head that needs convincing."

"I will do that."

Katie smiled then kissed Helen again. "I really need to go or I will start the day off late."

"Then get going and I will see you later."

"Count on it. I will have your mother in tow when you see me next."

"That's a long time. Will you at least call me when you can?"

"Of course. Depending on how the morning goes, I'll try to come by at lunch."

"Promise?"

"No, but I will give it my best shot."

"Come here." Helen kissed Katie soundly. "Now go and hurry back."

†

It was Friday and the third day of Helen's hospital stay. After speaking with Katie earlier her mood had improved from somewhat cranky to being happy and on an even keel. Sally and Fred came to visit near lunchtime and her sister wasted no time in starting her redemption plan.

"You need to go back to your home and job, Helen, and forget this deviant path that has twisted your mind."

"Sally, please, I don't want to discuss this with you anymore."

"I will not allow you to ruin your life. I did that once when I consented to your marrying that man and I won't do it again."

Arriving for a lunchtime visit Katie stopped in the doorway. She saw Sally and Fred standing by Helen's bedside and heard Sally talking in an adamant tone.

"Sis, you know I'm right. You need to go back to Highland Park, your job, the people who love you, and forget all this craziness."

"I'm staying in Austin. I already told you I really don't want to discuss this with you right now. Did you not hear me? I'm too tired and worn out to have any emotional discussions with you or anyone else."

"Remember, honey, she needs her rest and we need to avoid anything contentious," Fred said.

"I'm not being argumentative. I'm just trying to make her see the big mistake she's making."

Katie looked at the monitors and saw Helen's blood pressure and pulse rate rising. Moving into the room, she said, "Please leave the room while I evaluate my patient." Her tone was clipped.

"You again," Sally said. "I'll stay."

With her eyes fixed on the older woman, Katie moved into Sally's personal space. "You *will* leave this room now or I *will* call security," she whispered. "You have no say in this so go now."

"Fine." Sally turned back to her sister. "We'll be right outside the door."

Katie glared after the woman as she went out the door. She turned to face Helen and could see the sorrow in her eyes.

"So, it sounds like she is still on her mission to get you back to where you lived near Dallas and away from me. Is she succeeding?" Katie swiped at the liquid brimming in her eyes. "After our talk this morning I actually thought we had a chance. Now hearing her words again I'm not so sure."

"They are her words not mine," Helen growled. "Do you really think after all we've shared I'd believe one scintilla of anything she says?"

"No. Look," Katie sat on the bed, "I know we haven't known each other all that long, but for me being with you it's like I can finally see the life ahead of me. That is how right it feels when I am with you." Not being able to stop them, Katie let her tears fall. "I will always love you, Helen Dunham. You and you alone are the one bright spot in my life. But I cannot be responsible for tearing your family apart. It just wouldn't be right."

"The only one who will tear it apart is my narrow-minded sister. Let's just wait till Mom gets here and see if she can work her magic."

"She's that good?"

Helen smiled. "Even better. So there is nothing for you to worry over. It's all good."

Katie looked at the clock on the wall. "I need to get back to work. I will tell them to come back in."

"No, don't. Will you please tell them I want to sleep and to come back later this afternoon? I really am not up to listening to her plans for my return home, especially after I've repeatedly told her I'm not going back there."

"I can do that but she won't like it."

"I know, but Fred won't let her make a scene. If she does I will have them put the sign back up on the door."

"Okay." Katie kissed Helen and smiled. "Catch you later."

"You've given me a glimpse at the possibility of true happiness. I love you too," Helen whispered at the door that closed behind Katie.

†

Katie exited Helen's room, closing the door behind her.

Sally was glaring at her.

"Helen wanted me to tell you that she is going to go to sleep. She asked if you'd please return later this afternoon," Katie said directly to Fred. "I'm ordering her a mild sedative."

"Okay, sure no problem," Fred answered.

"Well, I have a problem," Sally said. "It sounds to me like you are purposely trying to keep me away from my own sister."

"I'm doing no such thing. Helen asked me to tell you she's going to take a nap. She also said if need be she will request the sign be put back on her door."

Sally bristled.

"Look, like it or not, your sister needs to recover and your constant badgering isn't helping that happen. Please come back later."

"We will." Fred took his wife's arm. "Come along, dear, we'll come back later."

At first it seemed as though Sally would balk. She glared once again at Katie. "I *will* be back, count on it," was her parting shot.

†

Helen spent into the late afternoon thinking about what she'd say to Sally. Although Katie hadn't told her everything she'd said, Helen had seen her sister in action in the past when she was filled

206

with righteous indignation. She needed to staunch what she knew would be a full-blown tirade against Katie and being a lesbian.

When Sally finally breezed into the room with Fred in tow, Helen steeled her resolve not to let her sister get to her.

"Did you get the sleep you needed?"

Helen shrugged. "Some."

"I know how hard it is to sleep when you are excited. Tomorrow is a big day for you. Let's talk about getting you back to your home. We went to your apartment earlier and I picked out some clothes for you to wear." Sally scratched her head. "I was surprised to see some of the clothes you had there. You've always dressed so respectably with an elegance that compared to no one else. Some of those things looked like something a slob would wear." She smoothed the sheet. "I don't know what's gotten into you but once you're back on your home turf you will get your senses back."

"Why did you confront Katie yesterday?"

Sally cocked her head. "She told you I did that?"

Helen nodded.

"Well, I saw no need to mince words or exchange niceties with her. It is clear she has corrupted your morals and she needed to know that."

"You didn't say that did you?" Fred asked. "She saved your sister's life, for God's sake. You should be on your knees thanking her not telling her she is a bad influence."

"Thank her for what? She's a deviant." Sally turned her attention to her sister. "Surely you know how destructive she will be to your life. Living outside of the norm is very difficult. Have you thought about that?"

Helen flexed her jaw and ground her teeth.

"Stop talking that rubbish. Can't you see you're upsetting her again?" Fred asked.

"No, I'm not. Am I, sis?"

"You had no right to speak to her like that. Katie is the kindest, most loving person I know."

"What you need is to get back to your normal life in Highland Park."

Helen shook her head as she digested what her sister was saying. "No, I don't. As I have told you repeatedly, I'm not leaving Austin. This is where I'm going to make a new home."

"You don't mean that."

"Yes, I do."

"Come on. Have you taken some more drugs? She said she was going to get you a sedative. Is that why you are talking so crazy? That woman prances around here like she is a real doctor when she is nothing more than a wannabe."

"That *wannabe,* as you call her, has saved my life on three different occasions."

"You mean two."

"No. Three."

"Are you sure you're not drugged? You aren't making any sense. She saved you when Bobby shot you and when Ingrid attacked you. That's two."

"She saved me when I met her."

"Don't be ridiculous."

"Ridiculous is your insistence to not listen to anything I say." Looking at Fred, Helen smiled. "I can't take any more of this. Can you please take her home?"

Fred took Sally by the arm. "Come on, dear. Let's get you out of here before she explodes. You know better than to antagonize her while she's still recovering."

"She goes home tomorrow and they've taken away the monitors. They wouldn't schedule that if she wasn't well enough."

"By the look on her face I think she is very upset. Let's go and come back after dinner."

Sally set her jaw. "I'm sorry I've upset you. It won't happen again."

"Sally, you can't help yourself. Go get something to eat and come back after that. Right now I need a break and some peace and quiet."

"Fine, but I will be back," Sally said.

"Lovely."

†

"Mrs. Dunham," Katie said. The tall blond woman was far more beautiful than her picture.

"Katie?" Carolyn said before pulling her into a hug. "I've been looking at your picture ever since I left Dallas." She grinned. "Helen was right. You are cute. Very cute indeed."

Katie blushed. "I can see the resemblance."

"Come on, let's get my luggage and go see our girl."

For a moment Katie was dumbfounded. "Okay. This is a small airport so it shouldn't take that long."

Carolyn laughed. "What kind of car do you drive?"

"A BMW."

"Small sporty one?" Carolyn looked her up and down. "No, you'd go for the SUV."

"Guilty as charged."

"Good 'cause I have a lot of luggage."

"Really?"

"For enough money you can have as many bags as you want."

Katie grinned. "Then we'd better get a porter." *I like this woman.*

Carolyn handed a twenty to the tall thin man who loaded all five of her suitcases in the back of Katie's vehicle. "Thank you." Her eyes twinkled when she looked at Katie. "Let's go see that daughter of mine."

Unable to help herself, Katie touched the woman's arm and smiled. "Yes, let's do that. I know she's excited to see you."

It was a fifteen-minute or less drive to the hospital and they had no sooner begun driving when Carolyn peppered Katie with questions.

"How did you and Helen meet?" Carolyn asked. "No, don't tell me I know. Last year around this time at Padre Island. Some flying group I believe."

"Yes. Did she tell you that?"

"I recall her saying the one bright spot of that adventure was meeting someone named Katie. I assume that was you."

Katie's heart skipped a beat. "Yes, it was me."

"So tell me about yourself, Katie."

"Not much to tell really. It sounds like Helen gave you all the highlights."

"That she did."

"I'm staying at the Wyndham and made you a reservation there for tonight."

"Is that where Sally and Fred are staying too?"

"No.

Carolyn laughed. "I don't blame you."

Katie nodded.

"I can see why my daughter loves you."

"She does?"

"Don't be coy with me, young lady. You know she does."

"I've hoped she does but the words have yet to be said."

"Have you voiced them?"

"Yes." Katie maneuvered her car into the St. David's parking garage. "Well, here we are."

Carolyn patted Katie's thigh. "Don't look so morose. You've got me on your side. Trust me that is where you want to be in this family." She winked and got out of the car.

†

After finishing her dinner, Helen was smiling. She had just received a text from her mother that she and Katie would be on their way once they collected the baggage. If Helen knew her mother, and she did, there would be more than the allotted number of bags.

"I wonder what they are talking about or if they are even talking." She smiled again. "No. Mom is definitely talking."

Her musings didn't last long—Sally and Fred were back.

"I see you did come back," Helen said in a flat tone. "If you're going to start in on me again you might as well turn back around."

Sally smiled. "Don't be ridiculous. I told you we'd be back after dinner."

"I'm expecting a visitor so you can't stay long."

"Who? That woman?"

"Just leave, Sally."

"Not until we have a talk about this insane notion of yours of staying in Austin."

210

Helen just shook her head.

"You can't be serious. Have you lost your mind?"

"No. I finally see what I want out of life."

The door pushed open and Carolyn Dunham appeared.

Sally turned and her eyes flew open. "Mom, what are you doing here?" She looked at Helen. "Did you know she was coming?"

"Of course she did. I am here visiting my daughter," Carolyn countered.

"With her?" Sally pointed at Katie.

"As far as I am concerned, Katie is a wonderful person who I am proud to know."

"You can't be serious."

Carolyn waved Sally off, went to her other daughter, and embraced her. "How are you feeling, darling?"

"Much better now that you are here." Helen's eyes tracked to Katie. "I see you found each other."

"Yes we did." Carolyn smiled. "And I heartily approve. She is a lovely woman."

Helen's eyes remained on Katie. "Yes, she is, and I'm privileged to have her in my life."

"You've got to be kidding," Sally spat.

Katie fished a hand in her pocket, pulled out a room key, and moved toward the bed. "Carolyn, here is the key to your room. It is an executive king room with all the amenities. The room number is on the envelope. I will have all your luggage put in your room. Text me when you are ready to go and I will come back to pick you up."

"You'll do no such thing. I will take *my* mother wherever she wants to go. It is not up to the likes of you," Sally spewed.

"Do not speak to her in that manner, Sally," Helen growled. "Fred, please take her away and don't come back. Go home."

Carolyn turned to Katie and took the key card. "You go on ahead, darling. I will take a taxi, it isn't that far."

"Please don't leave," Helen begged.

Smiling at her daughter, Carolyn nodded. "Don't worry I know where she'll be. Right now we need to settle things between you and your sister."

"I want her to stay." Helen was determined that Sally would not run Katie off. "She's a part of my life now and that means she's my family too."

Katie closed her eyes. "It is best if I go. There's a lot of history here that you all need to sort out." She smiled at Helen. "Don't worry, I will be back."

"You better because I know where you live and work and I will hunt you down if need be."

Katie shook her head and laughed. "You are such a goof."

Once the door closed, Carolyn sat in the recliner. "Fred, would you be a dear and give us some time alone?"

"Of course." Fred looked at his wife. "I'll be in the lobby," he said before leaving the room.

Carolyn pointed to a chair and looked at Sally. "Sit."

Sally sat.

"Now what seems to be the problem that has you two at loggerheads?"

"Don't tell me you condone this relationship."

"Approve? I most heartily do. Not only do I approve but I applaud both your sister and Katie for embracing who they love."

Sally laughed. "Love. Please, this is nothing more than a passing fancy."

"I beg to differ," Helen said. "There is nothing passing about this. Katie is in my life forever. I love her."

"You don't mean that. You'll come to your senses once you're back in your home and at your work."

"My home is in Austin now. I've told you that many times but it doesn't seem to sink in. As for my work," Helen shrugged, "I'm not sure what I'll do. Maybe I'll retire."

Sally looked at her mother. "See, Mom, it is that kind of insane talk that tells me she needs some sort of intervention. She wants to throw her life away."

"What Helen does with her life is her business. She is old enough to make her own mind up and choose who she wants to love." Carolyn leaned forward and rested a hand on the arm of

Sally's chair. "It is not your life. It is hers to do with as she pleases."

"You can't be serious that you'd let her go down this path," Sally cried.

"I'm dead serious. Why don't you go find your husband and go back to Dallas? I'm here now and I can take over caring for my daughter."

"I won't leave town until we've had this out. I won't let her make a fool out of herself." Without another word, Sally gathered her belongings and left.

"That went well," Helen said. "I should have never dragged you into this. I'm sorry, Mom."

"No need to be sorry. I've seen a side of your sister that I always suspected was there though I have never actually seen it until now." Carolyn shrugged. "The one lesson I tried to teach both of you was to be responsible for your own actions. Now it seems that your sister is going to put that to the test."

"I can't see her ever admitting she is in the wrong."

"Then it is her loss." Carolyn smiled. "From the time I've spent with Katie and the look on your face when you saw her, I meant it when I said I approve. If it is okay with you, I'd like to stay around and get to know her better."

"I'd love that, Mom."

"Speaking of love, why on earth haven't you told her you love her yet?"

"I was going to then I got shot and this whole mess with Ingrid erupted along with discovering my sister is a homophobe."

Carolyn yawned. "I hope you don't mind but I really need to find my bed and rest this old body. I've been traveling for a day and a half straight."

"Go get some sleep. I get released tomorrow."

"Not to worry. I will be here to help you."

"Thanks. Sally brought my clothes and Fred gave me the key to the new door of my apartment. So I should be good to go back to my new home. Mom?"

Carolyn paused.

"My car is in Sally's garage. How do I get it back?"

"Don't sweat the small stuff." Carolyn kissed her daughter's cheek. "I will see you in the morning."

†

The hotel room where Katie was staying was more than adequate since she opted to upgrade to one with a whirlpool bathtub. Bubbles floated up and around her and helped soothe her weary body but not her mind. Carolyn Dunham proved to be a pleasant surprise. Katie instantly liked the woman and was grateful for her support of the relationship she had with her daughter.

Although she told Helen it would be best for her to be with her family, Katie hoped Helen would pick her over her sister. The words she heard from both Helen and her mother gave her encouragement.

Earlier at work, Katie had worried about picking up Helen's mother at the airport and wondered if she'd get the same frosty reception that she had from Sally. Although Helen said her mother approved she still felt nervous. She focused only on her patients and that kept her mind busy while she was with them, but it was during the downtime at work that Helen and her family haunted her thoughts.

Now that the initial meeting was over, Katie could focus on other things, like finding someplace to live other than the hotel. "Hyde Park I think." The historical homes in that area appealed to her sense of nostalgia and reminded her of her gran. The cost of the homes in proportion to the size was astronomical. A home with less than thirteen hundred square feet would cost close to five hundred thousand dollars but the ambience of the area was well worth the cost.

Katie stepped out of the tub and looked back at it longingly. She imagined being in it again with Helen, holding her and making love with her. Her lover had a way of making her feel complete.

"Tell me, Gran. What am I going to do if she changes her mind?"

Choose a path and stick to it, child. Even when you encounter roadblocks you must overcome them so you can move forward.

Katie could hear her gran's words clearly. A half-forgotten memory worked its way into her consciousness...

A freckle-faced, ginger-haired, green-eyed girl stood on the porch of her grandmother's house. Six girls she went to school with were standing on the sidewalk pointing at her and laughing at how she was dressed. Soon their laughter turned into taunts as the nine-year-old began to cry.

All the while her gran was watching from the screen door behind Katie, never venturing out to defend her granddaughter. When her gran silently came out onto the porch the girls all ran away.

Katie turned around and when she saw Gran there her tears increased. "Why didn't you say something to them," Katie cried.

Gathering Katie into her arms, her gran soothed a hand over her unruly hair.

"I can't fight your battles for you, Mary Kate. You must decide what it is worth fighting for and what is not. If those bullies were hurting you with their words and you cried then they won. You never show a bully your weaknesses. You stand up to them and challenge them to stop or fight."

Her gran lifted the shoulder Katie was resting her head on.

"Sometimes they will fight, especially if they think you are weak. The next time they start, just fold your arms and stare at them." Her gran laughed. "They won't know what to do and will walk away. Never react, Mary Kate. Never let others get to you."

Katie smiled at the memory. "Gran was right. I never let anyone do that to me again until Sally got in my face and called me a pervert."

She made her way into the main room from the bathroom, picked up her cell phone, and noticed that she had a text message. It was from Helen.

Just wanted you to know I am thinking of you.

The words warmed her heart and she read it again only to be startled when the room's phone rang.

"Hello," she said cautiously.

"Hello, my darling, Katie. This is Carolyn Dunham. I want you to know I have arrived in my room and it is awesome. Thank you for arranging it for me."

Katie smiled. "You are more than welcome. I hope you enjoy your stay."

"Oh, I'm certain I will. Would you like to go with me to the hospital in the morning and spring Helen?"

"I would, but what about Sally. I don't want to be in the way."

Carolyn laughed. "Darling, you need not worry about her. There never was a contest. Helen would prefer you be there instead of her sister."

"Okay. What time? You must still be experiencing jet lag."

"I learned long ago how to beat jet lag so I am good. When do you need to be at work?"

"Seven thirty. If I have patients in the hospital I usually get there around seven." Katie could feel the grin on her face. "Since I do have a patient and she needs to be discharged by her surgeon I should check on her once more."

"In that case, I will meet you in the lobby at six forty-five."

"See you then, Mrs. Dunham."

"It's Carolyn. Good night, dear, sweet dreams."

"Thank you. I wish you the same."

Katie disconnected the phone and let out a deep relaxing sigh. She would sleep soundly.

Chapter Twenty-One

Carolyn Dunham, with Katie behind her, arrived at Helen's room finding the door partially opened. Sitting in a chair with her back to the door, dressed in her own clothes, Helen was apparently looking out the window.

"I'm here, my darling," Carolyn said in a happy voice.

No reply.

Concerned, Carolyn rushed to her daughter's side. "What's wrong? Why the tears?"

Helen had a worried look on her face. "Are you as disappointed in me as Sally is?"

"Oh, darling, I already told you." Carolyn embraced her daughter. "You have never disappointed me and certainly not now."

"Oh, Mom, I don't know what to do. What if Sally is right and I'm ruining my life with the choices I've made."

"Darling, why are you doing this to yourself? You had everything figured out last night and you were happier than I've ever seen you. Why?"

"I've been thinking that maybe I've been too rash in my decisions. I've been thinking with my overloaded baser instincts and not with my head. What am I going to do," Helen sobbed.

"Sweetheart, you will do what your heart tells you." Carolyn hugged her daughter. "What does it tell you?"

"I don't know." Helen scrunched up her face. "No, I do know. It says Katie is who I want."

Standing in the doorway, Katie had to grip the doorframe to keep from falling. Her worst fears were coming true—Helen thought they were a mistake. She was about to turn when she heard Helen's words and moved into the room.

"And I want you," Katie said softly. "But I won't stand in the way or break up your family."

Both Helen and Carolyn turned and looked at Katie.

"I'm going to find myself a cup of coffee," Carolyn said. "Can I get you some too?"

Katie smiled in the older woman's direction. "I haven't had my quota for the day. I take it black."

"Excellent. I will leave the two of you alone and find the cafeteria." As Carolyn passed by Katie she gave her a gentle squeeze on her shoulder. "Trust in your heart," she whispered before leaving.

"You don't need to go all the way to the cafeteria. Just ask at the nurses' station and they will show you where the coffee is."

Once her mother left, Helen sobbed, "Please come here."

Kneeling next to Helen's chair, Katie kissed her cheek. "I know you are anxious about going back to your apartment—back to where he shot you. That has to be coloring your thoughts."

Helen closed her eyes. "I don't know what to do. Everything is a jumble in my brain. Scenes keep playing that I know are not real or at least I don't think they are."

"Sweetheart, you've been through hell and back and the residual effects of all the drugs you've had are still having an impact."

"I didn't mean for you to hear what I said. I'm sorry."

Katie stood. "I won't lie to you and say that the overloaded baser instincts comment didn't hurt—it did." She looked out the window as a tear rolled down her cheek. "Maybe you're right. Maybe we are rushing into this. It is a total lifestyle change, and if there are doubts then we should step back and be sure before going forward." Tears were falling freely.

"Please don't cry. I'm sorry."

"Don't be sorry for your words. They obviously needed to be voiced. Your mother is a good sounding board for you since she doesn't seem to be opposed to how you choose to live your life." Katie's lips found Helen's, kissed her softly, and then pulled back.

"I will always be here for you. Take your time and be sure of what you want."

"I want you."

Carolyn stood in the door listening to the emotional exchange and decided it was time to interrupt. "I'm back. Here's your coffee, Katie."

Katie looked at Carolyn with a weak smile. "Just in time. I really need to get to work. Fortunately Saturday is usually a slow day."

Holding out the coffee cup, Carolyn passed it to Katie. "Be careful it is hot."

"Thanks I will." Katie kissed Helen's cheek before walking toward the door.

"Will I see you at the apartment later?" Helen asked.

"I'll do my best." Katie disappeared out the door.

Carolyn quickly went to her daughter's side. "Are you okay?"

"Yes. No."

"Come here." Carolyn pulled Helen to her feet and hugged her. "Follow your heart, my darling. It will never lead you astray."

"Oh, Mom," Helen cried. "Everything is crashing down around me."

"I know it is right now but have faith and it will all be as it should. I promise you it will be okay."

†

In the safety of her office, Katie couldn't stop shaking as she leaned against the door. Slowly she slid down, grabbed her bent legs, and began to cry. The possibility of losing Helen was so devastating that she was sure her heart would stop beating.

"I've got to pull myself together and get on with the day." Katie dragged herself up, straightened her clothes, and dried her eyes.

Ten minutes later, a soft knock on the door let Katie know her day was about to start. Pushing all her emotional turmoil into the deep recesses of her mind and devoid of any feelings, she opened the door and nodded to the woman standing there.

219

"I'll be right there. Room one, right?"

"Yes."

Katie remembered she promised Carolyn the use of her car to take Helen to her apartment. *Shit I didn't give her the keys.*

"Susie," Katie said to the retreating nurse.

"Yes."

"Will you do me a favor?"

"Sure."

†

"What happened to the *I'm settled and comfortable in my own skin* daughter that I left here last night?" Carolyn shook her head in amazement.

"I don't know." Helen shrugged. "All my life I've always been striving to succeed. I've never taken any time to actually allow myself to feel."

Carolyn gave her daughter a puzzled look. "Now you have. Right?"

"I thought so but now I'm not sure. I've always been about numbers and predicting the future. That's solid. That's what I know. That's who I am."

"What about your feelings for Katie?"

"I know my words hurt her deeply." Helen tapped her lips with her fingers. "How couldn't they? I know they would have hurt me. The worst part is that I can't take them back."

Carolyn hugged her daughter. "I don't think your words did irreparable damage. It is clear to me she is deeply in love with you. If I've ever seen two people more right for each other it's you two."

"I am scared, Mom." Helen looked away. "I can't believe that I doubted our love for even a minute."

"You've been through quite an ordeal. After being shot and attacked like you were, anyone would question their life choices."

"You're right. Katie said much the same thing. But after my overloaded baser instincts comment I can't help but worry that she will walk away."

"You think her love for you is that shallow?"

220

"No. I hope not."

"Why don't you give her a call?"

Helen looked at the wall clock. "She is into her day and won't be able to take a call much less talk. I will think on it and when we get to the apartment I will send her flowers."

Carolyn smiled. "Flowers are always a nice way to say I'm sorry. You are sending red roses, of course."

Helen nodded.

A small, blond woman entered the room. "Are you ready to go home, Helen?" the discharge nurse asked. "I will be back in about ten minutes with everything you will need so you can go home. You'll need you to sign some papers and I will go over your discharge orders with you."

Carolyn asked her daughter, "Has the doctor already been here?"

"Yes, about an hour ago. He said Katie asked him to see me first thing because I needed to get home." Helen sighed deeply. "All through this ordeal she has been there for me, calling in favors and making sure I was well taken care of. I repay her by saying words I didn't really mean."

"She did all that for you?"

"Yes." Helen was shamefaced and buried her face in her hands. "I've really made a mess of things haven't I?"

"Perhaps. But I doubt she did all that for you because she doesn't care about you. She loves you and love is paramount."

Helen looked at her mother and smiled. "She does, doesn't she?"

"Yes. I can see it in her eyes every time she looks at you."

Helen took out her phone.

"Excuse me."

Carolyn looked at a petite, dark-haired young woman standing just inside the door. "Are you here to take us down to the lobby?"

"No. Are you Mrs. Dunham?"

"Yes," Carolyn answered warily.

"This is for you." The woman held out an envelope.

"Thank you." Carolyn took the envelope then watched the woman leave. She could tell by the heft of the envelope exactly what it contained. She opened it and let a single key fall into her hand.

Helen closed her phone and asked, "What is it?"

"The key to Katie's car. We loaded my luggage in it this morning and she said I could use it to take you home."

"She's giving you the key just like that?"

"From what I've seen of Ms. Katie McGuire she is an honorable woman who always tries to do the right thing."

"That's her nature."

"It would seem that way." Carolyn pulled a folded sheet of paper out of the envelope and read it.

"What does it say?" Helen asked, looking over her mother's shoulder.

Carolyn smiled as she read, "As promised, here is the key to my car. Keep it as long as you need it. If it turns out that you need it to drive north please let me know and I will arrange for someone to ferry it back to Austin. Carolyn, thank you for your support. Regards, Katie."

Helen closed her eyes. "You know, I thought the biggest mistake in my life was marrying that man but I now know it wasn't even close to how I feel at this moment. She thinks I might go back to Highland Park."

With her hands on Helen's cheeks, Carolyn looked into her blue eyes. "You need to trust in her love for you and yours for her. It has always been so hard for you to trust anyone completely. Let all these questions go and follow your heart."

"While you were speaking to the nurse I called a florist and had a dozen red roses sent to her at the clinic."

"Excellent start," Carolyn said. "Anything else come to mind?"

"Yes, but I have to wait till we get to the apartment then I'll need a messenger."

"That sounds intriguing." Carolyn stretched. "Come on, let's get everything ready so we can leave as soon as possible. Then I will move into your apartment with you."

"You're staying?"

"Of course I am. You will need someone to take care of you during the day. After that there is Ingrid's trial that you will need to testify for." Carolyn smiled. "I can't just up and leave my little girl at such a significant time in her life."

"Thanks, Mom. I shudder to think what it would be like if I had to rely on Sally."

"She will come around, that I promise you. Right now she is struggling to hold on to beliefs she never thought would apply to her or anyone she loves." She took Helen's hand. "Love is the strongest bond of all and she will come around to that way of thinking. It will just take time."

"Will Katie too?"

"She loves you and I doubt that has changed."

"I've missed you, Mom. I can always count on you to be the voice of reason. You are the only one who can do that for me."

A hospital volunteer came to the door. "You ready for your ride to the door?" The elderly man looked at Carolyn and smiled. "Bring the car around to the front entrance and we will be waiting for you there."

†

With her hand trembling, Helen inserted the key into the lock of her apartment. Once the police released the apartment as a crime scene, Fred had hired a cleanup crew to remove all evidence of blood, fix the door, and change the lock.

"Go ahead and open it," Carolyn said. "The only way to face your demons is straight on."

Helen nodded, unlocked the door, and twisted the knob. She was terrified and could feel her heart beating hard in her chest. Her eyes scanned the room, focusing immediately on the area where she lay bleeding less than a week before. All evidence that a shooting took place there was eradicated. Wandering through the area she made her way into the bedroom. Her eyes focused on the bed and she could see, feel, and touch Katie as arousal coursed through her body.

"What am I going to do?"

Helen expected some sort of reply after she sent the flowers and was sorely disappointed when she hadn't. Of course, she forgot that working on Saturday meant that Katie along with one doctor were the only staff. "I need to put my thoughts into action then get a messenger."

"What did you say, darling?" Carolyn asked.

"I've made a royal mess of my life but I'm going to make it right."

Carolyn raised her eyebrows. "Mess in what way?"

"I need to make it right with Katie."

"I'm glad to hear that. I've never known you to be a pessimist. You usually take the bull by the horns and go after what you want."

"This isn't work," Helen laughed. "I was going for a gentler, more romantic approach."

"Wise move."

"Can I help?" Helen watched her mother move her suitcases into the spare bedroom.

"Didn't you hear what your discharge orders were?"

"Oh, yeah. I know. No lifting, but I'd be pulling since they have wheels."

"Same difference." Carolyn chuckled as she pulled two bags away from the front door.

Helen wandered into the kitchen and opened the refrigerator door. She was surprised to see it had milk, eggs, bread, and all the other essentials. The remainder of the meal she fixed before the shooting was gone. "Why did Fred do this? Didn't he think I was going back to Highland Park with him and Sally?"

Her hand wrapped around a bottle of water, took it out, and opened it.

Carolyn poked her head into the kitchen. "Because his career demands that he is an excellent reader of people. He knew you were never leaving here."

"He was right." Helen went to her desk, took out a piece of linen paper along with a matching envelope, and began creating her message for Katie.

"What are you doing?" Carolyn asked.

"Apologizing." Helen looked up at her mother. "Do you think you can find a messenger service and have them here within the hour? I'll need this delivered no later than two this afternoon."

"Will do."

The messenger came and went and Helen could feel her heart filling with hope. She wandered into the living area and slumped down in an overstuffed tan chair that she and Katie shared and made love in. She had to fix the damage she caused by letting Katie think she didn't want what they had. "I should have told her how much I want her in my life. That I love her." She bit her lip. "I hope my message works."

"It will. Count on it," Carolyn said from the kitchen.

"Damn you, Sally, and your outdated opinions. I can't believe that in a moment of confusion I took you seriously."

Carolyn walked into the room. "What's wrong?"

"Mom, I have a pain in my chest that is so intense and real that I think my heart will disintegrate into a million pieces. Is this what a broken heart feels like?"

Carolyn's heart went out to her daughter. "When your father died I had that same feeling. It was like I couldn't breathe and my chest was so heavy that I was certain I could not go on."

"What am I going to do?"

"Patience, darling, patience. Everything in life always works out the way it should. You and Katie belong together. She will forgive you and realize the words you said were made in a moment of emotional upheaval."

Helen was almost asleep in the chair. Carolyn smiled down at her as she covered her with a light blanket.

"Thanks, Mom," Helen mumbled before her breaths evened out.

Carolyn, watching over her daughter, settled on the couch across from her.

✝

Startled by an unfamiliar noise, Helen's eyes opened wide. She looked straight ahead—nothing. Not moving she listened for the sound again when it finally dawned on her what the noise was—Mom. With a slight move of her head she saw her mother sitting on the sofa looking at her.

"Sorry. Did I wake you?" Carolyn asked.

225

"No. Demons kept invading my dreams. Bobby was there beating me to death with his sister's help. Katie kept coming to my rescue, holding out her hand and telling me to trust her and everything would work out but Sally kept pouring coal dust on her and calling her a jezebel."

"What did that dream tell you?"

"That Katie has always been there for me and when she needed me the most—needed my reassurance—I let her down."

"Sounds like a good conclusion. So what are you going to do about the situation between the two of you?"

"I sent her flowers and a special message."

"That's a start."

Folding her hands, Helen rested both index fingers on her lips. "I need to find answers. I need Katie to know how I feel."

"Then tell her."

†

In her office during her lunch break Katie looked at the text message Helen had sent along with the vase of red roses sitting on her desk. *We arrived at the apartment. I am a fool to think for one minute that I could live without you. Please forgive me for my moment of doubt.*

It hadn't been lost on Katie that Helen's words had a ring of truth for her too. "Is sex clouding my judgment?" She needed to examine her feelings and decide what to do next. She could not deny her deep love for Helen but she wondered if it was enough.

A knock on the door had Katie looking up. "Yes."

Her triage nurse for the day, Susie Bennington, opened the door and smiled. "Those are gorgeous flowers." She held out an envelope. "A messenger just left this for you."

Katie frowned. "A messenger? Like the guys that ride on their bikes?"

"From what I understand that is exactly the kind of person who delivered it."

Katie took the envelope. "Thanks. I hope no one is suing me." Once Susie closed the door, Katie looked at the envelope. It was of the high-grade linen paper variety. "Can't be from a lawyer." She smiled when she saw the neat bold writing—Helen had sent it. With a letter opener, she sliced open the envelope. When she looked at the card her jaw dropped as she saw two red, hand-drawn hearts intermingled on the front of the card. Under the hearts was one word. *Maybe.* Opening the card she read the words. *We can rewrite history. Can you find it in your heart to forgive me for what I said?*

Her eyes brimmed with tears and she knew in that instant that forgiveness was a given. Katie took out her cell phone and texted Carolyn immediately.

I will stop by after work if that is okay.

It is more than okay. Should I tell her?

No. I want it to be a surprise.

That it will. See you then.

Chapter Twenty-Two

Carolyn was humming as she put the finishing touches on the meal she prepared as Helen took a shower. The text from Katie told her everything she needed to know. Her daughter and Katie McGuire had the possibility of a bright future. Hearing the knock on the door she smiled and walked quickly to open it.

"You're here just in time." Carolyn engulfed Katie in a hug. "Helen is in the shower, and I didn't tell her you were coming."

Katie was beaming. "Thanks. I hope the surprise isn't too much for her."

"Why did you decide to come?"

"She sent me a handmade card." Digging in her purse Katie pulled out the card with the entwined hearts and handed it to Carolyn. "I knew in the instant I saw it I couldn't live without her in my life."

A soft smile crossed Carolyn's face as she read the words. "That's my girl." She turned to Katie. "Do you still have your room at the Wyndham?"

"Yes. I came straight here from the hospital."

Carolyn held out her hand. "Good. May I have your key?"

Katie looked confused. "Yes, but why?"

"My darling, you and my daughter have a lot to talk about. Dinner is ready, the table is set for two, and the wine is chilling. I will collect a few things for tonight and be on my way. Tell Helen I'll be back tomorrow."

Just as the front door closed behind Carolyn, the bathroom door opened.

Helen looked toward the door and grinned. "You came."

"I couldn't stay away. Especially not after receiving those beautiful flowers and your heartfelt card." Katie gazed a Helen. "I don't want a life without you in it."

"With doubts and all?"

"Yes. If I'm honest I had the same thought."

After several long strides Helen stood in front of Katie. "It's been too long." She pulled Katie into her arms and kissed her softly. "I'm so glad you're here." Helen looked around. "Where's my mom?"

"She's gone to stay in my hotel room."

Helen frowned. "Why?"

"She said we needed to talk. She'll be back tomorrow sometime."

Helen passionately kissed the lips she had been dreaming about for what seemed like forever. It didn't take long for Helen to realize that before she went any further she had something important to say.

"Is something wrong?" Katie frowned as Helen pulled away. "I thought…"

Helen put her finger on Katie's lips. "I have something I need to say, but first I need to get something." She moved quickly into the bedroom then came back.

"What is it?"

"Katie, I love you more than I've ever loved anyone before." She held out a heart locket. "This is my heart, and my promise to you is to always be there for you. I'll never again listen to anyone who says our love is wrong. It isn't. It feels too right to be wrong."

"I love you too, Helen. I know it hasn't been long and we have a lot of the getting to know you kinda thing to do, but in my heart, I know you are who I've been waiting for all my life." Katie pointed to the table. "Your mother made us dinner."

"She knew you were coming?"

"Yes, I texted her after I got your card. I told her I wanted it to be a surprise."

A crooked smile crossed Helen's face. "I like your kind of surprises." She kissed Katie passionately. "Wanna forget about dinner and move this into the bedroom?"

Katie took Helen's hand and led her to the dining area. The table was candlelit with a vase of red roses in the center and two place settings next to each other.

"No." Katie saw disappointment filter across Helen's face. "It's not that I don't want to, because I do, but I'm certain your discharge orders didn't include making love. Why don't we eat and then we can talk about us and our future."

"Then you think we have a future."

"Of course we do, silly. There may have been a moment or two of doubt—probably on both our parts—but I don't think either of us ever doubted our love for one another."

"I agree."

Katie smiled. "Good. Now sit down and I will serve us dinner."

Helen watched as Katie went into the kitchen. She could feel her heart soar and knew without a doubt that her love for Katie would never waver again.

Long into the night, Helen cuddled with Katie as they talked. "I don't think I can stay here."

"I thought you loved this place."

"I did but not anymore. All I hear is him kicking down the door; all I see is his gun pointed at me and blood on the floor. I think I'm going mad."

"No you're not. What you're feeling is completely normal for anyone who's been through what you have. I wondered when you'd feel that way." Katie hugged Helen close. "Maybe we can find a house with a yard."

"Hmm, I'd like that." Helen sighed. "I wish you could see my house in Highland Park."

"You remodeled it right?"

"Yes, back to its original splendor."

"Do you want to move back there?"

Helen could hear the trepidation in Katie's voice. "No. My home is with you. Besides, that place holds too many bad memories."

"You know we have many historic homes here in Austin."

"Really?"

"Yes, there is Bryker Woods, Hyde Park, Aldridge Place to name a few. They are pricey for the amount of square footage but they are lovely old homes." Katie smiled. "I've always been fascinated with the Hyde Park area. It's quirky but in a good way."

"Would you like to share a home with me?"

"As long as it has a lifetime warranty the answer is yes."

That night, wrapped in the cocoon of Katie's arms, Helen slept without nightmares for the first time since the shooting.

✝

After eating a leisurely, late breakfast of eggs, bacon, and toast with jam Sunday morning, Katie and Helen sat nestled in the overstuffed chair talking quietly.

Helen, running her fingers down Katie's arm, said, "Are you sure we can't..."

Katie laughed. "You have a one-track mind. No, we can't until the stiches come out and even then we can't get overly rambunctious."

Helen's body trembled.

"What's wrong?"

Frowning, Helen looked at Katie. "Nothing really. I had a sudden flashback of him breaking down the door."

"Oh, sweetie, he can't hurt you anymore." Katie kissed Helen's lips. "The drugs you were taking might not let you remember that we spoke about you talking to a psychologist about what happened."

"I remember. I don't know why I can't just tell you about it."

"I will always be here to listen to whatever it is you're feeling but I may not have the answers you need."

"Can we at least try?"

"Absolutely. Tell me what you are feeling."

"Afraid. Unsafe. Violated." Helen quivered. "Ever since it happened I keep seeing the grotesqueness of his face gnarled in hatred just before his bullet sliced through my skin." Helen rubbed her neck with her hand. "The scene just keeps repeating itself like a never-ending reel of terror."

"What do you do when this happens? How do you feel?"

Helen's forehead wrinkled.

"I mean, do you just go with it and allow it to take over or do you fight it?"

"I feel helpless. Hopeless. Unable to move. It's like an abyss that I can never quite climb out of."

"It might help you to deflect the flashback when it starts by thinking of something that is not terrifying—something that makes you feel safe and happy."

"I can try." The door opened and Helen cringed.

"Good morning, darlings, did you have a good night?"

Katie felt Helen's body relax.

"Hi, Mom. Did you have breakfast?"

"Yes, I did, dear. How are feeling today?"

"Great, thanks to Katie." Helen looked at Katie and smiled. "We spent a long time just talking about our lives together."

"We realize there will be pitfalls along the way but we are willing to take that chance," Katie said. "To be with Helen is worth any sacrifice I might have to make."

Helen smiled. "I love you too."

†

A loud knock on the door had all three women looking in its direction.

"I'll get it," Carolyn said as she made her way to the door.

Helen's eyes widened when she saw Sally and Fred standing out in the hallway.

"Come in," Carolyn said. "The Marquis of Queensberry Rules apply here. If you do not comply I will ask you to leave."

Sally pushed past her mother and walked to stand in front of her sister and Katie. She shook her finger at the two women. "How could you let her talk you into being something you're not?"

"What are you doing here, Sally?" Helen asked. "I thought you went home."

"I'm trying to save you from this pervert."

Katie, trying hard to keep her mouth shut, began to get up but Helen stopped her.

"If Katie is a pervert then so am I," Helen snarled. "The fact of the matter is that Katie told me she didn't want to come between us."

"Yeah right. It was just a ploy to make you think she is so sweet and kind. But I can see through her and I can't believe you don't see that."

Carolyn stepped between her daughters. "What is your problem, Sally? Your sister is happier than she's ever been and here you are trying to convince her that her happiness is wrong."

"I'm trying to save her soul. She needs psychiatric help. An intervention." She looked at her husband. "Come on, Fred, help me convince her what a horrible mistake she is making. It is career suicide. No one will ever take you seriously in the business world if you continue down this path."

"I won't do that, Sally," Fred said. "Your sister is a grown woman with a brilliant mind and can make her own decisions."

"Don't be ridiculous. You will help me stop her from this path."

"Helen can do what she wants with her life whether you like it or not. Is this the mountain you want to die on? From where I'm sitting that is exactly what will happen if you continue to run at the mouth."

Katie couldn't help the low growl she made.

"He gives good advice, sis. Listen to his words and heed them. I love Katie. She's going to be in my life forever. I can't— won't go back to the life I once knew. Not now after I've found the meaning of true happiness. For me that is Katie. You can either accept that or not, the choice is yours."

"I won't let you ruin your life like this."

"Listen to your husband, Sally, because right now you're falling down the mountain and there isn't anyone at the bottom to catch you," Carolyn said.

Fred took Sally's hand. "Let's go. I've been in too many court battles to know you aren't going to win this one."

"But she's my sister. I promised I'd take care of her. The Bible says…"

"Let people make their own way in the world," Fred said.

"You must willingly let me go because I'm already gone and there is nothing you can say to me that will change that," Helen whispered.

"No. I won't accept that."

"I told you when you arrived what the rules were, Sally, and I've given you great latitude. You've crossed the line and it is now time for you to leave," Carolyn said in a firm voice.

Sally looked at her sister. "Is that what you want?"

Helen nodded. "You've given me no other choice. Please leave and don't come back."

"What is wrong with the two of you? Don't you see how perverted and demented that woman is?"

"Pervert is such a nasty word. It is reserved for pedophiles. I've spoken with Katie extensively and that's the last thing you should be calling her."

"If the shoe fits."

"Get out. Get out of here now and never come back here or in my life." Helen rose from the chair quickly then lurched and grabbed at her side.

Katie was out of the chair immediately and wrapping a supporting arm around Helen's back. "Let me help you back down then I'll look to see if you did any damage."

"Thanks. She made me so mad with her holier-than-thou crap that I forgot about my incision."

"Do you see what your narrow-minded views are doing to our family?" Carolyn glared at Sally. "I raised you to be tolerant and accepting of everyone, not to lash out at people who have different beliefs and lifestyles."

"It's unnatural and against God's teachings."

"I will not continue listening to you spewing your hate. I can do without you in my life," Helen said through gritted teeth.

Katie, crouching down, gently lifted Helen's shirt and took off the bandage coving the incision. "It looks good." She smiled up at Helen. "I'm with you," she whispered.

"You have a choice to make. Either accept Helen for who she is or stay out of her life. The decision is yours and yours alone to make. It is obvious from your sister's comments that you are no longer wanted or needed here." Carolyn resisted giving in to the tears streaming down Sally's cheeks. "You've done this to yourself, darling. Think about that on your drive home. I don't think this situation between you and your sister is irreparable, but because of your words the relationship that you've enjoyed with Helen is forever changed."

"You want me to give up everything I believe in to accommodate that slut? What will I tell the kids?"

Carolyn shook her head. "I may have been wrong. The damage you've done may never be undone. As for my grandchildren, I will tell them the truth."

"Have it your way." With one final huff, Sally, with Fred behind her, left Helen's apartment.

"Are you okay?" Carolyn approached her daughter. "Did you hurt yourself?"

"No, I'm good. As for Sally, she made her choice and I've made the one that is right for me. If she can't accept me then you were right, Mom, irreparable damage to our relationship will happen."

"Let's hope she sees how much she stands to lose." Carolyn shook her head. "It might take time but she will come around." She grinned. "I just have to give her my special mom treatment. It always has worked in the past."

"You do have a way with her, Mom." Helen clapped her hands together. "We were thinking of driving around various neighborhoods looking for a house. Will you please join us, Mom?" she asked.

Carolyn looked at Katie.

"Please join us. We really would like your input and thoughts about the home we will be sharing."

"I'd be delighted."

"I need to take a shower and change my clothes first," Helen said.

"No problem. I don't think we are in a hurry are we, Carolyn?"

"It is Sunday, the day of rest, so no I'm not in a hurry." She smiled.

Once Helen had left the room, Katie looked at Carolyn. "Why does Sally hate me so?"

Carolyn smiled. "You know, the first time I saw you and Helen look at each other I got goose bumps."

"You did?"

"Yes. The love you both exuded was undeniable. I think that is why Sally is trying so hard to break you two apart."

Katie frowned. "I don't understand."

"You presented a threat to her relationship with Helen. You are the enemy."

"I never wanted to do that."

"What you don't know, my darling, is that even though Sally is older, she adored her sister and was the one who followed Helen around." Carolyn sighed deeply. "Sally has always been somewhat of a loner who doesn't make friends easily. Helen, on the other hand, exuded confidence and although she shunned most attempts others made at friendship she always was there to give her sister a boost."

"Sally doesn't strike me that way. She has a business. Certainly that means she has to relate to the people in her workplace."

"All she knows about that she learned from watching Helen."

"Are you saying she is jealous of me?"

"Jealous? No. A threat. Yes."

"I don't want to be the cause of Helen losing her sister."

"You're not. Sally can either accept your relationship with Helen or not. The decision rests with her and her alone." Carolyn rubbed her hand over Katie's arm. "Helen loves you and that isn't something that I see changing."

"We spoke of that very thing earlier this morning."

"Is that why you're house hunting?"

Katie shook her head. "She can't live here with the memory of what happened."

"I wondered about that. She was terrified when we arrived yesterday."

"A new home and a new start. I can't think of anything better."

"Neither can I."

†

Their tour of the different historical neighborhoods in Austin had Helen smiling. "I love this. Look at the architectural design of these homes. I wish we could go inside some of them."

Katie guided her car down 16th Street. "I love the homes here but they are pricey."

"Stop," Helen said. "Do you see that one there? It is gorgeous, it is for sale, and even has an historical marker. I love the look."

Katie pulled the car to the curb and stopped. "Let me look it up." On her cell phone she entered the address. "Wow. It was built in 1899, and is in the Queen Anne style. It has three bedrooms, four baths, a mother-in-law suite," she looked at Carolyn and smiled, "a three-car garage, and has been completely restored to its original condition."

"Sounds perfect. When can we see it?"

"Um, you might want to get all the details first."

"Why? Is something wrong with it?"

"Well, it's over four thousand square feet and the cost is around two and a half million." Katie shrugged. "It is a bit big for just us."

"Mom, you can live with us when you're not traveling."

"Yes, it sounds big enough."

"So what's the problem?" Helen asked.

"It's a lot of money," Katie said.

"Can we at least make an appointment to see it?"

"Certainly. Maybe I can get a glimpse of what your house looks like." Katie winked.

"I know it is outrageous to even think about something like this but it is a start."

"Yes, it is a start." Carolyn gave Helen a conspiratorial grin. "Is anyone else hungry?"

"I am," Helen said.

"The Carillon is near here and has fabulous food. My treat." Katie smiled at Helen, who was sitting next to her. In the rearview mirror she could see a look of happiness on Carolyn's face. "It will be the end to a perfect day."

Chapter Twenty-Three

Rain pummeled the parking lot as Katie, huddled under an umbrella, trudged into the building. Her sleep the night before was anything but restful. She tossed and turned, never finding a suitable spot until Helen wrapped her arms around her and kissed her head. After living with Helen and her mother for the last three days, it was becoming harder and harder to leave the apartment and go to work. The rain only added to the ache in her heart of being there without Helen.

"It never rains in Austin so why is it today of all days," she grumbled. She shook the umbrella out before closing it and encasing it in one of the long plastic bags by the inside door.

"Good morning, Katie. How are you doing on this lovely rainy day?"

Katie looked at one of the front office women, Gail, who was showing her a toothy smile. "There is nothing about a rainy day that is lovely."

"Sure there is. It's a blessing. If it rains enough then the lakes will fill up and maybe one day they will be full and the drought will be over."

With a quick shake of her head, Katie gave the woman a half smile. "Let me have some coffee first before I think of the rain as lovely." She pushed through the swinging door and headed for her office.

Sari greeted her. "Looks like you have me again today."

"Good news, Sari. I always like working with you."

"Thank you. I like working with you too." The nurse smiled and opened Katie's office door. "Looks like another long day."

"Aren't they all?" Katie walked into her office and sat behind her desk.

"Do you need anything?"

Katie smiled. "No. Thank you for asking."

Over the last days Jack had called her frequently, asking her when she was coming home. Since she hadn't retrieved her belongings and a divorce lawyer hadn't contacted him, he assumed she had changed her mind and was coming back to him. *Never* she told him time and again but he was persistent so she stopped taking his calls.

Helen was all she could think about. No matter how involved she tried to be with her patients Helen kept invading her thoughts at the most inopportune times.

Looking at her schedule for the day, Katie knitted her brow.

Katie spotted Sari walking by and called to her. "Sari, I need to speak with you."

Sari came into the office. "Sure what can I do for you?"

"Do you know if there is a reason that my last appointment is at five?"

"I wondered that myself since the last appointments of the day are at four. Do you want me to find out what the deal is?"

"No." Katie shook her head. "There must have been some compelling reason for scheduling an appointment at that time."

"Are you feeling any better today?" Sari asked. "You've been looking distracted for some time now and it doesn't look like you've gotten much sleep."

Katie lifted a shoulder. *What do I say? I'd rather be with my lover than be here.* "I'm feeling worn out. I've slacked off going to the gym. I need to start again and get back into that routine." *Wonder if I can talk Helen into going with me?*

"I've missed not seeing you there. I'll look forward to seeing you at the gym again."

"Okay. Let me know when the first patient is ready."

"Will do." Katie looked at the time and calculated how long before she would see Helen again. She shook her head and laughed. "I've got it bad."

†

Each day at Helen's apartment, Carolyn would sit across from her daughter, keeping watch over her as she slept in the same overstuffed chair. Helen slept fitfully, often crying out, *no, get away from me*. It was her opinion that her daughter had to exorcise her own demons if she was ever going to get past the shooting.

Helen ate little and slept sporadically even with Katie there. She had spoken to Helen about seeing a therapist but she refused, saying she had her and Katie to talk to about it. "It isn't enough," Carolyn whispered. A plan suddenly erupted and she grinned.

Yawning, Helen opened her eyes. "Who are you talking to and why are you always there when I wake up?"

"I'm watching over you. That's what mothers do. They make sure their child is safe." Carolyn smiled. "What did you dream about this time?"

"Nothing new really. This time Bobby shot me and I looked at Katie who was turning blue as Ingrid choked her." Helen's eyes focused on her mother. "They say you never die in your dreams but Katie died in that one." She looked away. "I couldn't live if that happened."

"Now that you're awake I'm going on a grocery run. Is there anything special you'd like me to get for supper?"

"I have that appointment at the police station to sign my statement about the incidents with Bobby and Ingrid in an hour. I thought you were going to take me."

"It's time for you to venture out on your own, darling," Carolyn told her.

"No. Not yet."

Her mother patted her on the arm. "The first step is always the hardest."

"How will I get there if you take my Mercedes that Fred shipped to me?" She eyed her mother. "You certainly don't expect me to drive that clunker do you?"

"Well, I can't drive it. I know how to drive your car but not that thing."

"I can't believe you are doing this to me."

✝

Stepping outside her apartment building, Helen looked around the parking lot as she walked cautiously to her old junky car. When Detective Amanda Brewer called her the day before Helen asked if Ingrid would be there. The detective assured her that Ingrid was behind bars. Still, she was apprehensive about being out in the open even with her gun, which Fred had retrieved for her, tucked into the back of her jeans.

Once she arrived at the police station, Helen again looked around for any threat and saw none. With a sigh of relief, she stashed her gun under the seat, got out, locked the car, and went into the police station.

†

"Please, Ms. Dunham, take a seat," Detective Brewer said.

Helen held out her hand. She'd met the detective in the hospital but the drugs she was taking skewed her recollection of the woman. Now she looked at the detective much as she would a new client. The woman had a strong handshake and that was a positive in Helen's mind. Her hair was ginger like Katie's and Helen's stomach flipped. Her eyes were a deep brown, which contrasted with her porcelain skin. She never would have pegged her as a police detective.

The detective slid a piece of paper across the table to Helen. "Read this through and make sure everything is accurate. If it is, let me know then you can sign it at the bottom of the page. If not, note the changes and I will give you an edited copy."

Helen perused the document. "It is in order."

The detective tapped the bottom of the page. "Please sign it here and initial it here."

"What happens next?" Helen signed the paper. "I mean with Ingrid."

"The district attorney has assessed the case and deemed that we proceed to trial. The evidence we've gathered is strong and the eyewitness accounts are key."

"Will she get bail?" Helen swallowed hard. "She threatened to murder me and my friend. If she's out on bail I know she *will* come after us."

"She has a public defender. I was at the bail hearing and when the judge asked Ingrid Swenson how she pleaded she went off on the judge. Despite her attorney's attempts to silence her she sealed her fate. She ranted about how you were cheating on her brother so you killed him and she was going to do everything she could to make sure you paid for it. Her parting words were an eye for an eye and that she'd see you dead. Needless to say the judge denied the request for bail."

"Was anyone there for her? I only ask because I need to know if there's some kin I don't know about who might be out there trying to make me pay for Bobby's death. I'm fairly certain he didn't have any other relatives but I don't know that for sure."

"There was one man I saw her speaking with before the judge was ready for her. An older guy, tall, good-looking, fit. I did hear him say he'd put up her bail."

"Did he have a name?"

"The only thing I heard was Jack. No clue as to what the last name was. Do you know him?"

Helen nodded but kept her face neutral to belie her trembling insides. "Yes, Jack McGuire. He was Bobby's best friend." *Wait till I tell Katie he was there to bail Ingrid out. Can this get any more bizarre?*

"If it helps, the man left immediately after her ranting and didn't stay to find out if she got bail or not. I know you've been through a lot, Ms. Dunham. We will do all we can to keep you safe. If for any reason, and I don't foresee one, the situation changes you will be the first to know."

"Thank you, Detective Brewer. I trust you have my number."

"Yes, and as I said, I will let you know if anything changes."

Helen scraped back her chair and stood. "If that's all, I need to go."

"I will escort you out."

†

Katie stretched her back and rolled her shoulders. The day had been nonstop without a lunch break and barely enough time for a bathroom break. She had a patient that broke down during the visit and Katie made sure the woman had enough time to voice all her worries. That, of course, made her at least thirty minutes late for all her appointments for the rest of the day.

She did manage a moment to call a divorce attorney and set up a time to start divorce proceedings. It was like a weight was lifted from her shoulders when she put down her phone. *Now I can move my life with Helen forward.* She still needed to arrange a time when she could go to the house and collect all her things. Most of what was there didn't matter except for what she had of her gran's. The rest Jack could keep.

Standing outside the door before meeting her last patient, Katie hoped it wouldn't take long, for all she wanted to do was go home to Helen. She searched the chart for a name but saw none and looked around for Sari. "I guess she's left," she mumbled before opening the door. When she looked inside the room she couldn't believe her eyes.

"Helen," she whispered, "what are you doing here?" Quickly closing the door she walked over to her lover.

Standing, Helen wrapped her arms around Katie. "I had to see you and couldn't wait for you to come home."

"What did you do to make the appointment so late? I couldn't find anything out about who it was."

Helen grinned. "I told them I was your best friend and just came into town and wanted to surprise you. I showed them pictures of us together and they made the appointment."

"And someone fell for that?" Helen nodded.

"Once I told you that if I were a boy I'd never look at anyone else. Well, I'm not a boy but that doesn't change a thing." Katie breathed in the scent of Helen. "You are the only one for me. You're here." She placed Helen's hand over her heart. "I cannot let you go. If you think you're not going to have me in your life for a very long time then you are delusional."

Helen hugged Katie closer. "When can you leave this place and come home with me?"

"As soon as I am done with my last patient." Katie moved away. "Oh, that's you my best friend. I'll meet you outside after I check out your incision site." Katie patted the exam table. "Hop up here and take your shirt off."

Helen, with a glint in her eye, did as she was told.

Katie's finger palpitated the area around the incision. "Does this hurt?"

"A little. I bet if you kissed it I'd feel a lot better."

"Don't tempt me."

"Tell me…"

"What?"

"I'm madly in love with this beautiful woman and I want to make love with her in the worst way. How much longer do I have to wait?"

Katie scratched her head. "If you play your cards right you may just get lucky tonight."

"Seriously?"

"Oh, I'm very serious."

"Let's get out of here."

"I need to do some paperwork first."

"How long?"

"Fifteen minutes, tops."

Helen looked at her wristwatch. "I'm timing you."

"How'd you get here?"

"Mom insisted on going shopping so I have the junk heap."

"If I were you, I'd get what you want out of it, leave the keys in the ignition, the doors unlocked, and walk away."

"Just like that?"

"Yep. Otherwise I'll have to ride alone and I am not, repeat *not*, letting you get away."

"Good answer."

Katie fished in her pocket and pulled out her car key. "Here make yourself comfortable and I'll meet you out there."

"I'll be waiting outside for you."

†

That night as Helen and Katie lay naked next to each other they giggled.

"Are you sure you want to do this with your mom right across the hall?"

Helen rolled over on top of Katie. "There's no way I'm not making love with you tonight. I want you—I've always wanted you. I know deep down in my soul that I will love you after my dying breath. You are ingrained in my heart, my mind, and my body forever."

"Kiss me," Katie whispered.

The kiss sought out of longing and love was sensuous and full of promise of what was to come. They were finally free to love each other. No longer would they have to sneak around to be together for in that moment their lives truly became one.

About the Author

Erin O'Reilly

Erin O'Reilly was first challenged by a friend to write a story. Erin has since written numerous online and published works. Her story *Deception* was a GCLS Finalist in 2008. That book also garnered the Sapphic Readers Award in 2009. Her book *Fearless* was a GCLS finalist in 2012. Story creation, involving strong characters, always seems to dictate the story and invade her mind at all hours. It always amazes her when the characters she is developing suddenly take on a life of their own and lead the story down a completely different path. In her experience, the characters make a powerful impact on the storyline, thereby making the story better.

Other Books from Affinity eBook Press

Nesting—Renee MacKenzie   Macy Stokes, a divorced mother who is struggling with her sexual identity, jumps at a once-in-a-lifetime opportunity to help her friends. She doesn't foresee it will put her in jeopardy of losing her son, Jeremiah. Fresh out of high school, Cam Webber travels to Augusta, Georgia, to reconcile with her aunt. When she learns that's impossible, she determines to gain acceptance from her aunt's partner, Sharon. Meanwhile, Cam sets her sights on Macy, but Macy has other ideas. Kenny Brewer is a good old boy who loves his wife, Dorianne, even when he thinks she's gone totally off her rocker. Dorianne gets it in her head that a local woman is her long-lost half-sister. But soon, her obsession with that is eclipsed by medical problems that involve them all. Set in Augusta, Georgia, *Nesting* explores the age-old issues of guilt, regret, and redemption, and the part they play in driving people to create and protect family-at any cost.

Reece's Faith—TJ Vertigo   In the return of the main characters from the bestselling novel *Private Dancer*, we see the blossoming relationship of bar owner, Reece Corbett and actress, Faith Ashford. The two women explore new, uncertain territory together, using sexual intimacy as a glue of comfort, helping them become strong and whole. A trusting Reece shares with Faith the sordid tale of how she became *The Animal* and Faith finds herself newly empowered by Reece's ongoing trust and support. Jealousy arises when Faith has to kiss a man on her TV show and two amorous women stalk Reece. When Faith is outed on her television show, things get crazy. With the arrival of her parents on the scene, the craziness escalates. As Faith tries to justify her lifestyle and defend her love for Reece, she discovers that nothing about her parents is as she once believed. This, not to be missed passionate and erotic romance, will have you begging for more.

Starting Over—Jen Silver Ellie Winters, a successful potter, is living on a remote hilltop farm inherited from her parents. Her well-ordered life is shaken apart when her past meets her present. Robin Fanshawe, Ellie's philandering long-term lover, has a fragile truce with Ellie. The arrival of women from Robin's present threatens to break that tentative pact. Charming Dr. Kathryn Moss, an archaeologist and an old lover of Ellie's, arrives on the farm searching for a new site to dig. When she discovers a previously unknown Roman settlement and ancient burial site on Ellie's farm, Ellie allows her to start an archaeological dig of the area. Will Ellie also allow the rekindling of an old romance or will she stay with Robin? Can that long term relationship, albeit tentative, recover from this collision or will an old romance trump everything she knows? Will Robin, seeing the interaction between Ellie and Kathryn, leave her womanising ways behind? Will she take a chance on giving herself wholly to the woman she loves? These questions and the mystery of whose royal resting place is disturbed at Starling Hill are answered in this classic romance of simmering passions, anguished loss, and the wonder of love.

Twisted Lives—Ali Spooner A twist of fate leaves Bet and her daughter Kylie stranded at the entrance of the home of Alex Graves, as she flees the control of an abusive husband. When custom–homebuilder Alex arrives to find steam boiling from Bet's car and a beautiful child asleep in the passenger seat, her heart goes out to them. Alex offers shelter to the pair setting off a chain of events that bring both mother and daughter close to her heart and danger to her door. A heartwarming story of true love that will keep you smiling long after you've finished the book.

Malodorous—Del Robertson   Sequel to My Fair Maiden Something in Fairhaven stinks. Other than the mutton stew, that is. Gwen thought life after being a virgin sacrifice would be a bed of roses. Bodhi was just looking for a wench to bed. Neither less-than-dashing hero nor not-quite-so-pure maiden imagined they would meet again, much less be trapped together in a city the likes of the ill-named Fairhaven. There's a killer on the loose. Fairhaven's on lockdown, its citizens fearful for their lives. The local guards are corrupt. And, Bodhi's been accused of murder…

Desert Blooms—Dannie Marsden   Luce's story continues in DESERT BLOOMS… When we last met Luce Velazquez in Desert Heat, she went through hell and back to salvage her soul and reputation. Hoping to get her life back on track with lover Beth Ryan, a woman who understands her pain and can relate on every level. Instead, Luce is in the hospital, and Beth in protective custody. Jessica Sullivan, Luce's friend and ex, has big doubts about the sincerity of Beth's love, and is in no hurry to release her from custody. Can Luce's new found happiness last, or is Jessica correct in her doubts? A heart stopping romance that will fill you with the wonder of friendship, anger of betrayal, and the everlasting vision of love.

Finding Her Way—Riley Jefferson   Is it love or just great sex? After ending an abusive marriage, Jerrica Kerrison is finally alive and she's apologizing for nothing! She has a job with a financial firm in Boston, a townhouse in Newburyport, and a sports car she drives way too fast. Jerrica has everything except that indefinable emotion called love. Madison Jeffrey is a lost soul. A PR job in the south has always protected Madison from the pressures of her family. But one day, fate brings her back to New England, forcing

Madison to face her long buried demons, and a sister who despises her. When a chance meeting brings Jerrica and Madison's separate worlds crashing together, the attraction is instantaneous. After one passionate night together, Jerrica retreats into the safety of her world, leaving Madison to figure out what happened. Will Jerrica open up her heart to the idea of love? Can Madison finally believe that she is worthy of unconditional love? Or will a devil hiding in the shadows tear them apart?

HER—Lisa Ron Fox has been looking for that one person who will make her feel complete-her perfect match. Together with her friends, Megan and Tree, Fox continues her quest while dodging exes and clingers, laughing a lot along the way. When she meets Madeline, she instantly knows that she has found HER. Madeline has her own problems-notably a domineering husband. Can Fox win her heart? Can they make a life together? This story will make you laugh, cry, and hold your breath as the story unfolds. With the right person love can conquer all.

Bayou Justice—Ali Spooner Hell hath no fury like a woman scorned. When Kara, Sasha's new lover is taken hostage as a diversionary tactic to allow the drug dealing Bellfontaine brothers to escape justice, Sasha springs into action. Kara is released physically unharmed, however her emotions and budding career in the District Attorney's office are left in shambles when she is held to blame for their release, Appalled by the failure of the criminal justice system, Sasha exacts her own brand of justice for the acts committed against her lover. From the Bayous of Louisiana to the jungles of South America, Sasha plots her revenge.

Out of Retirement—Erica Lawson Melanie Stokes was a doctor—a very good one, or so she hoped. She was calm and cool under pressure, and very little fazed her. Until…Caitlin Joseph ran a small retirement home for older women in need. The fact that everyone in the house was gay was a coincidence, although it did cut down the number of women agreeing to live there. Mel took up an offer to do some relief work for a local community center when their regular doctor was away on holidays. As soon as she arrived at the home she knew something was different about the place. Was it the little old lady chasing the paper boy down the street or the sign saying "Dykes Retirement Home"? But there was something about the place that also appealed to her. Sure, Caitlin was cute as a button, but it was more the fact that she took very good care of her charges despite their rather bizarre behavior. The older women seized the opportunity to introduce a woman into Caitlin's lonely life, using any means possible to keep Mel coming back. Their plans were boosted by the introduction of another woman into the house, who set hearts a fluttering and blood pressure rising. Now if she was a lesbian it would have been perfect…

Letting Go—JM Dragon A failed relationship puts Stella Hawke's life on the brink of chaos. When her grandmother falls gravely ill in Ashville, Stella ends her army career to take care of the woman during her last weeks. Little does she know that an old army comrade, socialite Reggie Stockton, whose family owns the local newspaper, also lives in Ashville. Will she allow herself to accept Reggie's help to turn her life around and let go of the past? This is a journey where both women re-evaluate what they want out of life. Will that path lead to happiness or to a parting of the ways?

Through the Darkness—Erin O'Reilly Becca Cameron is a loner—by choice. She lives in a hundred year old farmhouse built by her great grandfather. A tragic accident in her home a year earlier drove away her lover, and Becca tries to accept what she cannot change and hang on to the belief that love can conquer all. Chase Hunter had a meteoric rise in the Eastman Corporation and was, at thirty-four, the youngest vice-president. To Chase, her work was all consuming leaving little time for friends or lovers. There was simply no place in her life for anything but her job. When Becca and Chase meet at their work place, the attraction is spontaneous. Life begins to look brighter for both women as work takes a second seat to romance. Unknown to either woman, someone is watching their every move... Will passion outweigh doubt? Can love conqueror fear?

Beginning of the End—Alane Hotchkin What happens when life doesn't go exactly as you planned and you must protect others from your own fate? Escaping a horrific childhood, Nikki longed to find happily ever after in adulthood. What she found was Hell. Or did it find her? Finding the courage to break the cycle of betrayal, she opens her heart one last time. Alex lived a childhood others dreamed of. Her father never once denied the young rebel a thing. All her life she dreamed of protecting others; to follow in her father's footsteps. Soon though she learned sex and fists made the most powerful of weapons. Alex controls the women in her life through fear and sex, will breaking the cycle be too much to overcome? Will loving Nikki be enough to change her, or is Alex beyond help? Alex would give Nikki the world, but at what price? When a person's tightly controlled reality snaps, what then...? This is the Beginning of the End for one of them and the ultimate sacrifice for the other. But who is who in this game of life?

Galveston 1900: Swept Away—Linda Crist On September 7-8, 1900, the island of Galveston, Texas, was destroyed by a hurricane, or 'tropical cyclone' as it was called in those days. This story is a fictional account of Mattie and Rachel, two women who lived there, and their lives during the time of the 'great storm'. Forced to flee from her family at a young age, Rachel Travis finds a home and livelihood on the island of Galveston. Independent, friendly, and yet often lonely, only one other person knows the dark secret that haunts her. Madeline "Mattie" Crockett is trapped in a loveless marriage, convinced that her fate is sealed. She never dares to dream of true happiness, until Rachel Travis comes walking into her life. As emotions come to light, the storm of Mattie's marriage converges with the very real hurricane. Can they survive, and build the life they both dream of? This second edition of one of Linda Crist's best-loved novels maintains the original story, while incorporating some reader-pleasing passages that were cut from the first edition. As an added bonus, the short story "Something to Celebrate" is included at the end of the novel, detailing further adventures of Rachel and Mattie.

Rapture: Sins of the Sinners—A. C. Henley & Fran Heckrotte A serial killer is targeting young lesbians throughout the state of Texas. Texas Ranger Cochetta Lovejoy is assigned to the case. Convinced she knows who is committing the murders, Ranger Lovejoy is willing to do whatever it takes to put the perpetrator behind bars--even if it means stretching the limits of the law by manipulating the judicial system. Detective Agnes Kelly-Elliott is one of Ft. Worth Police Department's finest investigators. When Ranger Lovejoy appears on the crime scene of a recent murder, Agnes fears a dark secret that, if revealed, could destroy her family ties and end her career. This is a dark, gritty, graphic tale of desire gone awry, and flawed characters looking for redemption in all the wrong places.

Absolution—S. Anne Gardner Games of the rich and famous, love, lust, and forbidden passions weave this tale that play out through decades and the world. The close ties the Alcalas have to the royal house of Spain provide them with an unspoken untouchable policy. Their passions and their secrets are about to come to light with a force that cannot be stopped. In this whirlwind is Cristina Uraca Alacala who is searching for a truth that has been denied to her most of her life and she must find. She is not unlike her family; Cristina does not stop until she gets what she wants. In the fog lies the truth that she must travel through to find. In this tale wealthy socialite Annais Francesca D'Autremond is a pivotal person of interest in Cristina's search for the truth. When these two women meet they find themselves drawn together by something greater than themselves. As the truth of a hidden past becomes clearer their passions grow beyond the realm of the no return instead of a status quo. Both tied together by destiny; will both survive the onslaught of past and present passions?

Denial—Jackie Kennedy Time spent in Somalia has Doctor Celeste Cameron accustomed to living and working in a war zone. Coming back home to America, Celeste is glad to see the end of the peril she has been in—or so she thinks. Danger seems to follow Celeste and she finds it in the shape of Amy. What Celeste feels for Amy scares her more than anything she has faced in war zones. Amy has the same feelings, but is in denial and vows to marry Josh, Celeste's twin brother, no matter what. When fate brings them together again, will they give in to their mutual attraction or will they once again deny what they feel?

Taming the Wolff—Del Robertson ONLY ONE WOMAN... As devastatingly beautiful as she is headstrong, noble-born Alexis DeVale abruptly finds her preordained life in upheaval. Abducted at sword-point, held for ransom, thrust into a maelstrom of lawlessness and piracy... HAS THE POWER... The strength of her passion, the depth of her love... TO TAME THE WOLFF... Mayhem. Brutality. Murder. These are the tools of the trade - and Kris Wolff is the master of her profession. Captain of the high seas, a roguish pirate, her heart hardened by life, her passion tightly controlled by the secret she's forced to keep. Faced with a new danger, The Wolff finds herself unable to guard her heart from the tumultuous desires that Alexis DeVale has awakened.

Private Dancer—TJ Vertigo Reece Corbett grew up on the mean streets on New York City, abused, used and in trouble with the law. Faith Ashford grew up wealthy, with all the creature comforts that money provides. When they meet fireworks begin.

Miriam and Esther—Sherry Barker Miriam thought her life would play out in the bustling metropolis of Dallas, but after a life-changing accident, she moves to the small town of Cool Lake, Texas to get her head on straight and regain her senses.

McKee—A.C. Henley Private Investigator Quinlan McKee has returned to Los Angeles after a three-year absence, only to find herself embroiled in a world of child slavery and police corruption.

E-Books, Print, Free e-books

Visit our website for more publications available online.

www.affinityebooks.com

Published by Affinity E-Book Press NZ LTD
Canterbury, New Zealand

Registered Company 2517228

Printed in Great Britain
by Amazon.co.uk, Ltd.,
Marston Gate.